Shadow Slayer

Flutterbye Trail Press
797 Sam Bass Road #2541
Round Rock, TX 78681

First edition

Chapter Art by Etheric Tales
Cover Design by Covers by Kellie Arts
Discreet Cover Design by Gombar Cover Design
Editing by Red Loop Editing
Hardback Case Design by Olga Sauchenia
Printed Interior Design by Enchanting Covers
Published by Flutterbye Trail Press

ISBN: 978-1-954582-12-5 (E-book)
ISBN: 978-1-954582-53-8 (Discreet Paperback)
ISBN: 978-1-954582-18-7 (Paperback)
ISBN: 978-1-954582-29-3 (Hardback)

Feedback: Encounter a problem with this book? Let us know at ellahendricksauthor@gmail.com

BOOKS BY ELLA HENDRICKS

Fated or Knot

THE ARCANE ALLIANCES UNIVERSE

House of the Sanguine
with Nicole LaBrocca
Dark Vampire Romantasy (RH)

Thirst

SHADOW SLAYER

MOONGROVE ACADEMY: WICKED SPELLS
BOOK 2

ELLA HENDRICKS

CONTENT OVERVIEW

This is a paranormal RH romance, meaning that the main female character does not need to choose between love interests. There are graphic sex scenes (some including more than one partner) between consenting adults. *Shadow Slayer* is book two of a trilogy with a cliffhanger ending.

Please be aware that this book continues to show depictions of grief because of the death of a friend. Also contained within are fight sequences that include death, gore, and magical violence. This trilogy is classified as dark academia because the main antagonists have magic that affects the souls of others.

This trilogy does not include a pregnancy for the FMC or MM content.

If you find anything in the contents of this book that should be added to this page, please let me know at ellahen dricksauthor@gmail.com.

1

CRESS

Though we returned to Northern Supernatural University in police vehicles, I was fairly sure my friends and I weren't under arrest. At least, not yet.

The Cress of yesterday would be worried about expulsion. Ever since I'd released an old and powerful dimensional from Moongrove Library, I'd constantly looked over my shoulder, expecting someone to realize my mistake and send me home for it.

Not too long ago, I'd thought leaving NSU was the worst thing the authorities could do to me. I'd only just discovered I was a witch and viewed the secret world of the supernatural as something straight out of my wildest imaginations come to life. The campus was like a melting pot, with mer, fae, vampires, shifters, and more all living in harmony without a need to hide their true natures. A place where I belonged, too.

But my recent encounter with the Hungering Darkness had ripped the fog from my eyes. Getting expelled was my worst fear? What a joke compared to the real possibility of my friends getting hurt. Downright laughable when Ben had just admitted to being magically enslaved to a vampire.

I was slumped in the padded, maroon-colored cushions of the couch I'd been shown to with Roe and Áine in the administration building's waiting room. My two friends and I had a few scratches and bruises between us but nothing compared to the beating Ben, Geo, and Phaeron had taken in the fight we'd barely survived.

Roe and Áine were leaning heavily into each other, dozing. Roe was an Ashbough, a storied guardian witch family, with the gym rat physique to match the physical requirements of magic that manipulated stone and made the user stronger and tougher. We'd done our best to fight side by side, but we knew maybe ten spells between us. "Baby witch magic," the Hungering Darkness had scoffed of our combined efforts.

Áine's healing magic had worked miracles when our efforts came short. She was a faun, a fae woman with warm brown skin and auburn-colored curls, plus a deer-like lower half that gave her a poofy little tail and a bouncy hoofed stride. Usually, she wove freshly picked flowers into her mane of beautiful hair, but after this evening, only a handful of bruised petals remained.

I should've tried to rest right alongside them. The lamps in the waiting room were off, and the overhead lights were dimmed to their lowest setting. A solitary owl hooted in the dark of night. I wondered if it was a true animal roosting on the building or a shifter giving in to their animal nature.

My thoughts simply wouldn't quiet, whether I was temporarily distracted by owls or just trying to pick out the murmur of voices down the hall. Dr. Melinda Aurina, the

University President, was keeping us here until she had the full story of what'd happened and why. Too bad the moment she'd seen Phaeron, she'd slammed him with crimson magic and rendered him instantly unconscious. The dimensional man was powerful—scarily so—but his weakened, bleeding self was no match for a cupid demigoddess at full strength.

Unfortunately for her, I think he was the only one who truly knew the whole story of what was going on. I had a gross, uncertain feeling brewing in my stomach. Had they believed us when we swore he wasn't the Hungering Darkness, as Dr. Aurina had immediately thought? She'd attacked him so quickly that she had to know exactly what he looked like and where he'd been for the last two hundred years.

I hoped he was all right. I'd despised the man, thinking he'd murdered my friend and roommate, Lanie, just to find out it hadn't been him this whole time. *Just like he'd tried to tell me.*

Just like how saying the Hungering Darkness's title aloud drew its attention, my thoughts of Phaeron seemed to summon him. The distant *ding* of an elevator preceded the clank of chains and gruff male voices. I locked gazes with him across the room, shocked at how dull his usually vibrant yellow eyes were when shadowed with deep hollows.

Heavy manacles restrained his hands together, and a second set caught the length of his tail between his cuffed ankles. He hobbled awkwardly without his tail lending him his usual extraordinary grace. A pair of campus police prodded him along toward the University President's office.

I hopped to my feet, startling my two friends awake. "This is completely unnecessary," I snapped.

"Peace, bright soul," Phaeron slurred.

"This is a good man you've chained up. He fought to protect me and my friends," I insisted to the leftmost police officer, a burly man whose aura had the fluid movements of a shifter. My tired eyes only caught a glimpse of his magic before losing focus.

The other officer, a green-skinned fae with leafy fronds growing from his arms and down his scalp like hair, gestured sharply. "Come along, then. Dr. Aurina wanted to speak with..." He consulted his phone and read off our names.

"It's pronounced 'Anya,'" grumped Áine, who bounded to my side within moments. Roe was still rubbing her eyes as she followed suit.

"Standard procedure," the shifter cop murmured to me behind his hand. "Don't you know how strong this guy is?"

All too well. I took in Phaeron again. He'd gotten a change of clothes that weren't stained with his purplish blood and shredded to bits from the Hungering Darkness's talons. His eyelids drooped, and he seemed truly out of it. "You think he poses a threat right now?" I countered.

"You never know with dimensionals."

The greater supernatural community would call this man backward or even racist for a statement like that. Dimensionals were people from another world, whose unique features were easily confused with the human idea of what demons looked like. And Phaeron was their prince, the man with enough magic to lead his people away from their dying, corrupted world.

His face was striking but attractive nonetheless. Sharp cheekbones, ashen-gray skin, and the pair of curling ram horns that cupped his pointed ears. His hair was a sleek and shiny black and held back by a fresh hair tie. When he smiled, he had vampire-like fangs, and when he wasn't so lethargic, his slit-pupiled gaze, colored as bright as cut topaz, seemed to see right through me.

He was the dimensional I'd freed from Moongrove Library. A devil with a deep, smooth voice that could instantly flutter my insides. But not a monster. He didn't deserve the criminal treatment he was subjected to as the cops practically hauled him to Dr. Aurina's office.

Roe put a hand on my shoulder. "It's not worth the fight. Let's just go," she sighed.

I muttered under my breath as I followed a pace behind them. Dr. Aurina's office wasn't far, and enough chairs had been dragged in across from her desk to accommodate for a large gathering. She liked blond wood and warm colors, especially the rich red of the upholstery and rugs.

The woman herself sat in a raised chair like a throne behind her desk, with her mates arranged to either side of her. I counted, thinking one was missing. Perhaps tending to the group's little daughter, who was also—thankfully— not here.

Dr. Aurina was easily the most beautiful woman who'd ever graced my eyes. Even wearing a simple woolen gown and a pinch between her brows, she had some cupid mystique about her that airbrushed over any flaws she might have. Her chair had special slits cut in the sides to account for her rose gold wings. Each feather glinted like molten metal even in low light. Her delicate fingers played with a lock of pink hair as the four of us sat across from her desk.

She nodded curtly to the two campus police. "I can handle it from here," she said. They left without a word of complaint.

I'd slipped into the seat next to Phaeron, noticing my

friends' discomfort with him, even with the state he was in. "The gargoyle and the blood witch should be joining us soon," said one of Aurina's mates after consulting his phone.

"The blood witch?" Roe echoed in shock. "Ben?"

"He nearly bled out," I said at the same time. Was he really going to be pushed into a meeting like this in the condition I'd last seen him in?

I'd also thought I'd have time to get my head straight before seeing him again, considering the massive gulf of secrets and lies I'd recently discovered between us. He had a lot of explaining to do, and I was not in the right mind to hear it all yet.

"As did the gargoyle, in his own way," Aurina herself answered. "They've been patched up in the student medical center for now. Once we hear the full story, they can go rest."

"I can tell you everything," Phaeron said with effort.

The demigoddess raised her brows. "Will you do so if I reverse my spell on you?"

"Yes."

Magic sparkled on the palm she lifted and aimed toward him. A cloud of sparkling pink mist blew from her skin and swirled around Phaeron's head, seeping into his nostrils until he'd breathed it all in. The links of the chains binding him clacked as he shifted and jerked.

Clarity returned to his expression, and he bared his teeth with a vicious, otherworldly growl. "These restraints won't hold me for long," he warned. I put a hand to my belly, trying to hide the relief I felt at hearing the smooth, seductive lilt return to his voice now that it wasn't gritty with forced exhaustion.

"Fulfill our agreement first," Aurina replied.

He muttered what sounded distinctly like a couple curses in an alien language that rolled off his tongue. Then he turned his head, inspecting first Áine, then Roe, and finally me.

"All of you are well?" he asked.

"As good as we can be," I answered.

The office door swung behind us, and in stumbled Ben, escorted by the same pair of campus police. At some point, the makeshift manacles Roe had created for him out of rock and clay had been replaced by real, metal ones. His golden-brown fall of hair was damp, and his skin pink, like he'd received a rough scrubbing of any blood runes.

At least he had some color. Last I'd seen him, he'd been covered in his own blood and deathly pale as his magic struggled to close several long gashes that split open his back. My lips fluttered into an uncertain smile as the butterflies in my belly grew leaden wings.

There was no hint of the easy charm Ben had used to his benefit through our short acquaintance. He snarled and cursed at the policemen, jerking his shoulders from their grip when they practically shoved him into the room. Yet he froze the moment he spotted me.

We stared at each other for what could've been two seconds, but it felt like an eternity. Did I ever really know this man? Despite the fact that our palms had matching anam cara marks, it felt like I was only just meeting the real Ben. I set my lips, trying to hide the pain that thought brought me.

"Cress—" he began to say, his expression falling. I would dare say he looked devastated, and I hadn't given voice to the betrayed thoughts crowding my head.

"Move," grunted one last person, pushing Ben further into the room. The promised gargoyle, Geo, walked stiffly behind him. He was in his human form, with several wounds up his arms and the exposed skin at the hollow of his throat. They glinted solid silver against his ebony skin, sealed with the enchanted oil that circulated his body like blood.

The tension hanging in the room could be cut with a knife from the moment Geo spotted Phaeron.

"Cress, kindly vacate the seat next to the dimensional." He spoke in a flat tone I'd once confused for robotic. Geo didn't have the best grasp on his emotions, considering he usually didn't have them in his true form of quartz and obsidian.

"No one's in danger here," Phaeron replied, though the way he stifled another growl made me wonder how true that was. They may have fought together earlier this evening, but I figured it was a temporary truce.

Slowly, I eased from my seat. Phaeron shot me an incredulous look. "Ben should sit here," I said, gesturing to it and avoiding looking at any of them. I dragged a different chair over to wedge myself between Roe and Áine. The faun nodded in approval, while Roe squared her shoulders and shifted to shield me from Ben's gaze.

Geo remained on his feet, standing in the space behind his two seated and restrained adversaries. He'd never liked Ben, sensing something was off about him from the moment he'd appeared in one of my classes, and had a longer, more complicated history with Phaeron.

"Well, now that we're all here, I would like to hear from you first." Aurina gestured with an elegant hand. "Ben, is it?"

"Who's asking?" he replied flippantly.

Her fingers balled into fists, and the force of her anger was like a physical blow, making me feel about an inch tall.

All of us leaned away from her, even her mates and Phaeron. The only one who watched impassively was Geo, who settled his lips into an unimpressed line.

"Be careful, assassin. I need little reason to harm you sevenfold for the pain you brought my daughter," she said through clenched teeth.

2

BEN

Accusing gazes skewered me from all directions. I swallowed with effort, my throat drier than the nearest fire fae. Even though a blood witch could heal the most devastating injuries with the power of a rune, as I already had this evening, my body couldn't go forever.

There were two furious cupid women in front of me, swimming in and out of focus. In my current state, I knew the next thing I said might be my last unless I could convince her of the truth.

"That…" I struggled to breathe under the pinning power of her anger. "That was my associate. She…she tried to make it a light cut."

"Light!" Aurina screeched.

One of her mates reached out, stroking her arm and murmuring in her ear. Her emotions drew back from their chokehold around my neck, and I filled my lungs gratefully.

Closing my eyes, I probed at the ruined blood rune tattooed on my side with my fingertips. It was tender to the touch, with a swollen ridge cutting it in half. I tried to say what I could, aware that the rune at full strength would boil my blood for daring to say a breath of Garroway's secrets.

"I was sent to NSU's Mabon celebration to collect a few cupid feathers with their magic intact. My associate, as I said, was tasked with, and I quote, making your daughter 'bleed.' When we're given an order from..." My fingers curled over the rune, which pulsed a painful warning. "...from the master, we have to obey."

"What master?" Roe asked.

"His name is Garroway. At least, that is the name he's used lately," Aurina replied for me. "I'm sorry, young man. It is not your fault he sank to new lows recently."

I cracked my eyes open to see her flashing me a brief pitying gaze. "This is the first opportunity I've gotten to talk to one of his witches without them immediately committing suicide."

"Not like any of us have a choice in that," I replied.

"If I don't miss my guess, you are speaking of a blood baron?" the dimensional asked.

Aurina nodded. "Indeed. We've played a song and dance for half a century, first with polite overtures and gifts from him. When I didn't climb into his coffers and allow him unfettered access to the pocket dimension that holds NSU and New Salem, then came the severed fingers and bloody knives secreted in my bedsheets. Obviously, he grows bolder still.

"Ben, you must tell me where to find him. I sense the echoes of your pain, like any of his witch assassins. His signature is unmistakable."

I knew before I even opened my mouth that I wouldn't just be able to tell her an address. The rune gave another warning pulse, and I tasted blood just from the thought of saying it, writing it down, or even leading one of the people in this room there.

"Now hold on," I hedged, also sure Aurina wouldn't take a deflection for an answer.

"What *can* you tell us?" Roe asked, a thread of concern in her tone.

The redhead's change in sympathies gave me whiplash. She was obviously protective of her friend, my anam cara, who had barely looked me in the eye since I'd walked in. My necessary lies had obviously fucked up that relationship. The moment I had to hold a dagger to Cress's throat, I knew I'd ruined one of the only good things in my life. But if our coven's mother hen was willing to hear me out, maybe not all was lost.

Before I died about two weeks from now, of course. The dark magic branded in my flesh still had a deadline ticking down for one last cruel mission Garroway had demanded of me.

"Let me show you why those witches all died," I said with effort as I stood.

I pinched the hem of my shirt and bent my elbows to expose the blood rune for everyone to see. A spiky, circular tattoo that covered most of my right side. The inside of the circle was one giant red glyph. An ugly, ragged slash bisected it now, still weeping, courtesy of the dimensional who nodded next to me and averted his eyes politely.

"This is my blood rune, carved into my skin by...Gar... the master himself." I huffed from the pulse of pain from it, but this time, Aurina, Roe, Cress, and the fae girl all gasped when red striations appeared around it as a visual cue to how much it hurt. I collapsed back into the chair from my wobbly legs. "All of his witches have one. If we speak of our missions or the master's secrets, the Agonia rune in the center activates and gives us a quick, terrible death."

"I didn't know," Aurina said quietly. Her beautiful face softened, dipping into a thoughtful frown.

"I've hunted a few blood barons in my day," the dimensional pitched in. "The runes are created by a shard of a dimensional weapon that was already illegal on Soiluire."

Cress spoke up, leaning past Roe's shoulder to address the cupid woman sitting across from us. "There are lines that branch from the rune too."

"Deadlines," I said. I pinched my eyes closed again. The room was spinning. If I taunted my damaged rune much more, it just might kill me anyway.

"Perhaps you can question the young man at a different time," the dimensional said in a cool tone. "And offer him something in return for the pain he suffers to give you information."

There was a long pause from the cupid demigoddess. "Well, let's hear your story, then, Phaeron. Or should I say—"

"Don't," he interrupted sharply. "His name was Endaeron. You may refer to him thusly."

Someone tugged at my shirt. I cracked my eyes open to see it was the faun, Áine, with a weak aura of green light haloing her earthen-toned fingers.

"Thanks," I mumbled, letting her touch the rune. Gentle warmth replaced the hot needle sensation prickling out from my skin. She was careful not to touch or heal the scratch that'd deactivated the deadly Agonia tattoo in the center of the rune.

"Don't mention it," she replied, but it seemed my story had softened her some. I just had to hope Cress felt similarly, as this wasn't the right time to pour my heart out to her about the true damage Garroway had done to my family.

"I have already told Cress part of this story, but it bears repeating so you all understand," Phaeron was saying in the meantime.

I was momentarily distracted from my brother and Cress as Phaeron described Soiluire and the mysterious goddess of light that'd shown up one day, Myuna, who'd turned out to be a parasite, transforming anyone she'd gifted magic to into monstrosities.

Phaeron's brother, Endaeron, had been closest to her and thus became the worst of the creatures when she showed her true face. He became the Hungering Darkness, a cursed being that eternally hungered for souls.

"The three tribes of my people combined their powers to come here. We sealed the way behind us, thinking we would be free of Myuna," Phaeron sighed. "Unfortunately, my brother had come along with us, hiding dormant in another's soul. Without a body of his own, he picks one victim to slowly corrupt and uses *them* to kill and consume other victims' souls. He is hard to detect and nearly impossible to stop.

"I recruited humankind to help, as the seal we created between our worlds was not as complete as we'd hoped. I personally taught the first librarian witch how to use dimensional magic, and together, we founded Moongrove Library, the first prison for unnatural beings and items too dangerous for mortals."

He turned slowly, glaring up at the gargoyle standing over the two of us like we were some kind of war prize. "We chased my brother from victim to victim. I'd vowed to end my brother's tortured existence, and in the process of learning from me and ascending to demigoddesshood,

Morgana Voidbinder became my partner and mate. We hunted Endaeron together."

"Again, I am not her," Geo said in his usual monotone.

"Trust me, I am well aware," Phaeron rumbled. "Morgana died two hundred years ago when we nearly had my brother in a containment room. We were *so close* to ensuring he was contained when he unexpectedly murdered the woman whose body he was occupying and lashed out at Morgana. Her last act was to seal the room—with both Endaeron and me inside. Presumably, she succumbed to her wounds minutes later. Had she waited a moment more, I would've been able to leave the room and get her treatment, but she didn't give me the chance.

"I just want to speak with her one last time, gargoyle. To ask her why," he said. "Two hundred years may have passed, but I've been in stasis for that time. Her death was a blink of time for me."

"That's rough," I muttered.

"You will not be speaking with her. She does not exist anymore," Geo replied.

"Her soul is clearly—"

"Phaeron, that doesn't explain recent events," Aurina interrupted.

He heaved a sigh and turned back to her. "Of course. Someone unsealed the containment room, and my brother latched on to him immediately. The boy I fought earlier."

"My brother," I said, swallowing painfully. "The master sent him to Moongrove Library. All he told me was it was 'a stop there for something.'"

"Was he the youngest assassin in the blood baron's coven?" Phaeron asked me.

"Yeah. There are some other kids, but Lucas is the

youngest who'd taken the blood witch affinity," I confirmed.

"But why unseal the room in the first place?" Cress breathed.

"Many reasons, I am sure," Phaeron answered. "But first, to escalate with you." He nodded toward Aurina. "All of the victims have been taken on the NSU campus. I do not know this man, but I know blood barons always have multiple irons in the fire. Until my brother takes over the boy's soul completely, he is leashed by the blood rune Lucas carries. He will fulfill any order the blood baron makes."

Aurina's flawless skin paled considerably.

"I'm not okay with any of this," Roe burst in. "We have to do something."

"Kill this vampire," Cress said in agreement.

"Get the monster out of my brother," I said.

"And throw him back in stasis, where he belongs," Phaeron finished with a nod. "Which means we are all on the same side. It is time we worked together, and there is one easy first step." He rattled his chains as he held his arms out toward Aurina.

"Seconded." I smirked at the cupid demigoddess as I mimicked his stance.

Her nostrils flared before she turned her face away. "There is one more piece of this puzzle to uncover before I decide what to do with you two," she said. "Tell me your story, Cressida."

"Me?" she asked, brows lifting.

"Were you not the witness that reported a dimensional standing over your roommate after her untimely death?"

Cress sucked in a breath, a pained gasp to have that memory unearthed.

"Yeah, that was me," she admitted.

"How did that get us here?" Aurina pressed. She steepled her fingers, inspecting the other two ladies in the room with her. "How did your friends get pulled into this situation?"

Phaeron reluctantly put his arms down, turning his attention toward her as well. I blew out a breath, knowing this was going to be hard to hear.

"Well," Cress hedged. She took several deep breaths. "You're right. The night of Lanie's murder, I saw Phaeron standing over her. I immediately assumed he'd killed her."

"Her distress activated this unit," Geo rumbled.

"And the university announced it was a blood witch's killing. I didn't understand it, but one of my professors told me to keep Phaeron's identity quiet to prevent widespread panic. He agreed to teach me librarian witch magic early," Cress continued. "I picked up a silver sword and started learning how to defend myself, and Geo became my bodyguard. But I have a confession."

She bit her lip, eyeing the cupid demigoddess and the unsmiling males on either side of her. "I released Phaeron from the bottom floor of the library. All this time, I thought the...I thought his brother's actions were my fault. I didn't tell anyone this because I thought I'd be expelled."

"Endaeron was long gone when you helped me shake off the disorientation spell keeping me in the library," Phaeron said, his expression softening. "You truly blamed yourself?"

She gave him a shy smile, a hint of color brightening her cheeks. "I did. Which was why I was so determined to handle you."

"You can handle me any time you like, bright soul," he practically purred.

I couldn't help a sudden and acute flash of jealousy. She

was really going to let him flirt with her right in front of me? Geo cleared his throat, a sound like two stones grinding together. With a flinch, Cress shifted with embarrassment.

"So, anyway, I kept it a secret, and around that time, Ben showed up. He was interested in me nearly immediately, and we found out we were anam cara, destined to be the closest of friends or maybe even lovers. In the meantime, another person died, and the university blamed a blood witch again."

"I thought it was Lucas being sloppy," I admitted.

"And I thought it was Phaeron because he'd been there at the Mabon celebration. Sorry, Geo," she said. His usual stony expression was twisted in displeasure. "I spoke to Phaeron while Geo was, uh, otherwise occupied. He warned me to leave the celebration early, and I did.

"I still hadn't told anyone about Phaeron, but he took me aside one evening after Ben left my dorm to tell me of Soiluire and his brother. I said the monster's name, and it came out of nowhere to attack me, which is how I then knew the…the Hunger, it wasn't Phaeron," she said, drawing a hand down her cheeks. "Lanie was an augury witch, and I finally read her last message to me. In it, she said she'd seen her murderer was a blood witch, so I started connecting the wrong dots. The university obviously thought a blood witch was involved—"

Aurina shook her head, muttering, "It was just a cover story. A lie."

"—Well, I realized a blood witch was involved then. And only one had come around at the same time of Lanie's death, pretending to be a different kind of witch, and been in the same place as each time the Hunger had appeared. I thought, if it wasn't Phaeron, it had to be Ben. I finally told my friends everything, and together, we set a trap for Ben, but instead of him being the monster, it'd been his brother all along."

"Hey, next time, you could just ask first," I said, trying to make a joke despite the tense atmosphere. No one laughed.

"And now we're here," Roe said.

"Indeed," Aurina said. She considered a few sheets of paper on her desk for a prolonged moment. "I'm glad to have had you all in the same room. It is, of course, disappointing that you did not come forward with your story earlier, Cressida, but in the scheme of things, it wouldn't have been all that useful without the other angles." She gestured to Phaeron and me.

"What will you be telling the campus?" Áine asked. "A bunch of mer saw the fight break out."

The cupid demigoddess pressed her lips together tighter. "To go to class on Monday, of course. We will continue to say that we have it under control."

I shifted uneasily but didn't point out that she obviously didn't have this situation contained. No one else seemed willing to challenge her obvious lie either, leading to an awkward pause until she nodded and gestured. "Ladies, you may go. You as well, Geo. I imagine you want to see your charge safely to her bed."

"Indeed," Geo said, taking a stiff step backward.

"He couldn't defend anyone from a fly right now," Phaeron remarked. "I will see Cress and her friends returned to their lodgings."

Aurina was suddenly twirling a keychain between her fingers, having the metal clink. "Well, I wanted to talk about your future first. And your freedom."

3

PHAERON

Before she left the room, Cress stopped beside my chair. My gaze traced the scratches on her face, left to seal themselves over. My brother had done this, marred her beauty. That was his nature, to ruin and destroy the prettiest of things. Especially if I was enamored with them.

Her shoulders were lowered with fatigue. This had been a long evening. By the time she retired to her room, the night may be over. "I just wanted to say, I'm sorry about ever thinking you were a monster." Earnestness shone in her wide brown eyes, and I cursed Aurina again for leaving me restrained.

I was so tightly bound I could not draw her hand to my lips to kiss the mark of protection I'd left amongst the bluish veins lining her wrist. "Let us put the misunderstanding behind us. Perhaps I will see you soon," I said.

She flashed a little smile. "I hope so."

With one last nod and an uncertain glance toward Aurina, she left the room. If she heard Ben softly hiss her name, she ignored it. She'd carefully avoided interacting with him. When I'd first chanced a glimpse of them together, I'd known he was concealing his true nature from her immediately, as his soul was stained with dark magic and twisted by the pain of the rune embedded in his flesh. One such as him didn't have anything to offer a bright, innocent soul such as herself, and it seemed she'd realized that.

Neither do you, I reminded myself. I strongly suspected there was more danger brewing in my own condition than I'd dare divulge to this group.

"Ben," Aurina said once we were alone with her and her mates. She cooed his name, weaving a thread of calming emotion in the single syllable. I'd felt her magic suffusing the room this whole time, feeling out everyone's emotional state with invisible tendrils.

Unlike me, Ben was unaware of her subtle manipulations, and he sighed as he struggled to focus on her rather than the door snicking closed behind us.

"Is this where you show me the secret dungeons you have under this building?" he asked. It might've been a snark, but his tone lacked any sharp edges, drooping like he did the moment Cress was gone.

She rolled her eyes. "No. You obviously need rest as well. How old are you?"

"Twenty," he said.

"Congratulations, then. In accordance with supernatural law, you are now enrolled as a student at NSU for two mandatory years of education in your magic."

"Whoopee. I better call home and tell them the good news," he mumbled.

"We will find accommodations for you that are safe and reinforced. I do not put it past Garroway to send some of his assassins for you if he realizes you are out of his control."

"Oh, guaranteed."

"Do you think he may still be able to send you orders and compel you to fulfill them?" she asked.

He hesitated. "Maybe."

"If I may," I interjected. Aurina's lips pressed together again, but she nodded. "I have an idea that may suit all our needs. You may remember how I just told you about teaching the first librarian witches and building the foundation of what became Moongrove Library."

"Mmhmm," she hummed suspiciously.

"It is time I claimed my position there as an instructor."

"I never said I trusted you with my students," she said.

I flashed my fangs and lifted my bound wrists. "It is clear you do not trust me at all. However, you have little choice."

My shadows had been probing at the manacle around my tail; the metal was inscribed with runes of containment. Most supernaturals would have their magic completely bound by such a thing, but my power was too much to restrain so easily. I picked it open and felt my shadowborn abilities flood back in like they'd never been locked away. In an instant, I'd transformed into a curl of smoke and back, holding the cuffs that'd been on my ankles and wrists dangling from one clawed finger.

The shadows themselves surged around me, overlaying my form until my hands were tipped with wicked-sharp talons. I let the shadowborn transformation go further than it had in a long time. Darkness enveloped my head, rendering me momentarily blind as thick shadows formed a wolf-like maw lined with jagged teeth and a canine skull protected by the circular shape of my horns.

"I have a few demands following my poor treatment this evening." My voice was an unearthly, reverberating snarl. "You will relinquish my rightful territory to me, Prince Phaeron Sudair of the dimensional travelers."

"Holy shit," Ben breathed. He was on the floor, inching away from me.

Aurina's mates were on their feet, reaching for weapons or magic as I sat there with my hands laced on my lap. She lifted her hand with a whisper of calming magic all around. "There's no need to fight," she trilled. "Of course you can go to the library. It's just...this is mid-year, and the students all have instructors... Perhaps you could be an assistant?" Her laugh was edged with nerves. "I could make you an assistant instructor? You would still have access to the library."

"I also require an instructor's lodging. One with enough room to comfortably house both myself and Ben." I pointed a single talon in the young man's direction. "I alone can see if his soul is tainted with more of the blood baron's black magic. Besides, his brother is currently victimized by what's left of my own kin. It would only be fair for me to look after him, yes?"

"N-no, I could make due somewhere else—" Ben was starting to say.

"Done," Aurina interrupted. "Consider all of that done."

I let my jagged shadows go, reclining casually in the chair and smiling just enough to show the edges of my fangs. "I knew we could come to an agreement."

She reached across the desk, offering me a key. "For Ben's cuffs," she said.

I took it and gave him a hand up before freeing him from the restraints. He tottered as if dizzy, and I steadied him with a hand on his shoulder. He flinched, a hint of fear in his hazy green eyes.

"Just step outside for a moment while I take care of a

few last details," I murmured, and he nearly tripped over himself to go.

I turned my full attention to Aurina, who was also standing now, just a desk between us. I was suddenly hyperaware of every inch of wood as her subtle magic drifted around me with another shift in emotional direction.

"Perhaps I can offer you a better deal, Prince Sudair," she purred. "You are clearly quite powerful. What if I told you my mating circle is always open for one such as you?"

It was hard to ignore the luster of her candy-pink locks, or the gorgeous lips she pursed at a coy slant. Every breath, I took in more of her lusty magic. "I will be in the library, awaiting my accommodations," I said, forcing my coldest tone. "Do not make Ben and me wait."

"Must you go so soon?" she asked. Brazen in front of her mates, but the same magic she tried to influence me with was drawing their attention too. They might all have her the moment I left.

I turned into a curl of smoke, thinking sobering thoughts as I drifted from the room and located Ben. He'd found a chair and promptly dropped unconscious the moment no one's eyes were on him. He seemed more hurt than he'd let on, so I didn't wake him, instead enveloping him in my shadows and carrying him on an incorporeal wind toward Moongrove Library.

It saved me the embarrassment of explaining why I was leaving Aurina's presence fully aroused and eager to catch a glimpse of a different beauty instead. Now that Cress knew she could trust me, I wanted to explore the draw between us, preferably with my tongue over every inch of her delicate skin. I could practically hear her breath quickening and feel her pulse ticking beneath my lips.

When Aurina had made lust circle the room, my first thought hadn't been for the curvy demigoddess. I wanted my fist wrapped around purple hair rather than pink. My fantasies had emptied Aurina's room in an instant, replacing her with Cress screaming my name while I pinned her to the desk and claimed her wet heat.

It'd been far too long since a woman had spread her thighs for me. My mouth watered for a taste of Cress. What would a little nibble of her sex—of her soul—taste like, other than the purest nectar? As sweet and bright as it was, it had to be delicious...

I let out a metaphorical gasp, realizing I was on the edge of the abyss that'd wash away my consciousness. I'd suffered from these blackouts far too much, especially around my brother, who seemed to know how to trigger them.

It was Myuna's corruption coming to root within me. Even as I lusted for Cress, I realized I didn't just want her body. I wanted *just a taste* of that beautiful soul that blazed around her and kept drawing me back like a moth to flame.

I'd watched dozens of my people succumb to a taste for souls, afflicted by the barest drop of corruption in our hurry to flee from Soiluire. One taste was never a "just," but the gateway to an addiction that could only be ended by the thrust of a sword.

In a panic, I slipped into the library that'd been my prison for two centuries, finding it just as modernized and alien as when I'd first escaped with Cress's help.

This time, however, a woman's voice reached out to whisper in my mind, *"My prince, have you returned at last?"*

"Braza. What a relief it is to hear you," I replied in kind.

"Do you mean that? Because last I heard, I was 'quite meddlesome,'" she teased.

I recognized the words I'd spoken in ire when Braza had forced me to seek out Cress and explain the Age of Decay to her. It'd been the best decision, in retrospect, but her offhanded comment also told me she was more aware of the world outside her library than I thought.

"Well, you are, but some meddling is for the greater good."

"Who's the boy you're carrying?" she asked.

"My self-appointed new charge. Do you have somewhere he can rest?"

She directed me to floor negative three, where there were small rooms for a librarian's occasional overnight stay. Ben was still asleep when I removed my magic and we emerged from the shadows. I placed him on the bed and turned back into a wisp of darkness, locking the door before flowing out of the miniscule gap on the bottom of the threshold.

"I'll keep an eye on him for you. Come visit me," Braza invited.

With her help, I found the stairs again and flowed down them until I located the floor where the mortals kept her nowadays, some thirty stories down. She was the powercore, after all, the beating heart of Moongrove Library. She siphoned from the ley line I'd identified centuries ago, creating a reservoir that was then tapped by the witches to keep order within the many levels of the library.

I took form again at the stairs, bowing to Braza. "May I approach?" I asked.

"Please. How I've longed to see you again."

I ascended, seeing the reflection of my shadowborn self in its dome of magic, its canine leer making it look like I prowled with lethal intent toward the jelly-like orb. I stopped short. The powercore showed me the truth, much as I didn't want to see it. My shadows lapped off my silhouette like flowing fur, pitch-black all over, save for the blaze of corrupted white taking over the yellow of my eyes.

"*Come in. It's still you,*" Braza whispered.

I stopped staring at myself and strode for the orb, taking a larger step up to where I knew there was a hidden ledge. Loose dimensional magic enveloped me and ran over my skin like a static-filled blanket. I absorbed none of it as I entered the hollow secret nook within the core.

A female dimensional stood there waiting for me. She was not flesh and blood like I was, but constructed of the same purple-black magic of the powercore's dome over us. Braza had the forward-facing horns and bat-like wings of my mother's tribe and the same youthful features she'd died with, having not physically aged a second in the last two centuries.

Static prickled the back of my neck as we embraced. Her body, such as it was, squished in my hold. "I've missed you, my prince. It's been torture knowing you were in stasis with Endaeron's remains."

"You knew, and yet you told no one?" I pulled away as if stung.

Her face fell. "I was well aware that to release you meant we released him as well."

"Of course."

I tamped down my resentment, eyeing her space. Braza could become a part of the powercore at will, but she was aware of every inch of the library and unable to rest. She had this stone platform with a bed and a couch formed of magic taking up most of the space, plus a chest where she kept who knew what.

It didn't seem like the kind of existence I'd be able to

endure, but Braza had preferred this to the uncertainty of death when her soul had been torn nearly in two. My brother was responsible, of course. She'd surrendered herself to power the library eternally as its custodian, maintaining everything as a stationary sentinel.

"How are you? Truly?" I asked.

She smiled and reached for me. I let her cool, electric touch drift down my cheek and the spiral of my horn, like she wanted to memorize every feature. I held my hands out and cupped her daintier clawed hands, letting her draw on my warmth.

"Lonely but well. The library has changed in your absence. Most of the mortal witches don't realize they can stop and chat at any time, and our kind have forgotten I exist."

"I will strive to change that," I promised.

"The new ones only know your name from a history book. We are not united anymore," she sighed.

"Do we need to be?" I asked gently. "If we have found our place here, I say that is better. The old ways brought us Myuna and her endless hunger for souls."

She lifted a shoulder. "I believe we all need a light to follow. Especially those who are shadowborn."

"Has anyone birthed a shadowborn since we came to Earth?" I asked, tilting my head curiously.

"Yes! It passes on in the family lines now. They're not nearly as powerful as the shadowborn from Soiluire, but the darkness is different here. Not as oppressive."

"It is," I agreed. Earth was far too bright, but beggars couldn't be choosers. "I have come to you with a heavy heart, Braza. I cannot be the returning prince you're hoping for. It seems that during our forced stasis together, my brother somehow infected me with his corruption."

"I see this," she said, leaning in to inspect my eyes. "I will give you raw power to resist. You cannot give in to the cravings to taste anyone's soul, else you are lost."

"Is there any hope for a cure?" I murmured.

She shook her head slowly, and my heart sank. "So, my days truly are numbered," I said, numb.

"I wouldn't say that! Those of our kind with similar afflictions have gone on to live fulfilling mortal lives with regular infusions of power. I am, after all, giving them parts of my extra-large soul." She squeezed my hands with a little laugh. "Don't go thinking you need to do anything drastic. Just stay in the library for now. Look, I saved something for you..."

She released me, and I rubbed my chilled fingers as I watched her unlatch the chest on the platform and rummage through it. What she handed to me were the perfect gift to lift my flagging spirits. Twin swords, perfectly maintained. Their sheaths were black, with ornate silver-colored filigree up the sides to match the oiled hilts. I drew one, admiring the pristine dimensional language etched into the metal.

The blades were edged in silver, a metal that wasn't native to Soiluire. It was deadly to me and anything else that originated from my home planet. They were the perfect unnatural-killing weapons, and I itched to plunge them both into my brother's husk to finally end the cycle of suffering he caused.

With Braza's help, I'd never follow in his footsteps and become a soul-craving monster.

I could court Cress without being constantly distracted by her bright soul. In time, I could trust myself to leave a mating mark on her without also consuming some of that light-filled aura she carried.

I resheathed the weapon and turned back to Braza. "Thank you. By the way, you are looking at Moongrove Library's newest assistant professor. I won't be far."

4

CRESS

After Lanie's passing, I'd asked to stay in my dorm room alone to give my familiars and me a peaceful haven. I'd never expected to have Geo out cold, sleeping off his injuries in the stripped bed while my three closest friends stuck around to offer moral support the next morning.

We ended up studying together. I sat cross-legged in my bed, cramming for midterms with an iced coffee in one hand, the other buried in Bella's fur. My tabby girl had tucked herself into a ball in my lap, purring idly. Milo, my other familiar, had stretched out next to Geo's sleeping form, acting like the stoic man's nurse again.

"I'm so going to fail," I bemoaned. After everything I'd been through lately, I'd completely forgotten to study for some of the most important tests of this semester.

"With that attitude," Áine commented. She had her hoofed legs stretched out on the floor between the beds, alternating between chirping to Jin in a fae language and doing her own studying. Jin seemed to like her, or maybe she was just coming back from losing Lanie. I had my friend's permission to make her my third familiar, but the small black cat wanted little to do with me.

Roe was at the desk closest to my bed, the two of us occasionally comparing notes over the class we had in common, Introduction to Witchcraft. While I was a true beginner, she'd already learned some of the details covered in the class from the special witch-exclusive private school she'd attended. She passed me some of the benefits as a patient tutor.

Meanwhile, my third friend, soft-spoken Willow Frost, sat at my usual desk. "Look at the bright side. At least you've learned some librarian witch magic ahead of schedule," she said. The brunette was always pointing this out, as her grasp on her oceanic witch magic was shaky at best. She'd wanted to help us fight the Hungering Darkness but had seen the wisdom of sitting it out until her control improved.

Bella pawed at my arm, looking up at me earnestly. She sent friendly warmth over our bond of witch and familiar. "Don't panic. You can do this," she squeaked. Where others heard her high-pitched meows, I understood her directly.

"You're right, ladies. It'll be okay," I said, meaning to return to my studies with those words.

That was when someone decided to knock on the door. Assuming it was one of the other witches rooming on this floor, I called, "It's not locked!"

The hinges creaked, and Ben poked his head in the room. I could practically feel the air shift as we all turned to look at him, cats included. "Oh, hi...everyone," he said, sounding like he'd rather just close the door and slink away.

I flushed hot and cold at the same time. "What do you want?" I asked.

"Shouldn't you be resting?" Roe added a breath later.

"I'm fine, mother hen," he said to her with a tight smile. "Look, Cress, can we talk?"

I could practically feel the disapproval rolling off the other ladies in the room with me. If Geo were awake rather than unmoving as a stone in his healing sleep, he'd probably toss Ben out himself.

But this was my decision, and I was unlikely to get another opportunity to get him on his own and answers out of his mouth. I gently nudged Bella off my lap and made to stand.

"Do you want me to come with you?" Roe asked in an undertone.

"We're just going to go out to the garden," I said, hitching my thumb over my shoulder.

"I'd feel much better about this if the *known assassin* would swear to me that he means you no harm," Áine interjected.

Ben's fingers dug into the cheap wood of the door where he held it open. "I swear I won't hurt her or let anyone else do so," he said.

"On your blood, honor, and true name?" she pressed.

"If I had anything sharp on my person—which I don't —I would pierce my thumb and swear it right now." He sounded honest enough.

I wanted to trust him and believe he'd come here without any bad intentions. "I'll be okay, Áine. He knows I'll never speak to him again if he dares to lie to me one more time," I said for everyone's benefit and to draw a flinch from him at my steely tone.

Her keen gaze inspected him for a moment before she nodded, and I left my friends to their studying as I joined Ben in the hall. I was aware of Bella following on my heels, a silent observer to how I gestured Ben toward the stairwell.

"I know I'm probably the last person you want to see right now." He stuck his hands in his pockets as we wound down the flights of stairs.

I didn't reply. It would be rude to agree, but I just didn't know what either of us could say to fix the chasm that'd opened up between us from the moment he'd held a knife to my throat.

"There are just a few things I need to tell you, and they can't wait," he continued in an urgent hush. "I'll be out of your life soon enough."

What was that supposed to mean? I slanted him a dubious look as we emerged into the afternoon sunshine. It was a calm autumn day, with a scattering of fluffy clouds flowing across the sky, accompanied by a gentle breeze that lifted a few locks of my purple hair sideways. Ben went straight to a bench within the small garden and sat with a groan. I settled on the bench's edge next to him, glancing up at my dorm window, where Roe's face was in the middle of disappearing from view.

"This isn't going to be easy for me to tell you, but I think you need to know," he said, drawing my attention back to him. He had a hand pressed to his right side, like he'd already aggravated the disc of dark magic that caused him so much pain.

"What is it?" I asked quietly.

"A politician...a man named..." He sucked in a sharp breath. "I guess I can't share his name."

"Can you call him by a nickname? Something like Bob?" I suggested.

His lips quirked into his usual sideways smirk. "Bob sought the master's services back when you were a baby.

Your parents...your real mother, was in his way politically."

"You know who my parents are?" I asked, sitting up a little straighter when he nodded. Some of my old friends had wondered if I'd ever sought out my "real" parents, not realizing I didn't care much past their names and the big question: why had they surrendered me?

I'd been raised by a good woman I considered my mother now, but that didn't prevent me from wondering about a few basic things I'd been too young to understand. Why hadn't I been wanted? Why had my—presumably witchy—parents let me get raised away from the supernatural world?

"Bob had them...ugh." He suddenly bent over with a pained wheeze. I muffled a gasp of surprise, reaching for him.

"Is this hurting you that badly? You don't have to tell me—"

"I do," he interrupted. "There isn't enough time." He pulled a paper towel from his pocket and dabbed at his nose as he straightened. It came away soaked in crimson.

I reached out and put my hand over his, feeling the heat rising from his side. That couldn't be pleasant, yet he was trying to endure it for my sake. The fact that it was active and harming him meant he was telling the truth, which meant my birth parents were...murdered, perhaps, at a politician's whims. It was the only thing that made sense, even if he couldn't say it aloud.

Ben's callused fingers entwined with mine, and he pulled me away from the overheated rune. I felt a jolt of awareness. Our anam cara marks had brushed, reminding me of the bond we shared. Two halves of a soul, destined to find and complete one another. I'd been drawn to Ben since the moment I'd met him, which made the twisted net of lies between us all the more painful.

I tugged my hand away from his. It didn't feel right to be holding hands like we used to, like nothing had changed. "You couldn't tell me anything before, could you?" I asked.

"Not without my blood rune ending my life," he murmured. "I'm sorry I kept so much from you. In the time I have left, I swear I'll make it up to you."

"What do you mean, the time you have left?" I asked. It seemed he was feeling some kind of time limit, as he'd mentioned it a few times now.

He sighed and ran a hand through his overlong hair. "My former master is an emotional vampire. He seems to enjoy feeding on fear and pain the most." He lifted the hem of his shirt again, pointing out a few lines rising from his blood rune. "Each of these is a deadline, a magical time limit for every mission I've been sent on. The black ones are successfully completed."

Ben's fingertip stopped right below a deadline that was as crimson as the center of his rune, stretching a couple inches long. "Only the master can declare a mission a success and stop an active deadline. Else it will reach the witch's heart and kill them."

I felt a chill creeping up my arms. "That's an active deadline, isn't it?" I breathed.

"It is. And there's no way he would ever stop it from killing me now that I have a taste of freedom," he muttered. "I have until Samhain."

"Ben—what?" I spluttered. There was no way he'd just calmly told me he was going to die in a couple weeks after also dropping the bomb about my birth parents. It felt like the world shifted a few inches on its axis, everything slanting in a new light. "What was the mission? If you complete it, won't the deadline stop on its own?"

He shook his head, pressing the paper towel back to his nose. "Never mind that. He has the tool to stop it."

"Well, we've got to get it from him!" I was ready to push from the bench and get started when he slanted me an incredulous look.

"In a couple weeks?"

"Where is it?"

Jaw clenched, he shook his head again.

With a sinking heart, I leaned back. Of course Ben couldn't say. His vampire "master" would keep his powerful magical tool out of easy reach, probably in the secret home Ben couldn't talk about.

"I don't think I can tell you much more today," he rasped.

I flashed a tentative smile. "Okay. You want to come inside and study with us? Midterms are about to destroy me."

His trepidation was unmistakable as he physically recoiled from the idea.

"It won't happen immediately, but you'll earn everyone's trust back faster if you don't hide from them," I said more gently.

"Maybe when Geo won't wake up and immediately try to make shish kabob of me. What about your trust, though?" His green gaze searched my face.

I found it easier to meet his eyes after this conversation. It was progress in the right direction, to see his pain and know he was a victim too. The evil vampire he kept referring to as his former master hadn't taken control of his mouth and lied for him, but it was obvious Ben had had to balance what he *could* say with what he felt for me as his anam cara.

"That will take time," I said honestly. While I empathized with him, I wasn't sure how close I could let him come to my heart anymore.

His gaze fell as he nodded with some reluctance.

"However, I want to make sure you have much more of it than just a couple weeks. Does Phaeron know?"

Ben paled some. "Why are you bringing him up?"

"Maybe a second scar over your blood rune will loosen the restrictions on you more," I suggested.

"You're probably right." His lips quirked. "I'll have to show you my new place sometime. Tall, dark, and terrifying has decided that he's going to look after me, so we're roommates."

Tall, dark, and terrifying? Well, if that was his new nickname for Phaeron, he wasn't quite wrong. "Then you'll have no problem telling him you need another scratch," I said.

"Maybe. I think you underestimate how painful his *scratches* are. But if it'll help me speak freely, I'll do it." He nodded, setting his jaw. I could feel the brush of heat from his blood rune from where I sat and flashed him a concerned look.

"I'd better go lie down." He lurched to his feet as he spoke, and I jumped up too, afraid he'd topple over from any stiff wind.

Ben reached for me, and I let him take my hand again. Those callused fingertips brushed against mine, and I felt a now familiar flutter lower in my belly. His little smile was less guarded, not like the mean smirk he wore like armor. This was the young man I'd fallen for, the Ben I'd daydreamed about, the one I'd taken to bed without hesitation.

Without the layers of pain and cruelty that'd formed the past he could still barely speak of, I recognized him, and I still liked the truth of him. If only he hadn't had to hide it under so much dishonesty and misdirection.

"Ben," I breathed.

He pressed a kiss to my forehead. I closed my eyes for a moment, flushing warm from the gentle brush of his lips. "See you soon, Cress."

5

CRESS

THE COZY STUDY group in my room kept going until late in the evening. My gargoyle guardian stirred in the afternoon, inhaling suddenly and cracking his joints like the quick snap of rocks tapping each other.

He startled the rest of us, but not Milo, who purred happily after Geo curled his stiff fingers and pet my cat's white belly. The ghost of a smile touched Geo's stoic features.

"How are you feeling, Geo?" I asked.

His quicksilver eyes tracked to my face. He still had the slow, uncanny movements that meant his gargoyle body was still in the process of healing from its trauma.

"I will make a full recovery," he replied. After a lengthy pause, he added, "I will be mended enough to return to my duty of protecting you tomorrow."

"Take your time," I encouraged. "You were banged up pretty bad."

A small crease appeared between his brows. "That does not mean I should laze in bed. I failed to kill that monster, and as soon as I am physically able, I will be seeking a means to improve."

"You and me both," I said. My three friends all nodded in agreement as well.

When Monday dawned, Geo was waiting in the garden in his gargoyle form, his stony arms crossed. His clothes had frozen to his form, taking on the same color of obsidian stone, with silvery veins lightly interspersed. A grand pair of carved bat wings was furled tightly to his back, and his chiseled expression was, shockingly, twisted with annoyance.

Ben was there next to him, leaning against his side as if the gargoyle were a real statue. The blood witch's smirk was mischievous. "Good morning, Cress," he said cheerfully.

"Good morning," I replied, gaze darting between them. "Are you bothering Geo?"

"We just had a chat, man to man. Well, man to stone," Ben said.

"He told me he is in need of my protection as well. I informed him of my primary directive, yet he has not left." Geo's voice in his gargoyle form was like the grinding of stone, deep and slow and a little abrasive.

I was worried to see him wearing his rocky form again, as he seemed to lose what little progress we'd made with him understanding and expressing his emotions each time he transformed. My biggest concern was that he would take his gargoyle form permanently and forsake the budding life he was forming for himself in the name of duty.

The problem was, *I* was his duty. I was his soul mate, according to Lanie's last letter, the duty that'd forced him from his rest and back into the real world. If he truly wished to embrace his duty, he had to figure out how to be a man instead of a statue.

I could see why he was confused. To a gargoyle, duty was protection. I was the safest witch with him never taking a break unless he was physically incapable of fulfilling the job. Which made things awkward for me with Ben right next to him to remind me that I had, essentially, two soul mates.

"Well, let's go, then," I said. I hoisted my backpack higher on my shoulders and set off for my classes. Ben walked by my side, with Geo just a few paces behind.

In the supernatural world, it wasn't unheard of for someone to have more than one partner. I was raised fully human, where the idea was more taboo, so it felt like a conversation and an unwelcome choice looming over my shoulder. I was feeling some contentment to return to normal with both of them here with me; I didn't want to ruin it by picking Geo's companionship over Ben's, as I would right now if forced to make a decision.

"So," Ben said, cutting into the silence that'd fallen between the three of us. "How do you feel about those midterms now?"

I breathed an uncertain chuckle. "It's just a couple of tests. How hard could they be?"

"Aw, don't jinx yourself there." He tisked. "Dr. Aurina wanted me to enroll as a student. If a registrar can find me, they can put me in real classes. Until then, I'm just going to Introduction to Witchcraft with you and hanging out with Geo or Phaeron."

I glanced over my shoulder at the gargoyle. Geo's expression had eased to a handsome carved mask with no emotion present. "Why?" I asked, raising a brow at Ben.

"Earlier"—he made a vague gesture—"I learned how to

fight anything, be it supernatural or unnatural. A blood witch can take advantage of nearly every situation and fight almost any being. But there are a few things we were taught to avoid at all costs."

He ticked off what he listed on his fingers. "Gargoyles, for one. No blood, just solid rock. For another, dimensionals with shadow magic. They *do* have blood, but if you don't get the jump on them, they turn incorporeal, and then your average blood witch is unlikely to survive what comes next."

I barely missed a beat this time, rather than puzzling over why he was mentioning fighting either man. "*Oh.* Others, uh, like you..." I said, stumbling over mentioning assassins when we were in the midst of heavy foot traffic in the heart of the NSU campus.

"Would be heavily discouraged by either of their presences," Ben finished for me. "More Geo than Phaeron, but only because he keeps his tall, dark, and terrifying act under wraps in public."

I smothered a little laugh. By the time we reached my first class of the day, Latin, Geo was transforming back to his fully human form. It was nearly seamless and gave him an opportunity to follow me into the classroom. I held out my phone to him but kept a grip of the other side when he moved to take it. "I know it's unusual, but would you mind staying behind to protect Ben?" I asked.

His scowl was quick to arrive. "My only duty is to you, not him."

I brushed my fingertips down Geo's arm. "I know. And it seems he likes to bother you," I said, slanting Ben a disapproving look when the blood witch began to grin. "It would, ah, make me happier to know that you would step in if any danger comes for him. And the least he can do in return is stop trying to get a rise out of you."

"That would be a requirement," Geo rumbled.

"I can promise I'll try?" Ben asked.

"Then I would *try* to protect you too," the gargoyle said.

Seeing that that was the best I'd get out of both of them today, I let Geo take the phone and unlock it with a twitch of his thumb. He went to sit on a nearby bench to get lost in one of his many Internet rabbit holes while I went to my Latin class to sweat through my first midterm.

Latin was one of my most difficult classes. I just didn't seem to get it, and my other friends didn't have to take this class to help with the practical aspects of casting their magic. Most of the people taking the midterm with me today were fellow librarians or celestial witches, who had the only affinity more complicated than librarian magic.

By the time I was finished, I wasn't sure if I'd done well or not. Usually, I chalked that feeling up to an inevitable failure, but I'd already learned a smattering of Latin words along the path to practicing librarian witch magic. Maybe my extra studies did me in good stead.

Ben and Geo went with me to Introduction to Witchcraft, but this time, they both came into the classroom with me. Geo stood in the back of the room to wait. I sat toward the end of our coven's row, with Ben leaning casually against the wall with his legs in a figure four. Seated in front of me today was the other oceanic witch in our coven, Heath Storm, a welcome change from the perfectly groomed blonde who usually claimed that spot. He nodded and murmured a good luck.

Wren Starsurge, said blonde, was up front today, putting a set of pens in just the right order on her desk in anticipation of today's midterm. I imagined she sat away from me, Willow, and Roe to avoid the distraction of coming up with some catty remark.

Most of my classes were having written tests in one long marathon, and this class was no exception. Heath seemed well-rested, and the back of Wren's head showed she'd had enough time to style it in soft waves.

I was sure I looked like a mess next to them. There were shadows under my eyes from my late-night cram session yesterday evening. I'd combed my hair and tied it back into a ponytail but otherwise ventured out of the dorm wearing no makeup and the last clean top at the back of my closet, the sky-blue turtleneck sweater Mom had insisted I take to NSU but I'd formerly sworn I'd never get caught dead in.

As I fiddled with its fraying cuff, I remembered that conversation as if it'd happened years ago. I'd tossed it on without a moment's thought this morning, more preoccupied with midterms, men, and monsters. And not necessarily in that order.

I fished out a single pen and set it down, breathing out a tense sigh. If I could push myself to learn my magic two years ahead of schedule, I could pass a few tests. I exchanged thumbs-up with Willow and pretended to fist bump Roe a couple seats up from me, then the whole room quieted as elderly Dr. Heartwood cleared her throat.

"Good morning, students. This test was designed to take you this whole class period to complete. Best of luck." She passed out thick packets whose contents looked like they were on their twelfth pass through the copier.

No one who knew me in high school would recognize the spirit that possessed me as I focused on this second test with everything I had. I'd always been a B student at best, knowing the limits of achievement that were required of me and coming in just a bit above average.

There'd never seemed to be much of a point, not when I spent my spare time working as a cashier at the fast-food place up the street. The only place I thought I'd go, at least in the short term, was to a full-time position there upon graduation. There was a purpose to the work, which was to take money home to support Mom and my younger sister, Carly.

My NSU coursework had purpose to me now, and for the first time, I wanted to be an A student. Key word: *wanted*. After the stress of cramming for this test and the others upcoming, I wouldn't get caught slacking on my studies again.

Which meant in the space between this test and the next, I needed to go see Dr. Voidbinder, if he was available. He'd agreed to wait in the library last Saturday, should I need a master librarian's assistance, and I'd left him hanging. I needed to apologize, explain, and ask to step up our training schedule even more.

If I wanted to truly tackle the joint problems of the Hungering Darkness and Ben's deadline, I needed to be a better witch yesterday. The practice of stretching out a curriculum and job path over the course of four years' worth of classes just wasn't going to cut it.

I turned in my midterm a little early and stood next to Geo to watch the muted video he played from my phone. It was one of those satisfying videos where an experienced soap maker cut finished bars of soap to reveal pretty patterns and details within. He made the occasional soft, impressed sound.

"What?" Geo whispered, realizing I'd stopped watching and was smiling up at him instead.

I lifted onto the tips of my toes to kiss his cheek, only confusing him more. "I'll be right back, okay?"

"Okay." He turned back to the screen and touched the spot where my lips had been. I smiled to myself as I slipped out of the classroom.

Hopefully, Dr. Voidbinder wasn't administering a test of his own, as I had a sliver of free time. My next class, Drawing for Fashion, didn't have a midterm, so I was going straight to Moongrove Library after this conversation to see what basic test of librarian knowledge I could ace in Library Science 101.

The door to Dr. Voidbinder's office was closed, but I heard muffled voices within. I lifted my knuckles, then hesitated. He was a director of sorts at Moongrove Library, as well as one of the professors who taught advanced librarian students who wanted to dedicate their life's work to their magical calling. Surely he didn't want me barging in on his meeting.

During my moment of indecision, someone else opened the door, and I took a step back in surprise when it was a tall dimensional on the other side of the threshold. "I thought I sensed you," Phaeron said, beckoning for me to step inside the room.

Dr. Voidbinder was seated behind his desk. I'd rarely seen the portly man red-faced and uncomfortable, but he was now. "Hello, Miss Cress. Speak of the devil, really. We were just discussing your training," he said.

"You were?" I asked in surprise. I eased myself in the second chair across from his desk, as Phaeron had already sat in the one closest to the door. It wasn't quite big enough for his tail, which draped over the armrest between us. I noticed the snap and flick of it, like the dimensional man was hiding some irritation under the polite smile he fixed on Dr. Voidbinder.

"I will be assuming your evening training," Phaeron

said. "In fact, with the piddling position the library has placed me in, I might as well take you aside during your librarian classes as well."

"Well, I'm only taking the one..."

Phaeron lifted a brow. "One?" he echoed in a low voice. Oh yeah, he was pissed.

Dr. Voidbinder cleared his throat nervously. "As I was telling you, Prince Sudair, most of our students aren't interested in becoming trained librarians after their time at NSU. Miss Cress, for example, is in the fashion design major."

Phaeron's yellow gaze followed the line of my body up and down, seeming unimpressed. "Did you design those garments you're wearing?"

I shifted, nearly as embarrassed as when the library's powercore had called my interest in fashion a "youthful endeavor." Then a flash of anger replaced it, and I set my teeth. "I've made plenty of clothes for my family when money was tight." And when wasn't it? Before I'd gotten a part-time job, sometimes ends just didn't quite meet. "While there's no need to be so judgmental, you should know that I was planning on changing my major at the end of this semester to take more magic-focused classes."

He dipped his chin in acknowledgment. "My apologies. The end of the semester is in how long?"

"Two months, plus a break for Christmas," I answered.

A fine line appeared between his dark brows. "Yule," Dr. Voidbinder supplied.

"Ah. Alas, we do not have the luxury of time."

"Can you promise you won't endanger her unnecessarily?" my professor asked. "Dr. Aurina won't keep you employed long if you involve any student further in your mission to capture your brother."

Employed? I turned to Phaeron for some answer.

There was a grim set to his lips. "I won't be the one to draw her into danger. However, Endaeron will return for her, and she must be prepared for the next encounter."

"All right. You can tell Aurina that yourself," Dr. Voidbinder replied.

"I will, from afar. If she uses her magic on me again, I doubt she'll enjoy the results." Phaeron scowled, tail lashing. He finally seemed to notice me waiting impatiently for them to stop talking about me while I was sitting right there with them. "After you left, I convinced Aurina to give me a job at the library and quarters for Ben and myself. I will begin earning the common currency shortly as an assistant professor."

"Dollars?" I ventured.

A flicker of shock passed over his expression. "Finally, something that hasn't changed in two centuries," he said dryly. "It turns out I'm an assistant to the basic librarian witch classes, and the course work is inexcusably slow. I will have you and your peers training on the sword shortly."

Dr. Voidbinder cleared his throat for attention. "Just a reminder, Prince Sudair, assistants still have to adhere to existing curriculums."

"I'm sure the proper curriculums exists in later classes," Phaeron said dismissively.

"If you don't, you run the risk of losing this job," he warned.

Phaeron bared his fangs in a dangerous smile, shadows flickering to life around his curved horns. "Let's see someone try to remove me from the library, then."

He got to his feet, signaling the end to the conversation, and offered me a hand up. I suppressed a swallow, but not because I saw him as tall, dark, and terrifying from that glimpse of what he could do.

It felt validating to know he had a poor reaction to perfect, airbrushed Dr. Aurina. Most men would salivate over a chance to see her again and let her magic wrap around them, but not Phaeron. As he looked down at me, his expression shifted, and he quirked his lips when he folded them back over his fangs.

I didn't like the idea of him and Aurina alone together in a room at all. Did that make me jealous? I had no claim on this man, just the stirring of warmth in my belly when he looked at me that way.

I took his hand up, following him out of the room. He rested the barest touch of his claws on the small of my back, standing closer than a professor probably should. A soft chuckle escaped his lips.

"What is it?" I asked.

"Geo looks like he wants to murder me," he remarked, motioning down the hall. "And Ben isn't sure if he'd help or run."

I looked up, startled to see the two men waiting for me at the juncture where the hall branched off to the elevators and the stairwell. Geo had frozen in place where he leaned against the wall, my phone forgotten in his broad palm as he leveled what could be labeled a death stare at my hip, where Phaeron had coyly slipped his hand. Ben was clearly noticing it as well, a line drawing between his brows.

Oh, hell no. I jerked away from him. "I'm not part of your male posturing," I muttered.

Only one of the library's silver swords could cut through the tension that threaded between the three of them in close proximity. Ben's charm hid behind a leery mask as he eyed the other two men, Geo could've pulverized my phone with one squeeze of his hand, and Phaeron smiled and relaxed against the stairwell railing in a self-assured way that said he thought he could win if this strained meeting boiled over into full conflict.

"I'm going to the library," I said, hitching a thumb over my shoulder.

"That's where I was headed as well," Phaeron said smoothly.

"Where you go, I go," Geo rumbled.

Ben shook his head slowly. "I guess we're all book enthusiasts here, because I'm coming too."

Books. Right. I was hyperaware of the reason these men had met at this junction, leering at each other like competition.

They all wanted a piece of me.

6

GEO

Cress had taught me that emotions didn't always have to be acted on. All people on the face of this planet would be criminals if they succumbed to every whim when they had one.

However, if I was accused of criminal behavior by finally getting two particularly untrustworthy individuals out of her life, I would just say I was doing my duty.

I hadn't forgotten how Phaeron had attacked me in the dark of night after I'd refused to allow him to speak to my honored witch, whose soul powered the stone heart which gave me life.

I also recalled vividly the moment Ben had drawn twin daggers concealed on his person and held the edge of one to Cress's throat.

They wanted to cozy up to her now? Well, they would have to get through me first. She was my duty; her protection my number one goal. My human skin tingled with the urge to turn back to unfeeling stone, better to fight them with.

The only thing that stopped me as we walked together to Moongrove Library was that I had a task of my own to complete. I wanted it to be done with utmost secrecy, so I spoke no word of it until Cress was comfortably seated in her classroom and focusing on the paper before her. I was in my customary position at the back of the room, such a fixture now that the other witches either greeted me with casual hellos or ignored me completely.

Phaeron had disappeared into a curl of smoke, going who knew where within the bounds of the library, while Ben apparently went off to nap in one of the overnight stay rooms. Now was my chance to query around the library for what I sought.

I started with the man who taught Cress's class, Lars Eriksson. He was a guest professor from another library in Sweden, but perhaps he could help me all the same. I didn't break the silence of the room, instead sliding him Cress's phone with my request typed in a quickly created note.

Where is the gargoyle keeper in Moongrove Library? I am seeking tempering.

Eriksson blinked up at me owlishly from where he sat on a stool at the front of the room. "I'm not sure what that is," he whispered.

Another emotion pressed up against my headspace. Frustration, I identified. A close companion of late.

He stood and stepped partway out of the classroom, flagging down a different adult librarian witch to watch the class, before he motioned for me to join him outside. "You see, new gargoyles haven't been created in some time," he continued at a normal volume. "You are one of the last."

"A status I am aware of," I replied.

"So, anything like a person dedicated to the upkeep of

gargoyles would be assigned elsewhere. What is tempering?"

This man had presented himself as a master librarian to the students, yet here he was, asking me a basic question. Either he was as much a useless flirt as he seemed, or knowledge of the upkeep of gargoyles had disappeared with the practice of making my kind.

"Magic tempering," I gritted. "My defensive capabilities are not where they need to be, so I need a gargoyle keeper or equivalent to strengthen my stone."

His eyebrows drifted to his hairline. "Aren't you an obsidian gargoyle? I thought you were already created to be above and beyond a common granite model."

"My current abilities are not sufficient," I answered firmly. The multiple gashes I'd had to heal in my flesh form were testament. If I'd been able to drag myself to the library while damaged, he wouldn't be looking at me like I was malfunctioning.

It was still common enough knowledge that I had a special soul within me. Morgana Voidbinder was her name, a librarian witch demigoddess who'd unfortunately been Phaeron's last mate as well as the woman to imprison him in stasis for two centuries. To honor her memory, I'd been fashioned to be unique, made of obsidian rather than granite, with quartz accents. I was the Quartz Gargoyle, one of a kind.

That didn't make me resistant enough to fight the likes of Phaeron or the Hungering Darkness. I could not successfully fulfill my duty to Cress if either were able to disable me with their shadowy talons.

"I will talk to the head librarian. Perhaps he can get you the help you need," he finally said. Frustration tumbled through me again, sure he was talking about Dr. Voidbinder. I could've just spoken with him when Cress had and chased off Phaeron before he'd had a chance to put his claws around her hip like he was staking some kind of claim.

"Very well. I need this done as quickly as possible. I appreciate your haste and discretion in the matter," I rumbled.

"Yes, good," he sputtered, caught off guard.

We returned to our posts in the classroom, and I waited with a neutral expression for Cress to finish her test. When she did, she turned to the side and met my gaze. "We need to talk," she whispered.

Were I a human with good sense, I'd dread those words. Instead, I simply nodded in agreement and waited with the patience of stone for her to turn in her test and gather up her things, stuffing them back into the backpack she swung onto her shoulders.

She didn't take me far, scoping out the other classrooms on this floor until she found an empty one in the corner. She closed the door behind us and settled onto the stool up front while I stood, as I was most comfortable doing.

"Hey, so, we had an awkward moment back there," she said.

Awkward: an uncomfortable or embarrassed feeling accompanied by a sense of not knowing what to do next.

Oh. I knew exactly what she was talking about. Awkward for her, perhaps, but I'd known exactly what I should've done in that situation.

"I am not sure why you allow either Ben or Phaeron so close to you," I commented, crossing my arms.

She blew out a sigh and let down her hair from its loose tail, combing her fingers through the violet mass in agitation. "There's something I'm coming to terms with still," she said.

I waited for her to elaborate, and for a moment, she seemed to pause, like she expected me to ask what it was on the tip of her tongue. But I was patient with her, as always.

"It seems, in the supernatural world, there's a way to have more than one perfect match. I feel a draw to Ben because we are anam cara, soul friends. A cupid's feather gave us these markings." She held out a palm to me, showing a maroon-colored symbol.

My breath caught. Something hot simmered in my core, like my stone heart beginning to overheat. "He is no friend to you. I saw him attack you. I witnessed him lie," I gritted out.

"You're right, and I'm not about to offer him easy forgiveness. But there's more to the situation than we know," she said, putting both palms up and lowering her voice to a tone intended to soothe.

"And how do you know that is not another one of his lies?" I asked heatedly, furious that she would entertain any more heartbreak with him.

"I mean, I've seen his blood rune. Haven't you? Someone cruel tattooed him with a rune to cause him pain and control him. I think he deserves more of a chance than he's gotten."

Wetness gathered in the corner of her eyes. I reached out, carefully wiping away a droplet before it could form a trail down her face. I cupped her cheek, forcing her to meet my gaze. "You truly care for this...boy," I said with distaste.

"I do. I can't help it any more than you can help how protective you feel over me."

"That is hardly equivalent," I rumbled. My hand moved

to the soft hair hanging partway over her face. I ran its silk over my fingers before tucking it behind her ear.

"Geo," she breathed. "It *is* the same thing. You're confusing your budding feelings for your duty."

"That's not possible. Duty is infallible," I said.

"And feelings are everything but that."

She stood and placed her hands just under the line of my collarbone. I stilled as she brushed a path of sensation down my skin. It didn't matter that I was wearing the cloth barrier of a shirt; I felt everything as keenly as if she stroked me directly. I tingled now just as I had all over in the wake of her unexpected kiss earlier.

"What do you feel right now, Geo?" she asked, the light in her brown eyes intense.

You, I wanted to answer. But she was asking about within, where her touch had turned my emotions into a tangled bundle of sparking nerves.

"I am unsure," I answered.

"Protective?"

"Yes."

"Anything else?" She pressed closer to me.

I rumbled wordlessly. There wasn't any way for me to describe what welled up within me and drew trembles through my body. I decided to show her with a gentle tug on her hair, pulling her head back so I could claim her lips.

Her hot breath mingled with mine in a soft gasp. Yes, this was right. Her smaller body fit perfectly into the line of mine when I looped my arm around her hips, tugging her against me. I'd never felt such a way before. My stone form would be incapable of feeling pleasure, let alone the softness of a woman pressed against me.

What did I truly feel? I'd been made for protection, her protection, but it was obvious she was my perfect match.

She was…"Mine," I practically growled when we came up for breath. "You are *mine*. And I was made to be yours."

Her kiss-swollen lips parted with something akin to surprise. "That is how I feel," I said earnestly. I had never lied to her, and I wouldn't be starting now.

"Geo—"

She began to speak in that tone that I knew would only upset me. I caught the words with a finger over her mouth. "No. Not right now. I know you're going to say you feel for Ben too. Maybe even Phaeron. But right now, it is only you and me."

"Okay. You know what, that's perfectly fine. This conversation is so much better."

I wanted to point out that we'd hardly conversed when she drew her pink tongue across the pad of my finger.

Right, she wasn't speaking literally. I liked where this conversation was going as well when she drew the digit into her mouth and slanted her eyes in a way that had my enchanted oil pooling lower in my belly on a rush of heat. My cock stirred.

In a century of service to the library, I'd heard plenty of jokes about how my kind must always be hard. But in my two hundred years of existence, I'd seen little use for my member. Its needs got directly in the way of my appointed duties. With it now pointing straight at the duty I'd come back to life for, I finally understood the humor.

Until she curled her fingers around its shape through my pants. She looked down between us, her smile eager. How she made me feel was anything but funny, and I came to full, pulsing life from the touch of her hand.

Of course, that was when the door to this classroom opened. "There you are, Cress—" the most unwelcome man interrupted as we both froze. She ducked backward to take my finger from her mouth, her cheeks stained brightly.

At least I had my back to Phaeron to disguise the wrath that crossed my face and stiffened my shoulders.

"I'll give you two a moment," he said, quickly shutting the door again.

I cupped Cress's face with both hands, asking seriously, "Are you certain I cannot kill him?"

7

CRESS

"Ben is awake after his ordeal and wants to speak with you," Phaeron told me once Geo calmed down a fraction. I felt like I was on the back foot. What ordeal? He read my expression and immediately explained. "He mentioned your idea of scarring more of his blood rune, and we took the opportunity to do it."

"Oh, did it work?" I asked. I cringed at the amount of pain it'd had to be to knock Ben unconscious.

"We're about to find out together." His tail lashed behind him as he turned, beckoning for Geo and me to follow.

Geo took his customary position a few paces behind us, and Phaeron walked just slightly ahead of me, slanting a look in my direction.

"Don't say it," I said tightly, recognizing the same expression he'd had when he'd witnessed me walking Ben out of my dorm one evening. One that spoke the words silently: *really, him?*

"It's not my place to voice an opinion," he said. His

usually smooth cadence was stiff with a reaction he was trying to hide.

I couldn't help a bit of whiplash. My lips were still tender from the way Geo had kissed me, like he'd bottled up every ounce of his passion to unleash it all at once. I was a little wet between the thighs at how incredible it'd been to finally break through to him that we might be something more.

Yet I had the sinking feeling I'd made some kind of mistake. Where were my relationships truly going? Though I hadn't quite forgiven Ben, I'd still slept with him before learning who he really was...something I'd just considered doing with Geo too, had we not been interrupted. Thank goodness we were before I could make a mistake that put everyone off.

We needed to have a conversation—Ben, Geo, Phaeron, and I—once I figured out what I wanted, and I'd better do that fast, before I might be forced to choose only one of them.

Geo was strong and steady, a comforting presence that was sometimes too protective. I worried he'd try to chase Ben away or come to blows with Phaeron. As much time and effort he put into keeping me safe, I had to admit that he was possessive, and our moment alone was only likely to make him more so.

And here Phaeron was, obviously hiding his own hurt feelings.

I'm new to this. I've barely held a relationship with one man before, I wanted to tell him.

The fact the three of them were all interested at the same time was the kind of new, uncharted waters that had me worried I'd pilot all of our budding relationships into a capsizing storm. The last thing I wanted to do was lead anyone on.

The tension was thick in the air as Phaeron guided us to floor negative three and to a hallway lined with small rooms. Within one was a shirtless Ben, who had a towel pressed to his side. My gaze traced the lean muscles of his torso, snagging on the series of dark lines that crossed from his blood rune toward his heart. One of the deadlines was dangerously close to it, but it was a fading black, like a real tattoo that'd been on his skin for years.

"Hey, all of you," he muttered. "Did you really have to bring Geology?"

"Geo," the gargoyle corrected in an irritated rumble.

"Yeah, that's what I said."

"No, you keep using these ridiculous nicknames. I tire of your impertinence," Geo said through gritted teeth. His earlier frustration hadn't cooled much.

"Gentlemen," I put in before a smirking Ben could make this worse, "we can't all be in the same room if you're constantly at each other's throats."

Ben worked his jaw, saying a clipped apology to Geo, who crossed his arms at his post by the door. He lifted the towel from his blood rune, letting us get a good look at what Phaeron had done.

I'd thought a second cut across it lengthwise would be ideal, but the dimensional man had taken it a step further. The outer ring of the rune, which was made of spikey, unreadable characters, was now ruined by several smaller incisions that cut through each one. "Garroway's blood runes attach to the nerves," Ben explained. "So, it's safe to say this hurt like fuck, but I think I'm really free this time."

"It's a shame it can't be removed from you completely," Phaeron said.

Ben traced the one crimson deadline still branching from the ruined circle; it was noticeably longer than the last time he'd shown it to me. "I'm going to put what time I have left to good use," he murmured. "Cress, do you still have your phone?"

Geo wordlessly withdrew it from his pocket and handed it to me. I checked the screen, eyebrow raising when I read a message already on the screen. I dismissed it with a flick of my thumb and made a mental note to ask Geo about it later. "You don't have yours?"

Ben shook his head. "Bugged. I ditched it."

I turned to Phaeron. "The first thing you're doing with your money is buying a phone so I can reach at least one of you."

He pointed to one of his wrists. "You can always reach me, bright soul."

I held my forehead. That wasn't what I meant, but I bet Phaeron was just as tech illiterate as Geo had been before he realized how entertaining the Internet could be. If anyone needed their own device, it was the gargoyle.

"Anyway, I was hoping you'd record what I have to say. There's no telling whether Garroway can feel that he's lost control of me completely or if he's positioned an assassin right outside to kill me before I can talk to Dr. Aurina," Ben said.

"Has she been demanding information?" I asked.

Phaeron answered for him. "She has requested to see him again, yes. Keep in mind that she is still one of our allies. If this blood baron operates how I suspect, her emotional magic could disable all of his assassins by over-loading their senses with pain and fear. Plus, she has the power to give us more fighters than us three." His hand gesture encompassed himself, Geo, and Ben.

"And me," I protested.

"I'll be damned if you get anywhere *near* Garroway," Ben said viciously.

"Or close to the assassin that carries my brother," Phaeron added.

I glanced toward Geo for some backup, but he had cracked a smile. "Finally, something we all agree on," he rumbled.

Wow. While I liked the moment of harmony, it was unfair they were probably right. A smart Cress would sit out a fight in the heart of a nest of trained assassins, plus whatever this Garroway vampire could do. Lump in the Hungering Darkness, and that was a battle meant for professionals.

"When were we starting training again?" I asked Phaeron.

His pupils narrowed to suspicious, cat-like slits. "This evening."

I started fiddling with my phone, pulling up the camera and getting Ben in frame. This wasn't his most flattering moment, and the camera seemed to fixate on his extra-pale skin and the shadows forming under his eyes. "All right. Let's start the recording, then," I suggested.

He nodded, and I hit the little red button. His green gaze lifted to meet mine, and he seemed to be talking to me alone. "I'll start from the beginning, even though I only just learned the extent of what Garroway did to my brother and me a few days ago," he began.

He told me the story of his mother, Marie Evenstar, a woman pushed toward financial ruin after losing her business partner and husband in two separate tragedies. She'd come to Garroway for a significant loan, which Ben theorized to be in the realm of five million dollars, as that number had been thrown at him several times over the years.

Instead of loaning her the money, Garroway had sent his assassins for her in the dead of night. He'd had Ben and Lucas stolen after framing their deaths so no authorities would come looking for them. I suppressed a gasp and looked toward the ceiling, trying not to cry. If Ben was starting this way, I had the feeling the rest of his story would be so much worse.

"Yeah. I don't know the stories of the other assassins, but Garroway is a creature of opportunity. His network of blood witches likely started as a bunch of orphans and unwanted kids with witch families. He forces all of us to take the blood affinity, but as you may have noticed, my parents were celestial witches, and I've gotten the feeling I've never been a particularly *skilled* blood witch. Just well trained."

He sighed, drawing a hand through his hair. Despite his freedom from the restrictions of the blood rune, the pain from his wounds seemed to be slowing him down all the same.

"We could do multiple takes," I suggested. Despite myself, I just wanted to hold him and soothe away some of his hurt.

He shook his head slowly. "No, I can do this. I want there to be a record of everything I know."

Ben explained the experience of growing up under Garroway's control to me and the camera. I snuck a glance at the other two men, who were listening just as intently as me. A muscle ticked in Phaeron's jaw, and his clawed fingers flexed. He looked ready to plunge into the past and save Ben and his little brother from the bloody, grueling training regiments they were forced into as boys.

Next to him, Geo still had his arms folded, but he'd resumed a patient, stony mask that showed no reaction to Ben's words. I was still glad he was here listening.

It sounded like Garroway took advantage of a blood witch's ability to heal to an obscene degree. He shattered bones for punishments or activated the Agonia rune on a whim to sear one of his witches from the inside out. Haunted shadows crossed over Ben's eyes as he described Garroway's favorite game, which was asking another witch what their peer's punishment should be.

"If it was bloodier and more gruesome than what he had in mind, he would make that their punishment. But if it wasn't as bad as he wanted to hear, he'd suggest things like making them eat their own pinky toes or whipping them until their backs resembled raw meat. 'Why does it matter? It all grows back anyway.'" He took on a slow, flat cadence as he mimicked his former vampire master.

"Disgusting," I muttered.

"Yeah...let's see how far we can push this. The clients that I can remember Garroway working with..." He started listing names. His breath hitched after the first few, and he clutched his side with the towel while continuing the litany in a rasping voice until it seemed he couldn't take it anymore. "It seems the blood rune still has some fail-safes to keep me quiet. That list isn't everyone, but it's a good start to unraveling the network of clients and informants.

"I want to talk about one man in particular, Blaize Star-surge. He's a politician appointed to the Crown Coven, the ruling body of witchkind." I had a sinking feeling from how he looked up into my eyes with a sympathetic little twist of his lips. "As I understand it, his closest competitor for his spot in the coven was a woman named Eris Darkmore, a fellow celestial witch who had the edge on him in every poll."

I forced a swallow, my throat suddenly dry. "Any relation to Wren?" I asked.

"Her father. I sincerely doubt he's told her any of this," he said. "Because to win his seat, he went to Garroway and paid to have his best assassin set up a murder of the whole Darkmore family. As I've told you, the only wiggle room we have to any of Garroway's orders is his wording. He instructed this assassin to 'take care of' the Darkmore family, so he did.

"What said assassin told me was that he hid the murder of Eris, her husband, and her sister by setting up an electrical fire in the house. But Eris had a daughter, a newborn, and he couldn't bring himself to kill her too. So, he took care of her by surrendering her to the local hospital, thinking she'd never reappear."

"Which hospital?" I asked from numb lips.

"Probably the one you were adopted from. Because recently, Starsurge reappeared in Garroway's manor all pissed off because, in his paranoia, a witch orphan had appeared, and he'd gotten an augury reading that she was *the* Luna Darkmore, sole heir remaining to claim the Darkmore hereditary power. He was so sure that was you, Cress, that he paid someone to sabotage your affinity test so you wouldn't pick the celestial affinity."

"Oh, shit," I said quietly. I swayed on my feet, my mind flashing back months in the past. The machine had seemed to malfunction, flashing the celestial symbol for a split second before lighting the one for a librarian witch instead. I'd second-guessed the decision, wondering if I should get tested again. But in the end, I'd decided that being a librarian fit my nature better.

Strong arms caught me before I could fall. Phaeron's topaz eyes glittered as he inspected me anew. "That explains it," he murmured.

"Explains what? That my parents—my whole birth family—were murdered?" I asked, voice gaining strength as the reality sank in. "That Wren's fucking *father* paid to have it happen? No wonder she was filming me when I was getting affinity tested! Her father put her up to it to make sure I picked the wrong thing."

"Peace, Cress. I mean the power lurking within you." Phaeron stroked my arm in soothing circles.

"My so-called bright soul?" I demanded.

He smiled slowly. "Indeed. I have noticed you've picked up and excelled at two of the basic librarian spells that utilize light, Lux and Luminaire. You may have bound yourself to the 'wrong' affinity for your bloodline, but it will lead you to being a bright spot in a dark world." The slow brush of his broad palm was starting to calm me down, just for my heart to leap as his gaze shaded with white. "*Beautiful*," he hissed.

His hand tightened around my arm, and he licked his fangs. He drew me closer, inhaling in the space over my crown with a low growl. "Uh, Phaeron," I said uncertainly.

I'd seen white fire in his eyes before, right before he'd started to claw at his face and disappear into a column of smoke. I slapped the mark of protection he'd left on my wrist and repeated his name, my fingers trembling all the while.

Phaeron jerked with his mouth open and shook his head. In a blink, he seemed back to himself.

Geo shifted closer, eyeing the dimensional man with suspicion, while Ben was saying, "I suppose now I better try to tell you where Garroway's manor is."

"Hmm, yes. That would be Aurina's first question." Phaeron sounded distracted. He stepped away from me, rubbing his forehead.

"It's…" Ben froze with his mouth open. "It's…"

He bent at the waist with a groan. "Another thing you still can't share?" I closed the distance between us and ended the recording when he nodded. Tossing my phone aside, I eased onto the bed next to Ben.

Meanwhile, Phaeron said something to Geo, and the two of them descended into the hushed tones of an argument.

Ben and I watched them. At some point, he slipped his hand into mine, and I gave our twined fingers a squeeze. "They'll be all right for a moment," I said.

"Yeah. It's…probably fine," he agreed. It felt like he'd caught my gaze in his, and after hearing his story, I couldn't keep pushing him away.

This man had gone through so much suffering and yet came out on the other end sane and still looking after the well-being of his brother and me. Garroway's evil had taken both of our families, yet somehow, it'd brought us together. I yearned to have Ben alone when he was recovered from his wounds, away from Phaeron and Geo and their drama.

My gaze dipped to Ben's lopsided smile. I pressed a little kiss to the slant of his lips. "I forgive you for a few lies to hide all this," I whispered in his ear before squealing when he banded an arm around my middle and hugged me to his side. I returned the gesture, careful of touching his wounded side.

"No more lies, babe. I promise," he said fiercely.

He cupped my cheek, drawing me into a longer, sweeter brush of our mouths. I got lost in it until I realized Geo and Phaeron's argument had lapsed to silence. Reluctantly lifting my head, I noticed Geo was leaving the room. Phaeron hadn't moved but began to blur at the edges, turning into wisps of black shadow. "When you're ready to train, Cress, find me by the library's powercore."

"Great, bye," Ben muttered and tugged me into another kiss. He didn't have much in him past a good make-out session and ended up falling asleep holding me to his chest. I lay there for a while, just thinking. I was feeling a little too hollow to rest with him, not after everything he'd told us. I ended up seeking out Phaeron after a few hours for the promised training.

8

PHAERON

I spent hours meditating at the base of Braza's power, communing with her to wash away the hunger still gnawing deep in my gut. I'd lost myself in less than an instant as I'd admired Cress's beautiful soul, full of the light of her celestial witch heritage.

As I'd looked into the depths of her light, my brother's voice had crept out to whisper in my ear. *"Just one bite wouldn't hurt her. Let yourself go."*

He was the trigger to my blackouts, but there was no way he was in the library. Braza had no sense that he'd passed anywhere near her territory. We were linked some other way, my monster of an undead brother and I, and the speed in which he'd tapped the kernel of corruption in me and compelled it to take control shook me to my core.

Then she'd called me back to myself. That could only mean one thing. Mix it up in the soup of jealousy that boiled within me at the glimpse of her intimacy with the other two men, and I had an explanation for my behavior that I couldn't ignore. My fixation on her soul was no accident. She was my True Light, and I, her Shadow.

To my people, those with the shadowborn blessing were considered powerful but incomplete. As beings born to protect others by being the biggest, baddest thing lurking in the night, we always sought the light for balance. A beacon in the darkness to return to, to defend, cherish, and pleasure. Only a mate can call a shadowborn back from the urges of their bestial side, as she effectively had twice.

On the heels of this revelation, I caught the sound of her footsteps before she cleared her throat and murmured my name for attention. I opened my eyes and stood, keeping my tail wound around my legs to show I meant no harm in the way of my people.

There she stood, haloed in the radiance of her own soul. She had no idea how beautiful she was with warm golden energy always washing her skin to my sight alone. How could I ever question my draw to her?

"Well, here I am. Ready to train," she said, stopping several yards away.

I could pinpoint several signs of stress and anxiety just from her expression and posture. *If I confess the truth to her now, she'll push me away.* But I still wanted to comfort her a lot more than I wanted to put a sword in her hand. Training could wait one more day.

She scuffed her foot. "Could I ask you a question?"

"Always."

"Isn't white fire a sign of corruption from your planet?"

I stilled. There was no hiding that I'd flashed my darkest secret in a moment of weakness earlier. "You saw it in my eyes."

She nodded and shifted back a step, angling herself so she could bolt if she needed to.

"I do not fully understand it," I said slowly. "But I am resisting a seed of hunger I must've picked up while locked in stasis with my brother." Her expression shuttered, and I breathed a sigh. "This isn't an either-or situation yet. I have the possibility of corruption if my willpower is weaker than my hunger for the taste of something I've never tried to consume."

She wet her lips. "So, you aren't corrupted."

"No. Not in the way that is a menace like my brother. I didn't bow to Myuna at the height of her strength, and I don't intend to bend to the temptation of her evil now." Slowly, I unwound my tail and approached her cautiously. "Some souls are more tempting than others. For the longest time, I've wondered why yours was so appealing."

She stiffened. "Its brightness?"

"Sure. If you could see the average librarian's soul, you would know it's full of the darkness of Soiluire. That's what I truly taught the first librarian witches—how to use the magical energy of dimensionals. What comes naturally to me." I manipulated a coil of shadows to dance around my arm. "Moongrove Library is built from the bottom up with the essence of my people. With our shadows. And yet, here you stand, one of us."

I held up a palm full of darkness toward her, and the tendrils of smoke naturally curled away from the light coming off her soul. She watched the effect with her mouth dropping into a surprised O.

"I'm a mistake," she murmured. "I don't belong here."

"No. You are needed, like the night sky needs its stars." I closed my fist, absorbing my shadows back into my skin. "There are more comfortable places to have this conversation. Besides, you are unprepared to begin practicing with me."

She scoffed. "What do you mean? I have my practice sword right here." She patted the battered hilt at her side.

"Yet where are your familiars? And your handbook? If you were assigned one," I pointed out.

"They're cats, Phaeron. They don't fight. And I do have one, but it's...special."

I shook my head. "Come, let us retrieve them all, and we can talk along the way. Can't believe what they're not teaching young librarians."

"Sure, I guess," she said with her brow drawn in confusion.

When we were in the elevator heading back to the surface level, she turned to me with an expectant look. "So, I shouldn't be worried if I see your eyes flash a different color?"

I considered how to answer without giving her a falsehood. "You seem to ground me, bright soul. Perhaps to the point where I should have you close when I next fight my brother." She could call me back again if he tried to send me away at a crucial moment.

She seemed hopeful, like I would invite her along to the dangerous battle that would follow when Ben finally admitted the location of Garroway's hiding place. It was likely Endaeron would be there, too. Before I'd consider that, though, she would need to relearn almost everything she'd already been taught about her magic. A daunting task.

"If I come along, my friends will want to as well," she said.

"The two young women who were there when Endaeron revealed himself?"

Cress had a genuine smile as she nodded. I'd barely glanced at their souls, but I'd been struck by how young and inexperienced they'd been to even consider fighting a monster of my brother's caliber.

"Then they will train alongside you," I said. She perked up further. That sunny expression would be my undoing, and she had no idea I'd do most anything to see it more often. "Where is Geo, by the way?" He would be the only one, I thought, who'd immediately try to thwart this idea.

"He's in stone form right now, waiting for Ben to wake up. He thinks I'm training with you in the library. I had to beg him not to follow me so he could pick another fight with you," she said.

"Good," I muttered. Finally, some uninterrupted time alone with her.

"Do you want to meet my friends tomorrow? We'd better start right away," she asked.

"Sure."

She pointed out a large building called the Witch Club-house once we entered the witchy side of the NSU campus. The women she trusted most were half of her coven.

"What of the other witches in your coven?" I asked.

"One's just a bitch." She affected a shrug but gritted her teeth hard. "Her father was the one Ben was talking about..."

I eyed her soul again, letting it dazzle my sight. I didn't doubt that the celestial affinity ran heavily through her family line. "Have you felt any of your hereditary power come in yet?"

"Uh, no. We covered the possibility of it happening in one of my classes, but I haven't had any dreams or anything."

"I know of a way to encourage the process," I told her.

"Oh?"

I nodded. "On Samhain, the night when the barrier between worlds is the thinnest."

Cress stopped abruptly, looking up at me with her lips

parted. The overbearing sun was setting, and at that moment, like everything around us, she cast no shadow. My instincts told me *I* was her Shadow and that I could earn her attention with a few flexes of my otherworldly power. "I can help you commune with the souls of the dead on that day only."

"Really?" she burst out. "Like, any soul?"

"Within reason."

Cress bit her lower lip. "What is 'within reason' for something like that?"

I waved my hand vaguely. "On Soiluire, such a thing wasn't possible at all. I've only done it a couple of times with the recently deceased. It was an excellent way to give my old friends some closure."

"Yeah." Her eyes moistened, and she cast her gaze away in a quick jerk. She started walking again. "You're thinking of drawing my potential birth mother back and seeing if that makes me start to inherit my family line's excess magic?"

I caught her wrist gently, tugging her back. "Cress, listen. I could see about calling back a different person, if you wanted."

Her shoulders hitched, and she sniffed. "Y-yeah. I'd...I would really love to see Lanie again."

I took a moment to brush back her hair and gently wipe her cheeks dry. That she didn't flinch away from my touch emboldened me to pull her into a quick hug. She clutched the front of my shirt and closed her eyes with a ragged sigh.

I remembered Lanie. More specifically, closing her eyes for the final time after my brother murdered her. *What do you mean, she's dead?* Cress had cried, catching me leaning over her friend. The echo of her sudden anguish resonated within me now. I had to give her the chance to say goodbye properly on Samhain.

"It has been a trying day," I said gently when we parted. "Let's begin your training tomorrow. I don't want you distracted with all the emotions of today rolling around in your mind."

"All right. But at least tell me why you need my cats to come along too," she said.

At some point, we began moving again, and I explained as we approached her dorm. "They are magically bound to you as your familiars. During day-to-day activities in the library, they are your scouts for danger. Most dimensional creatures don't recognize small animals like cats as threats to attack, and their souls are so tiny that they are not in danger of being noticed by corrupted unnaturals. In a fight, you can borrow an ounce of feline grace and their superior senses. The more you practice, the longer that moment lasts."

"Oh, I had no idea. I've been treating them like pets I can talk to," she said.

"It's a shame you weren't told, because most witches seem to see their familiars that way in this day and age. The fact that you have two cats is good. You'll have different bonds with each, but you can explore that over time."

"Three, maybe." She paused to get us into the building and took me up a few flights of stairs before letting me into her room. The perfumes of several women lingered in the air, as well as the earthier scent of Geo's enchanted oil. He must've laid across the other bed, as there were two in this cramped space.

Her brown tabby cat jumped atop the bed with a friendly chirp, tail straight up. I smiled and scooped her into a purring snuggle.

"That's Bella," Cress said. She had her chubby black and white cat in her arms and put him on the comforter next. "And this is Milo. Somewhere in here is...ah! That's Jin." A small, pure-black cat joined the other two and accepted a couple pets from Cress before edging away from her.

While I was distracted by her cats, she tapped on the screen of a device I'd learned to be a laptop. Technology had run laps around me during my forced stasis, but I had bigger problems than trying to learn how to use it.

"No emails. That's good." She closed the laptop and lifted the book resting next to it.

I put Bella down and took it, sensing the power within the handbook immediately. "Ah, an original. You said you bought such a venerated handbook?" I asked, inspecting it.

It was definitely from the first batch of books made by Morgana, animated by a minor dimensional creature called a wispfly. I gave the wispfly within this one a jolt of power and watched its front and back cover crack open and close on their own.

"What's happening?" she asked, staring as it tentatively flapped, hovering midair.

"Hooooo boy," the wispfly said, flying the book into a curlicue. It had a squeaky voice, like a toy, emanating from the pages. "No one's trusted me with a lil' pip of magic like that in decades!"

"Why is *The Librarian Witch's Handbook* talking and flying around?" Cress asked in an insistent whisper.

"Cressie-poo!" it exclaimed. "I can flap my pages like you flap your fleshy lips! Isn't that great?"

"I told you not to call me that," she said, her cheeks starting to heat.

"C'mon! We're friends, right?" It perched its spine on her shoulder like an odd bird.

I stroked my chin, watching it go with a grin. "You didn't tell me you claimed a malfunctioning handbook."

"I'll show you malfunctioning, you—wait, Cress, who is that?" the book asked.

"Phaeron."

"Eek!" It clapped itself shut and fell off her shoulder, causing her to fumble to catch it.

"How did you not see this?" she asked. She and I were both laughing at this point.

"I'm a nearsighted handbook. All those years of humans squinting close to my pages does a number on the magical sight, you know?"

"Sure," she chuckled.

"Are you still..." It dropped its voice to a dramatic whisper. "*Trying to kill him?*"

"Noooo. He's a friend now," she said quickly, flashing me an apologetic look.

I touched her arm with a little smile before taking the book from her. "Okay, good, because he's like—oh, hello, big, strong man hand."

I held its flapping pages up to my face. "Be quiet," I ordered.

"Hah, it's funny, because you're definitely the strongest dimensional to ever hold me and all, but I don't have an on-off switch like an electronic, you see—"

Shadows gathered around my head, lengthening all of my teeth into ebon fangs as I spoke with a deeper intonation. "*Stop* talking."

It quieted at last with a little squeak.

I passed it back to Cress. "We could get you another book, if you desired. It's a simple process to break the bond between witch and handbook," I offered.

She shook her head, holding it to her chest. "I love my snarky book, actually."

"I was on sale," it whispered.

"Well, this is unusual. Handbooks are supposed to wait in silence until they're needed, but fully empowered ones fly and can speak their knowledge aloud." I didn't think even I could convince this one to shut up for long. Not without adding a sturdy clasp over its pages, which was another option.

She shrugged before yawning hugely. "Ah. Let me send a message to the library so Geo returns to you," I said, reaching out to Braza's energy to do so. "Once he's in place, I'll leave you to rest."

She didn't argue, only sitting at the foot of her bed and placing her book aside. I sat next to her, tempted by the scant space between us, but let her be the one to reach out and brush her palm against mine. Our fingers twined, and I traced the shape of her blunt little thumbnail as I waited to hear the telltale thump of a gargoyle landing somewhere close.

I forced myself to be content if this was all I could have of Cress right now. We'd come a long way to get to this moment, even if I only wanted more from her. I imagined her resting her head against my solid shoulder and her not flinching if I were to put my arm around her waist and draw her closer.

I could be patient. When she was ready, I'd be here for her.

9

BEN

Phaeron returned to the library by evening to help me return to the modest faculty house where we now lived. Neither of us had left much of a footprint here to make it "home." I'd been saved with the clothes on my back and a nearly empty wallet, while it seemed the other man had little to his name.

The house had a basic set of furniture in each room, else we wouldn't have any. We both settled in the living room. The threadbare couch creaked when I dropped my weight into it, and I made a similar sound from the way my side's throbbing doubled. I was used to pain, but it was exhausting to carry it for a day and know it would be worse tomorrow.

Luckily, NSU staff got to eat for free from the campus dining halls, so we had a couple takeout boxes laid out on the battered coffee table between us. I barely knew the guy, but Phaeron seemed quieter than usual this evening, and his gaze was distant. As he leaned back in the armchair set at an angle to our couch, his tail drew restless patterns across the rug.

I shrugged to myself and began eating while it was still hot. One didn't wait when it was dinnertime in the manor. The strongest assassins would edge the rest of us out and eat the best parts of each meal. I'd made a habit of getting to mealtime early to have a chance at some protein and only ever shared with Lucas and Bianca.

Until she'd really come into her magic, Bianca had joined my brother and me in dreaming of freedom and quiet nights like this one, without the cutthroat atmosphere encouraged by our vampire master. I slowed my chewing as my shoulders dropped.

I'd left both of them behind with Garroway. Even now, my brother and the woman I saw as my sister were still in the manor and under his complete control while I slurped free food. I *had* to share the manor's location, but even the thought of it replaced the taste in my mouth with that of copper pennies.

My body was telling me not to push it any further. Tomorrow, then. I'd try every tomorrow until the deadline stopped my heart. Not just my own life was on the line here.

"Hey, dude," I said.

Phaeron cracked his eyes open, raising a brow in my direction. It was not quite the reaction I was hoping for, but he'd proven himself harder to pester than Geo.

"What happens when we see my brother next?" I asked, setting aside my empty box. I knew I couldn't have this conversation over food unless I wanted it to taste like ash on my tongue.

He seemed to see through me immediately, answering the core of my concerns. "He is still alive right now. Endaeron is not interested in inhabiting the bodies of his victims unless their soul is intact and aware."

I cringed. It reminded me of when Garroway took complete control, which he'd done to me a time or two. It'd felt like a second person inhabiting my mind, pushing me aside to take command of my body and its movements. I imagined the same happening to Lucas, but with him aware and screaming on the inside, banging his fists against the walls of his mind as they closed around him like a cage.

"Our best course of action is to capture Lucas and bring him to Moongrove Library. It'd be safest to remove my brother there and throw him into a stasis room."

"I'd say great, except he kind of cut you and Geometry to ribbons a few days ago," I commented.

He nodded slowly, looking as worried as I felt. "With access to a blood witch's healing, he was able to outlast us both. The good news is that he will want to prolong his time with Lucas because he knows we will avoid causing fatal harm to him. It is something he'd do, shield himself with the body of a boy to gain an advantage."

My hands balled into fists. I wanted that monster out of my brother by any means before the Hungering Darkness could leave any lasting scars on his psyche. There were some things worse than physical pain, things that couldn't be healed away with the application of a rune. "I'd do anything to have him out of Lucas."

"I know. I will do everything in my power to separate them. Just a word of warning...my brother is not a living, reasoning creature anymore. He has clever instincts and a bottomless pit of hunger to tend to. When threatened, he's been known to abandon his host. A sudden explosive exit from his host's soul is fatal."

"So, you're saying..." My stomach soured, and I shook

my head. "Thank you for the warning, but I have to get my brother back. There has to be a way."

Phaeron's tail had stopped its restless coiling, lying flat on the ground while he leaned forward to pick up his own dinner. I caught the pitying look on his face before he glanced away.

Maybe it was naïve, like I was an ostrich with my head buried deep in the sand. The odds of Lucas's safe return were obviously long, but I couldn't just give up and accept that he was lost forever. I would not bow to the inevitability of his death, not when he'd never had a moment of freedom in his entire life.

"The manor is...is..." I started to say. "...not in..."

I pretended the *thunk* noise that sounded nearby was the reason I stopped talking, but the pain in my side was nearly debilitating. Damn Garroway for making sure I couldn't breathe a word of his most important secret.

Phaeron shot to his feet first. "What was that?" he asked in a low growl.

He started to walk toward the front door while I was still in the process of standing while clutching my side. "Wait—"

But he was already opening the door. He stiffened in surprise before turning into a cloud of darkness. A crossbow bolt sailed through him, disturbing the shadows in its wake before it struck the far wall with a similar noise to the first. I cursed as Phaeron took physical form and charged outside.

Our front door had a piece of paper attached by a still-quivering bolt. I tore it free to read what was written on it. "The next one won't miss. –B"

"Still a bitch, I see," I muttered. Bianca's signature weapon was a crossbow, and it chilled my bones to know Garroway had sent one of his best for me first.

If I were Bianca, I would have taken that shot from as far back as possible while wearing runes of accuracy and speed. She'd be ready to take off running should she miss, despite the ridiculous flex she'd left on the door.

Was Phaeron faster than her? No matter what the answer to that was, I was clearly standing in the open with one of Garroway's assassins nearby. I turned to go back into the house.

"Do you know this person?" Phaeron's smooth voice sounded behind me.

Startled, I whipped back to see him standing over Bianca, who was bound in coils of shadow magic. Her muffled voice shouted around a ball of darkness stuffed in her mouth, and her reddening face had an expression promising painful death.

"Yeah, actually," I answered. "Think you could give her some blood rune surgery?"

In response, he extended his shadowy claws to their full, pointed length. Her eyelids lifted to show the whites of her eyes.

I couldn't help a little smirk. "By the way, Bianca. You missed."

"Fuck you, Ben," Bianca muttered on our way to Dr. Aurina's office the next day. She'd passed out when Phaeron's claws cut through the magic of her blood rune and had woken on our couch in a spitting fury the next morning.

It'd been nice to see her, too.

"Do all the women of this age curse so much?" Phaeron asked from her other side. He had her hands bound behind her with a coil of shadow since she'd said good morning with two kitchen knives and a whole litany of foul language.

"Fuck you too," she answered.

"No, thank you," he replied politely.

She rolled her eyes hard.

"Are you ready to listen yet?" I asked, doing the same at the exchange.

"You do know I'm still on deadline, right?"

"I am as well."

"Great. So we're both going to die," she muttered.

I'd done my best not to dwell on it, but she was right. Our only hope was if we could share where Garroway's manor was and infiltrate it with a team of professionals to get his black knife. The fact that I now had Bianca, willing or not, to talk to was enough to lift my spirits. One of us would muster the strength to tell Dr. Aurina where the manor was. Unless...

"How much time did Garroway give you?" I asked.

She lifted her chin. "Until Samhain, the same deadline he said he gave you. But he was sure I wouldn't need that much time."

I hid my relief with a crooked smile. She and I had the same amount of time left. "Uh huh. Yet you tried one of your most overdone tricks."

"I was trying to warn you," she muttered. "And how was I supposed to know this fucker would run me down despite my speed runes?" She tilted her head toward Phaeron.

"Sounds like poor planning to me," I needled.

The look Bianca swung on me could make milk curdle. She'd get over it soon, though, once the reality of her situation really sank in. At least, I hoped so, since she was a prized assassin who was treated relatively well by Garroway's standards. Unlike me, she'd seen the upside of working for him—preferential assignments and praise. But she'd still been a dog at his beck and call, sicced at his command and forced to heel at his whims. Surely she'd still prefer her freedom and turn to our side.

"For all your appreciation, maybe I'll knife you in the back for fun," she said with faux sweetness.

Phaeron cleared his throat. "I was under the impression you two were friends?"

"We are," she and I said at the same time.

"Just checking," he said with a chuckle.

We were soon in the administration building, speaking to a wide-eyed secretary who looked at Phaeron like he was the menace of our trio instead of my stabby friend. Most people would be forced to wait for the attention of the University President, but not us. We were soon in Aurina's office again, speaking with the demigoddess alone this time.

"A second assassin," she remarked from the moment we sat down. "Not nearly as saturated with pain as you, Ben, but she still stinks of Garroway's influence."

I glanced toward Bianca, expecting her to tell off the cupid too. Instead, the color had drained out of her face as Aurina inspected her more closely.

"I take it Cress has sent you Ben's story from yesterday?" Phaeron asked, briefly drawing her attention.

There was some unspoken tension between the two of them. His sharp face was set in a guarded expression of dislike, while Aurina avoided looking at him directly even with him speaking. *Interesting.*

"Yes, she emailed it, and I've reviewed it several times. While I empathize with the horrors that have been committed against you, Ben, I need facts. I need to know where he is hunkered down," she said, her gaze cutting to me. "Preferably before the Samhain Ball."

"The manor?" Bianca asked. "It's—" She cupped her hand over her mouth, coming away with blood coating her fingers. Aurina reached over to offer her a tissue box.

"Yeah, I was worried that'd happen. I can't say it, either." I frowned, knowing we desperately needed to get around this.

"Try one more time," Aurina ordered. Her aura lit up with her pink magic, inspecting me closely as I attempted to disclose the location again and came to a stuttering stop after a couple words.

Her brows lifted, and she pursed her lips.

"We cannot push them too hard. If this is the rune's doing, it's clear it'll kill them before they can say anything," Phaeron said.

"We are running out of time," she replied.

I considered her for a moment. "What does some ball have anything to do with finding Garroway?"

"Every major event this year has had an attack of some kind. The Samhain Ball is nearly as universally loved as the Mabon feast. Yet I had to cancel the ball. What better way to show that we've ended the threat than reinstating it and allowing students out past curfew again?" She gave a wide, magnanimous gesture but hadn't quite hidden a quaver in her words.

I narrowed my eyes. I wondered how long she could

stay at the helm of NSU if students kept getting endangered on her watch. Her job could easily be in the balance along with everything else.

"Before we go any further, I have a question for you, girl," she said abruptly.

"My name is Bianca," my friend gritted.

"Bianca, you wouldn't happen to know who harmed my daughter at the Mabon celebration, would you?" Aurina leaned forward, her fingers steepled as she focused intently. If there was a flare of magic, I didn't see it, but Phaeron loosed a soft growl beside me.

"Yeah, that was me," she answered. Carefree, like sharing what the weather was outside.

I jumped to my feet with a shout when Aurina slammed her palm down and Bianca's chair toppled over as the latter woman jerked backward. "I thought I recognized you," the demigoddess snarled.

Phaeron's shadowy claws extended. "Stop this. I thought we already discussed how it was a light cut."

I ducked to help Bianca right herself and her chair despite her restraints. "Why'd you tell the truth?" I muttered.

"She cast some spell on me," she replied just as low.

"...and that she did it as Garroway's slave," Phaeron was saying.

"All the same, she will be the one to disclose the manor's location. I will assist." Her cool gaze fell on Bianca again, who lifted her chin a notch in defiance. "I will take your pain away. Where is it?"

Working her jaw, she took her time saying anything at all. The Bianca I knew would say something flippant like, "At the corner of Third and go fuck yourself."

Instead, she said, "Sorry about your daughter. I didn't want to do it. Principles, you know?" Following that, she gave a whole address for the abandoned house in Salem that hid the pocket dimension where Garroway had his manor.

Then she passed out.

10

CRESS

I DID my best on my second round of midterms before showing up at the Witch Clubhouse midday with a coffee in one hand and the other firmly clamped around the pages of my handbook. It wiggled in protest the whole journey from the café to here, but I appreciated the moment of quiet.

It was obvious why no one had given it the magic to talk and fly. I'd had to hand it to Geo to take it out of the classroom when it'd whispered in a pin-silent room, *"Psst! The answer to three is A."*

It would be a wonder if I passed that test. Regardless, I set it free in my coven's room in the clubhouse, and it shook itself in disgruntlement before flapping to a corner of the room to sulk. I held the door a moment longer to let my cats slip in before securing a seat at the couch before anyone else came in. I was a little early, for once, and took a moment to catch my breath.

Unless I was sleeping, lately, it seemed I was never alone. Geo was keeping watch at the front of the clubhouse today—in theory, to tell Phaeron where to go—so I had some time just to sprawl and pet my familiars. Jin had come along with us, tentatively sitting on the opposite arm of the couch, just out of reach. We were making progress...I think.

Just like I'm making progress in my relationships with more than one man? I asked myself. My mother had taught me not to lead anyone on, that love was meant to be kept between two people. She wasn't a supernatural, though. She'd also stopped believing in true love a long time ago, saying soul mates were firmly the realm of fiction.

But I had *two*. I'd woken Geo from pure stone when I'd first been in trouble, and my connection to Ben was undeniable. Ben was the man I hoped walked through the door first. I yearned to see him again, but it was more than that. I wanted his hands on me, his sweet whispers in my ear, and his hard body between my thighs.

Yet when I closed my eyes to visualize it, it was the texture of Geo's palm that I practically felt skimming up my thigh. He'd hesitate at the apex of my legs before skimming his thumb up my wet seam. I imagined he'd want to explore my sex fully.

I leaned my head back. In this fantasy I built, the ghost of warm breath skimmed the shell of my ear, and goosebumps rolled over my skin. The smooth, seductive voice behind me was Phaeron's, though. My hand tensed on my knee as he just breathed, "bright soul," as clearly as if he were in the room with me.

My eyes shot open and darted around, heart leaping like he'd caught me. I was more flushed than mortified at the idea. But he wasn't there, just the lingering sense that I *wanted* him here with me.

Make that three men, because despite everything, Phaeron and I had some kind of draw, too. He'd been a perfect gentleman last night, holding my hand as the sun set. I really appreciated it, because I'd been at my emotional limit, and I think he was well aware of it. He knew when to push. My belly tingled with the idea of him trying again soon.

I could curse my traitorous thoughts, though. I'd originally been thinking of Ben, yet my mind lumped in Geo and Phaeron immediately. I wanted Ben most, though, and it wasn't just the lust talking. Just to see that he was okay and to hold him again following his confession yesterday. He needed to see that I accepted him despite the lies that'd first brought us together and that I trusted him to give our relationship a second chance.

The deadline ticking down to Samhain stood in the way, though. My words were air if we couldn't save him from his former master's cruel send-off.

If my friends were true, they would feel the same way. I'd sent Ben's confession video to Dr. Aurina first, but soon it was in the hands of my trusted coven mates, who drifted in one by one and filled this space with color as we awaited the men. Roe had blasted my phone with rapid-fire texts, all in capital letters.

She arrived first for once, seeing me and exclaiming, "Training is my middle name. We should be fighting as a coven anyway!"

"I doubt the dimensional can teach me anything more about my magic," Áine said in her shadow.

"It'd still help if we knew everything you could do," Roe said. She was dressed in her workout gear, clearly expecting to go straight to the library for the group sessions Phaeron had alluded to yesterday.

The faun shrugged, her gaze falling on my sulking handbook. "Is that book flying?"

Uh oh.

The handbook twitched, flapping over to hover too close to her face. "Hi! Who are you? Wait, you're the faun, right? Áine?" it asked rapid-fire.

"Last time I checked," she replied.

"Coolio. I'm *The Librarian Witch's Handbook.* I've taught Cressie-poo everything she knows!"

I tried to cover my embarrassed blush. "Cressie-poo?" she echoed with a wicked look my way.

"Noooo, don't call me that," I complained. I explained how it had the magic to fly around as Willow arrived and was quickly enamored with the talking book. She chased it around the room for a few minutes, giggling all the while.

We were soon settled and restless, though, chatting idly about midterms and magic while Bella visited with each of us for scratches and Milo napped in my lap. I was beginning to think the men weren't coming after all when Jin lifted her head and cocked one ear like a tiny radar.

Geo's voice preceded him. He held the door as Phaeron slid in sideways, supporting an unfamiliar woman around the waist. Roe hopped to her feet first, helping support her from the other side and guide her to slump upright on the other side of the couch. Her head leaned against the backrest, spilling dark hair around her pale face.

Ben closed the door after them, his expression set in a displeased line.

"What happened?" I asked.

"Aurina." Phaeron's reply was a low snarl.

When I set Milo aside and was on my feet, I realized all three of the men who'd been on my mind turned to me at the same time. I went to Ben for a quick kiss but didn't miss how Geo uttered a sound somewhere between a growl and the rumble of a distant rock fall.

"She didn't hurt you, did she?" I asked, searching the lidded eyes and little smile Ben flashed just for me.

He shook his head. "Just Bianca. She extracted the address of Garroway's manor from her."

My next breath caught in my throat. I turned toward the unfamiliar woman, torn between elation and concern, with more questions piling up behind my lips with each moment that passed. Bianca's gray gaze met mine, and her pale lips quirked in the cocky manner I always associated with Ben.

I suddenly recognized her from Mabon, but she'd been dressed much differently, with her dark hair braided and crowned with turning oak leaves. For a moment, she'd seemed to be there with Ben when I arrived, and I'd been struck by a pang of jealousy that he'd been chatting with the slim, stunning woman who'd exuded self-confidence.

"It's nice to finally meet Ben's crush," she croaked. She was significantly paler now, her olive-toned skin white with the trauma she'd undoubtedly gone through if she was another of Garroway's assassins and forced to say something Ben hadn't been able to past shredding pain.

"Uh, yeah," I said, hesitant. Who was she to Ben? He was obviously concerned for her.

"So, we know where the manor is now," Roe put in. "What's the plan?"

"We all may as well be sitting for this." Phaeron reached out and curled a tendril of shadow around the edge of a chair, pulling it over so he could lounge in it. Geo remained standing behind him, arms crossed, while Ben and I settled on the couch with him between Bianca and me.

He put an arm around me, and I sank into his side with a sigh. Bianca lidded her eyes, draping her arms around her middle and making no moves toward him.

When we were settled, Phaeron spoke. "Everyone in this room has a reason to go on this raid to Garroway's manor, which is not scheduled yet. We left Aurina's office quickly after she stabilized Bianca and ensured that she'd wake following the trauma of sharing such a protected fact as Garroway's address. Certain details were not decided, but Aurina will allow anyone I can muster and vouch for to come, while she will be summoning a force of professionals and accompanying us personally to assist.

"Blood barons thrive on corruption, however, so Aurina will keep her moves secret until it's time to go. We can trust very few people outside of this room, so what we discuss must remain a secret." He met everyone's gaze in turn, and I had tingles. It was like he'd erased the secretive, shadowy Phaeron and come forward with the prince and leader of the dimensional people. I appreciated the change more than I could say.

"That being said, I don't think we all *should* go," he said. His topaz eyes landed on Willow, whose shoulders slumped. "Perhaps some introductions are due."

Roe jumped in to facilitate that, and Bianca sat up with a groan to pay attention and say, "Bianca Cross, blood witch," when her turn came.

Phaeron asked a few questions of the other women. He seemed most impressed with Roe, I think, who was undoubtedly the best fighter of the freshmen present. When it was Willow's turn, he inspected her again. I recognized the way she reacted and sympathized. His gaze was particularly intense sometimes; I think that's when he was looking into my soul.

"Do you have trouble with your magic?" he asked her.

"Um, yes. No spells have worked quite right for me," she mumbled.

"Curious. The magic in your soul is quite strong, but the two sides are at odds with each other."

"Sides...?" she echoed.

"Storms and winds versus scales and song. Were you aware that you're half mer?" Though he asked it casually, he had a knowing look as she gasped and clapped both hands over her mouth.

"No way!" She turned to Roe, joy flashing over her face. "You were right. I'm not broken!"

Roe reached over to hug her fiercely. "I told you something else had to be up, girly."

"That's great news! If you end up growing a tail, I'd love to make you some new clothes," I said, already looking forward to it. I admired the mer for their natural beauty and grace, both in and out of the water. There were a few in my fashion design classes, unmistakable with the patterns of scales on parts of their bodies and the iridescence of their skin.

All traits Willow didn't have. I wondered if she'd pick them up if and when she unlocked this secret side to her.

"Do you think I might?" she asked, glancing over at Phaeron.

"I suspect so. But we can discuss it later, yes? Right now, you don't have control over both sides of yourself," he said. She nodded in acceptance, as this had been why she'd sat out our first fight with the Hungering Darkness. Raiding Garroway's manor would be so much more dangerous. "However, I don't see why you couldn't join us to train your magic. You *all* need it."

Phaeron's plan was pretty direct. We had two former assassins now, who could teach us how to fight Garroway's trained blood witches. If we could prove ourselves capable, he would take us on the raid, but we only had a week to do it. Everyone agreed, even Willow, whose face was set with new determination, and Bianca, who'd regained some of her color.

We were finalizing when we'd be training every evening when the door opened and in fell Wren Starsurge, her lips locked with another of our coven mates, Heath Storm. *I knew it*, I wanted to crow. Those two had totally been into each other from the moment she got over not matching to the same coven as her best friend.

The air turned icy, as I wasn't the only one glaring daggers at her from the moment she and Heath sprang apart. She looked around and huffed, adjusting her top and bra with a dignified lift of her nose. "I guess this room's occupied today," she said and dragged Heath away.

"Damn. I was looking forward to telling her the truth," Ben muttered.

"Time and place," I said. I wanted to see her knocked off her pedestal with the truth of her father's dealings, but like all revenges, it had to be delivered at the right moment.

PHAERON TOOK us to the heart of the library, floor negative twenty-six, where a padded space awaited. Weapons straight out of a medieval armory were racked along the wall, which made the bright red modern first aid kits stand out where they were posted at regular intervals.

With Bianca resting out of the way, Ben was busy for the whole time we were here, sharing tips about fighting blood witches and sparring with anyone interested in trying their luck. I resolved to talk to him later, distracted by Phaeron, who spent most of his time that evening teaching me directly.

Geo remained apart from everything, watching with his arms crossed. I had a sense of his disapproval when Phaeron stepped behind me, helping teach me better form with my silver sword in hand. But I quickly forgot about the gargoyle when Phaeron's hands drifted to my hips.

"You shift your weight like this," he said close to my ear.

I was all too aware of him, goosebumps rising on my arms when he leaned in further to whisper, "Just like that, bright soul." And in that moment, I was no longer preparing to sword fight an invisible foe, but instead about to shift back to rub against him.

No, bad Cress, I chastised. "Got it," I said aloud. I had just as much to prove as Roe or Áine. If I wanted to help Ben and go on this raid, I needed to get my mind focused on what mattered.

It was just, his fingers seemed to tighten like he wanted to pull me against him before he continued critiquing my form. Soon, we reached the end of my limited training, including the few spells I knew. He ended our training session with a neutral hum, and I turned to see his gaze intent on me, eyes narrowed to slits.

"What is it?" I asked.

His lips lifted into a confident smile, flashing his fangs. "I'm just thinking, we can work with this. Let's try one more thing." He slid a little closer to me, and my gaze slipped to his mouth. All he'd have to do was lean a little closer to my level...

"Call over one of your familiars," he murmured.

I gave myself a mental slap and turned, spotting Bella first. She, Jin, and Milo were across the training room, taking turns playing with my flying handbook. Jin was currently perched on its spine as it labored to stay in the air, so it seemed the little black cat had won the game already. When I called her name, Bella came running and leapt into my waiting arms.

"Hi, sweet girl." I giggled as she purred and headbutted my chest.

Phaeron walked me through checking the connection that linked us as witch and familiar. My bonds with both Bella and Milo were strong enough to work with, but apparently, they could be even stronger.

"Familiars are more than pets. They're lifelong companions, here to help with whatever you need. This will tire her out, but if she's okay with it, let's try to have you borrow some feline senses from Bella," he said. I asked her if she was okay with it, which she squeaked an affirmative to. "Focus on your connection with her," Phaeron continued.

I closed my eyes and did so. Other than being able to understand her meows as her witch, I could feel her simple emotional state, which was a deep contentment to be in my arms. *Aww.* I loved this silly little cat. She purred a little harder in response as she felt that back from me.

"Now, the tricky part. You have to communicate to her that you need to borrow from her. When you're more experienced with it, it's as easy as reaching out over your connection in a split second and taking some of her grace or her senses, but right now, you should simply ask for what she can give and know what it feels like."

I clenched my eyelids and tried it, wordlessly asking Bella over the familiar bond for her senses. I understood why it seemed Phaeron couldn't explain it fully. It just happened. My face tingled, and I was suddenly overwhelmed with the scent of sweat and metal in the air. I wanted to clap my hands over my ears, but that would mean dropping Bella, who was frozen in a state of concentration.

It only lasted for three seconds at most, leaving as abruptly as it arrived, but in those moments, I had the same senses of smell and hearing as Bella. My nostrils were still full of the closest smell other than mine—Phaeron's. His shadows carried a particular signature scent that I'd caught here and there, like clean earth and night air. It left me with the impression that I'd just gone on a walk outside in the dark.

"That was amazing," I said, glancing down at my cat, who yawned hugely. "But...I don't understand how that was possible at all."

He smiled and shrugged. "Familiars are a little magic, which is how they bond with witches in the first place. I doubt you borrowed all of her senses or really wanted to. With practice, you'll be able to do this more for longer and be able to specify between her sense of smell, or her grace, or her reaction speed."

"We'll definitely be practicing," I promised. I could already see where this could come in clutch in a fight.

He rubbed her ears, dropping his voice to a gentle coo. "Just not too much. This little girl needs to rest first." She leaned into his touch with a smug kitty smile.

My connection with her was stronger than ever, so I sensed firsthand that she approved of Phaeron quite a bit. I smiled up at him with an echo of the same feeling, and it took him a moment to notice. His sweet talking of Bella faded, but that more tender side of him remained. He tucked a few strands of hair behind my ear and cupped my face.

His gaze dipped to my lips, tracing the path of my tongue as I wet them in anticipation. When his thumb tipped my chin up and he slid closer, my heart leapt, and I rose to my toes—

"Dimensional." Geo's voice startled us apart. "The witches need to leave now to make it to their dorms before they stop serving dinner." His stoic features curled at the corners as Phaeron lashed his tail with a poorly concealed growl.

I had no doubt this was supposed to be payback for interrupting Geo and me in the classroom yesterday, but *damn*, couldn't a gal get a kiss around here?

11

CRESS

Frustrated, I invited Ben to walk back to my dorm with me, ignoring whether or not Geo followed. Phaeron had stayed behind to get Bianca set up in one of the overnight stay rooms in the library, the safest place for her to sleep off her trauma, while my friends walked ahead of us, giggling at some story Willow was telling. I sensed my cats frolicking in the grass, keeping up with the group.

"I have a question," I said while they were giving us some privacy.

He'd fitted his hands in his pockets and raised a brow at my tone, which had come out more tense than I'd meant. "Uh oh. What'd I do this time?" he asked.

"Who's Bianca to you?"

I knew Ben could be an effortless liar, so this was the first real test for our trust. He seemed honest when he met my gaze and said, "She's another witch who grew up in the same situation Lucas and I did. She's more of a sister than anything—you haven't seen her real personality yet, but she's more likely to stab me than ever want to kiss me. She's not your competition, babe."

I couldn't hide how my shoulders lowered with relief. "Okay, I just wanted to be sure," I said.

"You're cute when you're a little jealous." He winked, and color rose to my cheeks. "Honestly, no one could be your competition. I should be jealous instead, with how much attention you're getting from Geo and Phaeron."

If there was a sign hovering over my head right now, it would be flashing *hypocrite* in big neon letters. "About that..."

Ben saved me from putting my foot in my mouth with a casual shrug. "When you come into your family's power, no supernatural will be surprised that you have three men."

"*If* I do," I replied. There was still no guarantee that I was secretly a Darkmore and the sole inheritor of the family line's hereditary power. Anxiety prickled its way up my spine at the thought.

In class, we'd discussed how magic was inherited from our ancestors, but it was magical theory. Like science had its theory of relativity, witches had a theory of inheritance, and it would remain a theory, as the only beings that knew exactly how it worked were the deceased. As far as we understood it, when a witch passed on, they left a piece of themselves behind to protect and support their children and their children's children. Witches across the ages reported dreams of the past, ghost stories, and tales of impossible feats, especially when their lives were in danger.

If I were, in fact, Luna Darkmore, miraculously saved while the rest of my birth family was murdered, the concentration of power in the whole Darkmore line would fall to me. The problem was, I didn't know what I'd inherit, because I was a librarian witch, while the rest of the family line were celestial witches. If I were to borrow lingering magic from, say, my grandmother, would I be able to cast spells outside of my affinity? Or would I simply be haunted by all the ghosts down my family line? There was no way of knowing until it happened.

I swallowed past the sudden dryness in my mouth. "Phaeron was going to help me figure this out on Samhain, but I'm nervous. It might not turn out to be a net positive. Instead of being a stronger supernatural, I might just turn into an overwhelmed one."

"You're letting doubt take over too much," he said. He held out his hand, and I took it, lacing my fingers with his. "See what happens when it happens."

I squeezed his fingers. "Yeah. And you're going to be there too. Maybe inheriting from your own true family line," I said.

"I sure hope so. If we're waiting a week to attack Garroway, it's going to be my only chance." He placed his free hand over his side. "Can I tell you a secret?"

There was a serious shift to his tone, which struck me as unlike him. "Of course," I answered.

"My extended family, the Evenstars, probably think Lucas and I are dead. Garroway made them sound like callous rich people, but it's not like I can trust anything he's said. I just wonder if they looked for us or if they bought the entire setup." He looked into the distance, where we were coming up on my friends' dorm. Troubled shadows played in his green eyes as we passed under a streetlamp.

"You wonder if they'd care," I said quietly.

He nodded slowly. "If they knew what'd happened, would I have a family, or just a group of strangers who pity me?"

"There's only one way to know."

"Yeah, that's true. But if they met me right now, I'd just be a penniless beggar—I don't have anything to offer but my story and my name. I want to meet them when I've made something of myself, you know? If this deadline doesn't kill me first."

He released my hand when my friends stopped before their dorm, waiting for us to catch up. Ben's vulnerability retreated behind the mask of his smirk. "Well, here we are, huh?" he said. "It's too bad I'm not a real student. Guess they'll let me starve while you all eat."

Áine rolled her eyes. "We'll bring you something, drama king."

"Actually," I ventured. "I'm feeling pretty beat. I'll take care of Ben back at my dorm."

As I was hugging Willow goodbye first, Áine and Roe exchanged a knowing look. "Bye, girlie. See you tomorrow," Roe said, crushing me in her arms next.

"Have fun," Áine said in a laughing tone, twinkling her fingers.

Ben and I turned away when Roe called, "Hey, Geo, come get a bite with us!"

I glanced over my shoulder, knowing exactly how this would go. Geo wouldn't leave his duty. But the gargoyle was frowning over at Ben and me. He eventually dipped his chin in a reluctant nod and followed the young women up the steps to their dorm.

"I'll be damned," I muttered.

"He's probably hoping I get assassinated on the way there," Ben whispered back.

"That's definitely *not* it. We had a talk earlier," I said.

Well, it didn't seem Geo quite *accepted* anything at the end of that chat except that his duty was something more than passionless servitude, but it seemed he understood that he and I didn't always need to be sharing the same space.

He smirked. "I'm not going to complain."

Of course he wouldn't. As soon as we were half a block down the street, he warned me before drawing a concealed dagger and twirling it in between his fingers with practiced ease. Ben was busy scanning the shadows, his stance more guarded now that we didn't have a gargoyle ready to come to our defense, but he kept stealing glances at me, too.

I admired him in the same way. This was a side of Ben I'd barely gotten to see—the trained assassin alert to any potential threats. He probably still had runes under his long sleeves from our time in the library. While I'd been occupied with Phaeron, Ben had been demonstrating what each rune did and how to counter them.

Luckily for us, he didn't need to give me a firsthand demonstration of him using those runes in a real situation this evening. I took him in the back way and let him into my room before doubling back to grab dinner for us both.

That was the first time I realized I'd left my handbook in the library, as I usually spent my meals quizzing it for random knowledge, but I shrugged it off. It was probably off bothering Bianca or Phaeron with its endless chatter. My cats had followed us without issue and were getting their daily scratches from the cafeteria manager, who looked the other way when I loaded up my to-go box a little too much.

When I let myself back into my room, Ben was lounging on my bed, arms behind his head. He slanted a coy look at me when I stopped dead in the threshold. He'd tossed aside his shirt, leaving his leanly muscled chest on display. I was glad to see his color was back.

I hesitated for an extended moment before closing the door behind me, knowing where this would lead. It was a choice I made as I turned the lock and set dinner aside. My heart picked up speed in my chest as I turned and read the hints of uncertainty that lingered on his face.

Mere hours after the first time we were intimate, things went right to hell. I still chose to climb into bed with him again despite a nagging sense that there was no guarantee that any pleasure we shared wouldn't be followed by more peril.

He was still on a time limit, after all. At some point, he'd bandaged over his blood rune, leaving only the active deadline to peek out from under the white linen. I was glad to see it, considering how I'd been afraid I'd hurt him by brushing over his wounds by accident.

I kissed him first, grabbing a handful of his longish hair and pouring all my frustrations of the last couple days into the slant of our mouths. It felt like true forgiveness to give myself to him again and feel his arms tighten around me. For all I'd had budding thoughts of intimacy with Geo and Phaeron, it was Ben I chose to be with tonight.

His tongue pressed against the seam of my lips, and I opened to him, letting our tongues duel and twine. He was already working the button off my pants. Callused fingers brushed the line of my hip and down to cup my ass, pushing my panties down in the process. I lifted and kicked the clothes off, sighing into his mouth as cool air caressed my needy sex.

He'd woken something in me the last time we'd been alone in this room, and I was only just realizing it. The moment my anam cara mark turned blood-witch maroon, I should've known I would crave him again. I straddled his waist, breaking our lip-lock and rolling my hips against him. His hard length pressed back, trapped within the meager barrier of his jeans.

"Hey, babe," he said, husky with arousal. "Why don't you have a seat up here?" He tapped one of his cheeks.

I flushed at the suggestion. He wanted to put my pleasure first. Even still, I was hesitant to spread my legs right above his face until I saw the glimmer of eagerness in his eyes as he took in the sight of me.

"You're so sexy, babe," he murmured. He guided my hips down and angled them just right above his face. My belly quivered, nerves and anticipation clashing for the moment it took for him to move. He ran his tongue up the seam of my pussy before delving deeper with a groan I felt through the tender petals of my sex.

I didn't know what to expect; he was still my first lover, and this was the only time I'd let another use their mouth to bring me pleasure. I followed his lead for the grind and roll of my hips, sighing with a growing smile as his lips and tongue stoked the pressure in my core. His hands kneaded my ass and held me steady when he laved my clit in a sudden shock of bliss.

He tugged at the hem of my shirt, and I pulled it over my head before releasing my breasts from the confines of their bra. Our anam cara marks brushed when he took my hand and placed it over one of the nipples pearling from his darkening gaze. We moaned together from the brief shock of pleasure and *rightness* that came from those little magical symbols.

It took me a moment to realize he wanted to watch me play with myself. I fondled my tits, flicking the tips, and watched him smile by the lines around his eyes before he closed them to savor the moment. He licked and sucked on me like he couldn't get enough of my taste.

When he transferred his lips to my clit and sucked, I came apart with a sudden cry. I wondered if I drowned him for a moment when he lay back before noticing how smug he looked with my slick shining on his lips.

"I have a bit of bad news," he murmured. "I don't have any condoms."

Panting, I rested a hand on my chest. I didn't want to hear about *bad news* when I was naked with him. But he'd presented a problem I had the solution to.

"Well..." I leaned over him, only saved from falling when he caught my hips. My legs were akin to jelly, leaving me to fumble at the end of my reach to open the first drawer of the bedside table next to us and withdraw a condom package to toss to him.

He walked it between his fingers before squinting at it. "The student center has a whole bowl full of them," I explained as confidently as I could.

I'd gone out of my way to find them and make sure they were on hand after forgiving him. Just in case he'd share my bed again. I cleared my throat and added, "Someone told me recently that it's sexy to be prepared."

He shifted to sit up with a wince. "Damn straight."

We shared a look, silent understanding passing between us. First, we worked together to free him of what remained of his clothes. He fumbled the condom package when I went for his balls, giving them a testing roll in my palm while claiming his lips. His mouth held traces of its usual mint, mixed with lingering, sweet musk. It hit me suddenly. To have this strong, confident man at my mercy felt *good*. It was satisfying to know I was his world, his full focus.

He was *mine*, as fate intended.

Then he grabbed a fistful of my hair, sending a shock of pleasure through my scalp. "Get on your hands and knees for me," he whispered into my ear.

I gave his balls a parting squeeze that had his cock twitching before swinging around and getting comfortable in the suggested position. His roughened fingertips ran up my waist and back down to grasp my hips as he shifted his weight behind me.

I expected to feel the head of his cock at my lower lips, but instead the heat of his shaft pressed along the length of my slit. There was a subtle shift of the condom's plastic, the smallest of possible barriers between us. He rubbed against me, holding my hips to keep me from angling them.

My lips parted as he pressed...no, grinded against me harder. With a glance over my shoulder, I caught the playful smile on his face.

"You want this, babe?" he purred.

I moaned in reply. My body language clearly said, *take me.* I could barely think with how much I wanted him inside me properly.

A sound of denial escaped my lips when he pulled away instead. "Let me hear you," he said.

Tease, I wanted to accuse. I found my voice to reply, "I want you."

"Tell me what you want me to do to you."

"Come back," I whimpered.

He hadn't gone far, but watched me with the kind of anticipation that required a response. A deeper flush took over my face, but I was aflame with need, far past any kind of modesty. I exclaimed, "I want your fat cock in my—oh!" In one swift motion, he'd pulled my hips into him, pushing his cock deep. This angle made him feel thicker than ever.

Something told me he'd had mercy on me this time. He was definitely the type to draw out the moment, but I felt how he pulsed within me—he wanted this just as badly.

"That better?" he asked as he withdrew, forcing the air

for my reply right out of my lungs with the next drive of his hips.

I let out a breathy laugh. "Ben!" And by that, I meant, *you know it is, you tease.*

He was grinning as we rocked the bed. "Yeees?"

"Don't stop."

He had my toes curling and my hands feeling out a more stable place to hold than two fists in the blankets. I grasped the edge of the bed to push back against him as we found a rhythm together. I kept stealing glances at him, enamored by the play of pleasure on his expression, an echo to mine.

He listened well sometimes—he didn't stop, not until I came again and so did he with a jerk of his shaft within me. I breathed out with relief as we curled up together in the afterglow, cuddled up until our breath settled, trading little kisses and soft words. I enjoyed gazing into his unguarded eyes and counting the little flecks of gold within the evergreen while he traced his fingertips over my skin.

It was a relief to have him back, and in these moments, I would've done nearly anything to have his deadline miraculously pause. Especially when he peeked into the drawer I'd left half open.

"Did you take the whole fucking bowl?" he asked with a laugh.

"I wanted to be *really* prepared," I said.

I'd taken a couple handfuls, enough to fill the small space. It was a private wish of mine he'd uncovered—I wanted him here until we used them all up, and then some.

He took one and turned to kiss the tip of my nose. "Well, you're *really* sexy."

12

GEO

She'd barely looked back before disappearing into the night with Ben.

As much as I wanted to understand emotion, I found I had a basic misunderstanding of *her* feelings. What else could explain why she'd slipped off with Ben, of all people, instead of with me?

It got under my stone skin, needling within my tender flesh. I was made for her, and she was mine, as she had just convinced me. What need did she have for another man? I'd had the feeling she was trying to ease me into the idea earlier, but I couldn't help but feel...inadequate.

While I'd watched Cress and her friends train that afternoon, an unfamiliar librarian witch had slipped into the room briefly to pass me the note now crumpled in my hand. I turned to Roe, the young woman who'd invited me to dinner. I'd pretended to accept for Cress's sake, but my flesh form did not have hunger pangs tonight.

"Will you send a message to Cress for me later?" I asked her.

She hung back to talk while the other two headed

inside, likely drawn to the promise of dinner. "As long as it's not a hurtful one," she said, raising a brow. I liked Roe. She reminded me most of myself—solid, strong, and loyal.

"No, never," I rumbled. I showed her the note, which had details for a place and time tomorrow to begin my tempering. It would start earlier than she usually woke. "I must leave her side for a time to temper my body."

"What does that mean?" she asked, her tone lowering as she read the message.

"It is a process I thought the library had lost. Our foes have magic my stone body is not impervious to, so I am going to strengthen myself. The process takes time. I do not wish for Cress to worry, so now seems like the right time to leave," I said.

"Well, big guy." Roe tilted her lips aside. *Skeptical,* I told myself after a moment of studying the expression. "It'd be for the best if you told her yourself."

"I do not wish to...interrupt her," I muttered.

She propped a fist on her hip, really looking me in the eye. "Fair point. Tell you what, I'll share what you've told me, but only if you promise to explain to her later why you chose *right now* to leave with that heartbroken expression on your face. Okay?"

"Heartbroken," I repeated without emotion.

"You might think it's subtle, but this time, it's not. Just don't be a dick to my friend because she chose to go home with a different guy, that's all I'm saying. She's going to be upset when you're not there tomorrow morning."

My first thought was, *Perhaps she should be.* But it wasn't my duty to be cruel to Cress. "That is why I am leaving the message with you, since I don't have a phone," I said on a sigh.

"All right." She sounded reluctant. "You want to talk about her before you go?"

"I do not have the words. Nor the emotions."

"Consider it an open invitation, then. Cress isn't the only one who can help you work through what you're feeling, and it seems like you need someone else," she replied.

Her offer stirred some appreciation in my stone heart. I dipped my chin in acknowledgment, knowing she was likely right. If I was confusing my duty and my affection for Cress, then I had to be making other mistakes. Pushing her away. This evening's events reminded me of the time she'd tricked me just to have time away from me. The memory stung nearly as badly as when I'd first realized what'd happened.

"I appreciate your assistance in this matter." I stepped away from her and transformed back into my gargoyle form. She waved in farewell, and on a delay, I returned the gesture and flared my wings.

I flew back to Moongrove Library in a fraction of the time it took to walk to the girls' dorm. Without Cress or her friends, I had no need to shift back once I arrived. The librarians were used to a few still-active gargoyles coming and going from their missions.

I arrived for my tempering appointment several hours early. The master librarian they found for the task had chosen the same level where the others were training earlier but bade me wait in a second room. It was more enclosed and had fewer weapons available to use, ideal for close-quarters combat or the focused assault of magic I'd need to strengthen my stone.

Satisfied with the choice of location, I exhaled a soft gust from my stony lungs and let myself rest like a true statue.

NOW THAT I'D experienced sleep in my flesh form, I knew there were a few key differences between the sleep the people around me needed versus the motionless stone of a gargoyle.

I preferred what I knew, because I was still somewhat aware of the occasional voice nearby or the thumping of footsteps on the stairs. Sleep reminded me too much of stasis, where I'd been akin to a real statue for far too long. Unaware. A shade of existence close to death.

So it was an unpleasant surprise to be rapped on the forehead by a set of gray knuckles. My resting gaze focused in an instant on my least favorite being, Phaeron, who'd crept into the room without detection. I rumbled deep in my stone throat, straightening from my slouch.

I had the sense that it was early morning, hours still before my tempering appointment. "What do *you* want?" I demanded.

"You're early," he commented.

Were I more flexible in this form, I would have narrowed my eyes at him. "Explain."

"You're here for tempering, yes? A process the librarians of this time have forgotten."

"But you have not," I said. That was logical.

I hated it. The emotion heated my stone heart, where the soul of my honored witch animated me. A heart Phaeron had already tried to rip from my chest once.

He nodded. "When you started seeking tempering, they asked if I would help you. It makes sense that you want it. You were built with the best enchantments and advancements of your time." In a blink, he vanished into curls of smoke. I whipped toward the sound of his voice behind me. "Your reaction times are fine. It's your defenses that are lacking when faced with a creature such as my brother."

"Or you," I gritted out.

"Or me," he echoed more mildly. "So, as unlikely as it seems, I'm here to help you."

A dubious silence hung between us. I inspected him for signs of untruth: fidgeting, looking away, even a desire to fill the air. His tail had its usual casual sway, and he had an expectant air as the seconds rolled by.

"What do you want?" I said.

"You've already asked me that," he pointed out.

"In exchange for your help."

"Oh, I think you know the answer to that." His yellow gaze dipped to my chest.

"I told you. I'm not her!" My raised shout echoed back around us in the small space.

Phaeron's brows rose. "I know. And I must apologize—for earlier. I was not in my right mind." If he thought I was going to accept and forgive, he'd be waiting far into his immortal lifetime. But he wasn't done talking. "Samhain approaches. On that day, I just want to call her spirit out of its...your heart for a talk."

"You wish for an explanation. I remember."

"I did. But the more time that passes, the less I desire to vent my grievances with a long-deceased woman. Morgana made her choice, and now I must make mine. All I want to do is say goodbye to her." He cleared his throat, stepping forward slowly with his hand outstretched. "Let us make peace, gargoyle. If we are to have the same woman, we must find some common ground."

Instead of staring at his hand, I took a few moments to transform into my form of flesh and bone so my emotions wouldn't be so muted and dissonant. I took my time opening my eyes.

My feelings pushed and pulled in at least three directions, becoming a tangled skein that I picked at as quickly as I could. I recognized the rage first. Anger was easy to come by, alongside its cousins, frustration and unwelcome surprise.

I realized it was his comment about Cress that displeased me most. His apology, even his offer to help me with my tempering, were all wrapped around the idea that we needed to get along better because we had to share her. When I finally looked at him again, he still had his hand out, waiting with a knowing glimmer in his otherworldly eyes.

I would find no one else who could make my stone resistant to the Hungering Darkness's claws. If he did not help me, I would be unable to protect Cress when it returned for her soul. And it *would* return.

"For you to speak with Morgana…it would not damage me?" I asked, shocked to be even considering this.

"Your heart would stop beating while she is outside of it. It'd be a lot like stasis. Asleep without the soul, your same self when it's returned as your heart."

Odd, shivery bumps crawled up my skin. *Stasis.* Cold, unaware. Unfeeling. I didn't want to return, not when I could spend my time with Cress.

"You have my word that I will return the soul quickly," he said.

"Then…I accept." Finally, I shook his hand.

He grew and flexed shadowy talons over his free hand's fingers. "Let's begin. Do you know your power level?"

"It's a six, all in defensive ability," I replied, assuming my stone form again.

Power levels were determined by three measures: offensive capability, resistance to magic, and the level of magic one could hold at one time. Gargoyles of my time had a standard power level of four, which was concentrated in defense and magical resistance. I'd been tempered far more as a special gargoyle to honor my witch and set me apart as one who carried the soul of a former demigoddess.

It didn't prepare me for the pain of being tempered anew, though. The process was one of exposure, and by the time I started to withstand power-level-seven spells from Phaeron's shadowy magic, I was sheened from my oil leaking from hundreds of tiny cuts...and forced into the nothingness of stasis to rest and recover for the next round.

TIME LOST MEANING after that first session. I'd wake, allow Phaeron to damage me further, return to stasis, and repeat. My stone didn't part like butter for his talons anymore, which meant when I faced the Hungering Darkness again, it would not be able to stop me so easily.

At some point, I shook off the clinging fingers of unwelcome sleep to see that Roe was standing across from me, inspecting the oil that stained my obsidian body like splashes of silver paint.

"Who did this to you, big guy?" she asked. My rigid lips curved at the corners to hear her tone, like she'd take on the aggressor herself.

"It's what I asked for," I replied in a low rumble. She only calmed herself once I explained I was improving myself one spell at a time. She hadn't realized what the strengthening process looked like in reality.

"So, you're done with this tempering thing and ready to say sorry to Cress for making her worry?"

I stared at her, unblinking. "I am not yet ready to leave this room."

"Dr. Aurina wants the raid to happen in two days. You're out of time," she replied.

Two days could mean one more tempering session and hours to recover before facing the true threat.

"Besides, there's someone I want you to meet. He's here now, waiting for you," she added.

"Oh?"

"You'll have to come with me. I promise it'll be worth it. He'll help you with what you're going through."

I was...nervous, perhaps, to see Cress again after leaving her so abruptly. A part of me knew I didn't have the tools to have that conversation. Perhaps this mysterious visitor did.

"Who is it?" I asked.

"Someone you used to know." She smiled mischievously. "C'mon, Geo. Come out of that rock form and live a little. Have a conversation with an old friend."

I sent her out of the room and cleaned off the worst of the oil before becoming human as she requested. If this were to be a quick chat, perhaps I could continue preparing my stone to withstand the Hungering Darkness's magic afterward. Before we even took the elevator to the surface level and I spotted him, I had an idea of what, if not who, this old friend was.

Another gargoyle. And once I saw him, he seemed familiar, even if he was in human form and looking older than I remembered. "It really is you, Geo!" He waved a pale arm.

"Marl?" I guessed. He had the same features as the

common granite gargoyle I remembered, though I'd never seen his lips stretched into such a big smile.

"In the flesh." He laughed and slapped his thigh. I suppose it was funny, since we both were in our flesh forms.

Roe beamed. "I'll let you two catch up! I've got a class to get to."

"Thanks again, young lady," Marl said as she bustled by him. He turned back to me and let me have a few moments to inspect him.

Granite gargoyles were not blessed with a human form that looked fully human. Some retained the ugly, exaggerated features found in gothic architecture, or others, like Marl, simply were too gray to overlook. His pale skin held undertones of rocky marbling, and his short-cropped hair was the color of wet stone. He had a more pronounced gut under his casual clothes, and wrinkles were slowly invading the spaces around his eyes and mouth.

"Last I heard, you were a decoration in the University President's office," Marl said quietly. "It's been a while, Geo."

"What..." I hesitated. It would be rude to ask what happened to him, and something told me he was in tune with himself enough to be offended.

He inclined his head toward the library's exit. "Let's take a walk, shall we? It looks like you have a lot of questions."

"Sure." But I didn't ask, unsure of this new, jollier Marl.

He picked the path, and we walked at an aimless pace. When I didn't speak, he filled the space between us. "My daughter is a senior here. When Roe learned she was half-gargoyle, she reached out to tell me a little bit about you.

We're rare now, you know. Most gargoyles who've served a long time go into stasis and never return."

"Duty compelled me to awaken," I replied. "You have a daughter?" What I meant to ask was, *It's possible for a half-gargoyle child to exist?*

"Sure do." His gray eyes twinkled, and he pulled out his phone to show me a couple pictures of him making silly faces at the camera beside a young woman doing the same. "Took after her old man, too. She's a guardian witch about to graduate with a degree in Criminology. I've worked with the SPDI for about thirty years now."

"I have heard the acronym before but don't know what that is," I admitted.

"That's because it's a mouthful. It stands for Supernatural Police Department and Investigations. The only time I need to shift anymore is when a criminal gets it in their head that they can use their magic to escape the long arm of the law."

"And that is common?"

"Eh. Once a month, maybe."

Hmm, no wonder he was aging. Stone didn't wrinkle and shrivel up like humans do at the end of their life cycle. He would eventually expire if he continued to remain out of his gargoyle form.

"I...don't understand. Why wouldn't you spend more time as a gargoyle?" I asked.

"Well, duty had me waking up from stasis too a few decades ago," he said. He veered toward the coffee shop Cress liked. "First, let's get a sip. My treat."

"My body does not require—"

"Trust me, it does," he interrupted. "Once you start eating and drinking regularly, you'll feel so much better."

I eyed him skeptically. I felt fine, if a little sore from my recent tempering.

"I can give you all the tips I've learned from my transition. Once you realize how good it feels to be alive, you'll never want to return to stone unless you absolutely have to," he promised. His words echoed common gargoyle knowledge. Many of those who caught a fancy for their flesh form and the pleasures it provided veered away from their duties to the library.

Transition was an interesting word, implying that he'd moved from one lifestyle to another. Marl was no longer the gargoyle I knew. It was his happiness, and the way it radiated from him, that had me open to hearing more about *transitioning.*

He placed a complicated coffee order, and we settled at a small table with the steaming cups between us. "Tell me of your life," I invited.

Marl nodded and began speaking of the moment he woke from a long period of stasis. He'd felt a new duty pulsing in his stone heart, which had led him to serve a verdant witch. It sounded quite familiar thus far.

"There was no danger to her, though, other than herself," he shared. A fond smile was aimed toward his coffee cup before he picked it up to take a cautious sip. "The clumsiest woman I've ever met. My first emotion was confusion at being called to the side of a woman after she tripped over a curb.

"Of course, out of an abundance of caution, I stayed with her for a time to be sure she wasn't threatened by something unseen. I ended up carrying cupcakes and other orders to her clients since she was always afraid she'd fumble and drop them. She's a baker—an artist with icing, really—and she'd tempt me into my flesh form so I could sample her treats."

Marl patted his belly with a laugh. "I grew a taste for them. Once all the dust cleared from my lungs, I enjoyed them even more. I carried emotions like joy and love with certain flavors, and that was how I eventually realized I loved my clumsy baker and wanted to make a life with her. Everything about her made me *feel*, and that was better than years and years of being alone. On my own, I'd chosen to sleep, to leave the world. Now, the idea makes my skin crawl."

"I would rather not go back to stasis, either," I said.

"You must've found your own woman, then. Do your instincts call her your duty?"

I pictured Cress with a wistful twist of my lips. "Yes."

"It sounds to me that you've found your mate, too. Congratulations," he said warmly.

My expression didn't shift from stony concern, and his expression fell after a few seconds. I felt I could confide in Marl, though. If anyone would understand my deepest concerns, it would be a fellow gargoyle who'd been through this before. "I am not her only male, and no matter what I do, she clearly prefers the company of other men."

"Hmm, I want to hear more, but let's try something first." He gestured for me to pick up my coffee cup. "Take a smell of it."

I did as he bid, taking in the aroma of rich, warm coffee blended with milk.

"You may not realize it, but you're building a memory right now. It's normal to pair memories with tastes or smells. Have you had coffee before?"

"Only sips," I replied. "Cress...my duty, she enjoys coffee that tastes very sweet."

I tasted the blend he'd ordered, which was not nearly as sweetened. With more of the flavor of the coffee apparent, I didn't mind it or the heat that traced its way down my throat as I swallowed.

"Coffee is great post-shift. I have a particular drink I always get after having to take my stone form that reminds me of leisurely Saturday morning wakeups and my family." He inhaled the vapor above his coffee with a sigh. "It grounds me and reminds me of what's most important in life. I suggest you find something that does the same for you."

I took another sip and closed my eyes. I was at my most relaxed right now; no wonder this shop was so popular.

"You're human now, Geo. You're alive. Do you feel alive?"

I took in a deep breath and let my eyelids lift more slowly. My emotional state was stable. No, content. For the first time in a long while, I felt fully in control and ready to take on the problems that followed a messy, living existence. Even like learning to coexist with the men who intended to share Cress with me. "Yes."

13

CRESS

My DAYS FELT HOLLOW without Geo's presence. It was almost funny how much I noticed one person's absence with how often I was surrounded by others.

The spirit of motivation had taken hold of me, and I didn't struggle within its claws. I did my best in my classes, staying at or above a passing grade in them all. However, it was a relief to get my ass out of a seat at the end of the afternoon to head back to Moongrove Library and pick up my sword. Its grip and weight were becoming as natural to me as an extension of my own arm.

Without Geo, I saw a lot more of Phaeron and Ben. They didn't walk me to every class, but early morning and late evening trips across campus were usually colored by Ben's humor or Phaeron's wit. They'd both taken places in my friend group, too. Well, Ben more tiptoed back into the spot he'd already made for himself, while Phaeron was cautiously accepted as a mentor figure.

Bianca, too, fit easily in the group, despite her origins. She just seemed to keep some of her thoughts firmly sealed behind her lips, especially when Ben wasn't around. Once she was recovered, she'd started helping him train the rest of us for what we'd potentially see in Garroway's manor.

It was Phaeron I had to thank for most of my bruises. On Monday, Wednesday, and Friday, I trained with him twice a day thanks to his assistant professor job, which meant he now co-taught my Library Science 101 class. He'd "abandoned pretext," as he called it, and used Mr. Eriksson's obvious fear of him to steal me away from the classroom for private tutoring sessions.

Though white fire occasionally flickered in his gaze like embers trying to set something ablaze, he was strictly professional during these times. Too often, he had me flat on my back and a sword to my neck. It wasn't fair—he had two of them!

"No one will hold back against you in a real combat situation, bright soul."

Speaking of unfair, though, as a librarian witch, I had a huge disadvantage against a blood witch in a fight. The first time I trained with Ben, he'd swept my sword aside with one dagger, stepped into my guard, and held the other blade to my throat. *Without* any blood-drawn runes for strength or speed.

"There's no such thing as a fair fight, babe."

Five days did not make me an expert duelist, but I learned several new spells and every blood witch trick Ben or Bianca could drill into my skull. Phaeron had called the level one through three spells I was learning "foundational" and wouldn't test my magic further with more advanced techniques until I was ready. The librarians I saw working in Moongrove Library every day had to at least have a grasp on power-level-four magic, the spells of which were geared toward controlling and commanding the dangerous forces contained in the lower levels.

In what little free time I had, I experimented with my familiars. Bella was better at lending me feline senses, while Milo, despite being my chubbiest cat, always preferred to give me enhanced reflexes. Jin watched but remained a little apart.

When I got exasperated one time too many at my flying, babbling handbook, Phaeron borrowed it for an evening and returned it with a thick leather clasp over the pages. "This way, it can talk when you permit it," he'd said.

He also gave me a modified belt made for fully trained librarians, to which I could attach a book and my sword's scabbard on either hip. I'd been so thankful and posed in the mirror with the belt on and loaded, feeling official.

The one thing we didn't notice was any sign of Garroway himself. After we'd freed Bianca from his control, I wondered if he wanted to keep the rest of his assassins away from us, just in case. I didn't want to consider the other possibility, that he'd packed up his people and things and moved his operation now that it was compromised.

Ben had less than a week left of his deadline. He spent most of his evenings in my dorm room, where other activities gave me too many peeks at the red line creeping ever closer to his heart like an insidious blood infection. We had to get the magical weapon that'd made this from Garroway, no matter what.

It was Thursday evening when a tiny winged person delivered news of Dr. Aurina's plans in a sealed envelope addressed to Phaeron. "We're going this Sunday, midday," he told us, then took another glance around the room. "Some of us will, at least, be joining volunteers from the campus security team and Dr. Aurina's private contacts, along with the cupid herself."

Willow and I exchanged a glance. She started to wilt,

knowing he had to be talking about her staying behind when he referenced "some of us" going. Her grasp on her magic was shaky at best. The bubbles of water she worked with would either inflate into too-big domes and explode in her face or fall to the ground like she had no magic at all. I went to put a comforting arm around her.

Roe, Bianca, and Áine were the only obvious choices to attend alongside the friends Phaeron had found on short notice. I'd met them all briefly over dinner last night. Mostly a couple of dimensionals old enough to remember Soiluire, who'd been keen to discover their prince returned from his wrongful imprisonment. There were more dimensionals who *hadn't* wanted anything to do with our fight, however, too afraid of the Hungering Darkness to pick up their weapons and fight. And then there was David.

David, unlike everyone else, had greeted Phaeron with an effusive hug that nearly dragged the big gray man off his feet. "I got the job!" he'd exclaimed. "Campus security."

I'd peered at his aura and nodded to myself. Shifters were still the hardest supernaturals for me to identify at a glance if they didn't wear features of their animal sides openly, but their auras didn't lie.

"Congratulations, friend." Phaeron had slapped him on the back. I'd learned that David was a bear shifter and apparently the first friend Phaeron had made upon waking up in the modern day.

With all the allies we'd come up with, I was more than aware that a stony one was missing. We couldn't stall for time, not with Ben and Bianca both on a deadly deadline due to expire on Samhain. I just couldn't help but feel that it was my fault that Geo was spending so much time away from us.

When presented with the choice, again, I'd picked Ben

and our immediate physical connection over the deeper, slower, forming emotional bond that linked Geo and me. I hoped he was all right, whatever he was doing. Roe had shared that he was undergoing tempering to strengthen the resistance of his stone to magic. While I recognized it as important, I wanted to see him again.

The group agreed to have one last training session Friday evening so we could recuperate and recharge our magic before the big event. I intended to ask Phaeron if he still needed me to come along to ground him. As hard as I'd worked, I didn't have a lifetime of grueling training and an affinity for magic meant to fight other people, like the majority of the witches we'd face in Garroway's manor. Yet I still wanted to go and support Ben.

I entered our training room in the library, waving a hello to Roe already doing some warmup stretches, and stopping dead as I saw who else was already here. Geo was standing against the wall like he'd never left. My heart leapt to my throat.

"Geo," I said in surprise.

There was something different about him. Maybe it was his smile and the way it carried an air of confidence that had his silvery eyes twinkling. He closed the distance between us in two long strides and had me securely in his arms the next moment. Nearly a week's worth of tension fell from my shoulders in one whoosh of breath. Though I tilted my head up for a kiss, he cupped the back of my neck to draw me further into his hold.

My protector was back. I held him just as securely, murmuring into his shirt, "I missed you."

"My absence was necessary." He cleared his throat. "I mean...I'm sorry for my abrupt disappearance. I needed some time to improve myself."

"I heard about it from Roe." I turned and realized that she was no longer in the room with us. In fact, neither was anyone else except for my cats and handbook, which was hovering in a corner at a safe distance from cat paws. Roe was outside the room, chatting with Ben and Phaeron's less distinct voices and proving why she needed an award for being the best friend a gal could ask for.

"Did she tell you about the process?" he asked. I shook my head no. As he described it, my eyes widened. It sounded a lot like torture, but he'd promised that was how tempering worked.

"You didn't have to go through all that. Or make such a big promise to Phaeron," I protested.

He touched a fingertip to my lips. "I did. I had to, for you," he said. My breath caught as his fingers brushed my cheek. "Truth is, I needed time to think and be away as much as I needed to temper my body." It was clear what he'd been thinking about, too, which made me hyperaware of each touch.

He cupped my face and gazed down at me with a sparkle of adoration. "I needed to realize what you mean to me and how I can show you." He read my face, memorizing it, before lowering himself to finally meet my lips in a slow, tender kiss. I basked in the way his hold made me feel so safe and shielded from the rest of the world.

My heart could've busted right from my chest. "Don't leave me like that again. Without saying goodbye," I murmured.

"Never," he promised. "But perhaps...I would be willing to share your time more."

Who was this man, and what had he done with Geo? I smiled hopefully, thinking maybe we could begin setting more healthy boundaries not just between us, but also between the other two men who rivaled him for my time.

"We will have to discuss that very soon." I knew now wasn't the time when the others began filtering into the room and Phaeron approached us, his gaze lifted over my shoulder at Geo. *Uh oh.*

They exchanged nods of acknowledgment, and Phaeron said, "Welcome back. Shall we start training?"

"I have a quick question for you," I said to the dimensional, trying to step to the side to have a more private conversation with him. I leaned in close and whispered, "Do you still need me to come along to help you fight?"

"What?" Ben exclaimed, having not moved far enough away to miss the question. He whipped back toward us. "I thought we agreed that she was staying behind." This drew Geo's attention, whose expression showed he hadn't changed his mind, either.

Phaeron's keen eyes darted. He was thinking quickly, which gave me hope. "The agreement was that the young ladies who proved they could handle themselves could go. Cress has."

Fear bleached Ben's face. "Bullshit. You saw how that... that *thing* in my brother wanted to eat her. She's the last person who should be going." He stepped forward, catching my hand between his. "Cress, please. You know you should be sitting this one out."

"She won't be fighting unless she has to," Phaeron interjected. His tail lashed, betraying some inner turmoil, and he avoided my gaze when I turned a look of betrayal his way. "She will be with Geo and me, acting as bait."

Ben's eyes bugged wide. "Bait! Fuck that."

"Bait?" I asked more calmly. He'd mentioned that he'd needed me there to ground him, not that I would be a draw for the Hungering Darkness. But if it meant I could join them and help Ben, I would. I could take care of myself.

"If Endaeron is there, he will sense Cress, Morgana's soul within Geo, and me in one place. I don't know of any better trap than that. You do want us to capture your brother alive, yes? This may be our only chance." Phaeron's tone was as hard and cold as stone.

The three men had the kind of stare-off that made me worry they'd spark an actual fire.

"I consent to this. I've learned from the best, and I'll run if things become too dangerous," I said first. Phaeron tipped his hand my way as if that concluded the matter.

Ben was about to argue when Geo responded, "I will only tolerate this because I've been tempered and prepared for the fight ahead. We will lure out the biggest danger to Cress's safety and dispatch it."

"Fine," Ben sighed. He ran a hand through his honeyed hair, leaving it in a tousle. "We'll be a happy unit, because I'm coming too."

"Fantastic. I'm glad we could all agree on something... for the second time ever." Phaeron's lip quirked with humor.

14

BEN

We gathered early Sunday morning in a building on the outskirts of campus, the office and training grounds of NSU's campus police. The bulk of the group going were professionals with affinities or powers that matched up well against blood witches. I was exceptionally nervous around all these guardian witches and shifters and the scattering of cupids.

Dr. Aurina was here, meeting with Phaeron and the head of security, and her mates and a couple of her friends were coming along. I understood the strategy—we might have an easier time if Garroway's enslaved coven were crippled by an overload of pain and fear, magnified from the magic of multiple cupids.

I had a sour feeling in my stomach, regardless. My deadline was up in a few short days, and the pain from the magic was a constant pulse reminding me of what would happen if this raid failed. Garroway was too clever not to be prepared for us.

I'd put my limited affairs in order, just in case. I'd enjoyed my taste of freedom to the highest—I had the opportunity to make friends, to have Cress in my arms again, and even mailed off a message to one of my estranged Evenstar aunts with a carefully worded explanation of where Lucas and I had gone and what had really happened to our mother. Bianca had helped me track down what was left of my family online, and I'd picked this aunt in particular because her smile on various social media posts seemed kind.

But as I faced down my own mortality in the wait we had to endure before the raid started, I knew it wasn't enough. I was not ready to check out. I'd do nearly anything to stay, to keep this nice little life I'd started to form for myself.

I wanted so much more.

My gaze traveled the length of the room we all waited in. Cress stood against the wall with Geo, his dark arm wrapped around her hips. She giggled at something he said and leaned her head against his shoulder. I loved that laugh...actually, I simply loved that woman, enough to share her, which I never thought I'd be willing to do for anyone.

I hadn't told her how I felt, not wanting to cause her more pain if I didn't live past this evening. Instead, I'd tried to show it through every tender kiss, each stolen glance and brush of our fingertips. I'd followed her back to her dorm night after night, and she hadn't hesitated to let me in so I could show my love skin to skin with her. In that, I'd indulged in the selfish urge to keep her to myself and out of anyone else's bed.

Cress came to see me before long, greeting me with a brief kiss. "Hey. How are you holding up?"

"Just fine." I may have promised not to lie, but it sure felt like one. "It's not too late to go back to your dorm."

Her lips pressed into the stubborn line I was familiar with. "No, Ben. I'm coming along to help you. And Lucas."

My palms were a little sweaty at the reminder. I'd face down my demons with a smile on my face, but to think Cress would be there too...used as *bait*, no less.

She placed a hand on my chest, right above my heart. "This is everything I've been training for. Don't try to leave me behind." She batted her lashes up at me.

"Okay. Right," I relented. If only her charms worked on the people we'd be facing as well as they did on me. At least she'd be well guarded, whether she wanted to be or not.

Phaeron gathered us around soon after to tell us the plan. "Given that our two main targets are going to cower inside away from the sunlight, we will be heading into the manor and going straight to the vampire Garroway's quarters," he said. He spoke to a team made up of the people he'd personally recruited—myself, Bianca, Roe, Áine, Cress, Geo, David the bear shifter, and a group of four grim-faced dimensionals.

Phaeron unfolded a map, a photocopy of the sketch Bianca and I had made, and explained that we'd be going in last, through the back entrance. Aurina and her cupid companions would enter first to cripple with their emotional magic, and then the campus police would engage anyone still standing while handcuffing and removing any blood witches they could. I was glad to hear that we might have a chance to save some of the men and women enslaved to Garroway's will.

I put an arm around Cress, holding her protectively. If all went well, she would see very little of the place I'd spent most of my life. I could have Lucas back by this evening, and we'd be freed of Garroway forever by dragging him into the unforgiving sun.

I just hoped I wasn't dreaming while the bulletproof vests and weapons began being passed around.

When it was go time, we loaded into unmarked vans and came screeching to a sudden stop in front of the dilapidated lot in human Salem, where Garroway hid the pocket dimension to his grand manor. The sun was high in the sky as Bianca cut her palm and opened the doorway to the pocket dimension wide for the rest of us to pass through.

We piled out of the van, waiting tensely on the cracked sidewalk. No one lived on this stretch of road, but that didn't mean a mixed group of armed supernaturals wouldn't bring immediate alarm if we were spotted. Despite the autumn chill, sweat dripped down my back as I imagined everything that could go wrong in the minutes that passed.

Phaeron crouched a foot ahead of me, his voice hushed as he turned to the crimson-skinned dimensional woman next to him, who hid her face from the sun with a lift of one of her wings. "I sense a disturbance. He's here," he said.

"We'll follow your lead, my prince," she replied. "Let's get him contained swiftly."

He nodded and looked past me, sharing a meaningful glance with Cress, who was toward the middle of our group. I made a note to ask what that was about if I had the chance.

There could only be one "he" they were referring to, and I struggled to calm my racing heart. I'd soon be face to face with the monster who thought he could use my brother for a puppet. This time would be different, I vowed.

A whistle went up, the signal to enter the pocket dimension. I twirled one of my blades between my fingers and kept one eye on Cress as we approached the rip in reality Bianca had opened.

The manor's roof was smoking, with fire flickering along the upper levels. I stumbled over my own feet, staring.

"Uh, I don't remember this being part of the plan," Roe commented.

"It was," Phaeron said. "A backup if Aurina thought her magic wouldn't be enough. We're now on a time limit—let's move."

"Shouldn't we have known about this?" Áine grumbled, her deer-like ears folded back.

"This is a little unexpected for me as well. But we must adapt," the dimensional answered calmly.

Out on the lawn, guardian witches and familiar faces were locked in deadly dances of blades, stones, and the occasional gunfire. Most of Garroway's assassins preferred edged weapons that required an up close and personal touch, all the better to steal someone else's blood and magic, but we were prepared for projectiles as well.

We skirted the edge of the battlefield. Cress summoned her magical barriers, layering one atop the other, while Roe formed a solid shield of rock from stone pulled from the ground and carried it along. She'd slam it into the ground to give us a wall to take cover behind, if we needed it. Filling the gap between them was Geo in his gargoyle form. His shiny stone body didn't even flinch when a bullet ricocheted off him.

Winged shapes circled over the manor, fanning the flames. I didn't see any distinct rose gold wings, but it had to be Aurina and her mates smoking out the place. We reached the rear door and slipped inside. An assassin jumped out at Phaeron, dagger whipping toward his neck with enhanced speed.

He flinched and turned his body into smoky shadows, which were disturbed by the path of the weapon. It was the winged dimensional woman who reacted first, blasting the assassin's side with a superheated gust of air from her palm. If I thought I was sweating before, between her magic and the crackling flames overhead, I'd soon soak through my shirt under the bulletproof vest I'd borrowed.

The assassin hit the wall hard, his head clunking against it with an audible *thump*. He sagged, unconscious, and Roe clamped handcuffs of solidified dirt and rock around his wrists.

"Calling in. One neutralized," whispered David into a radio while we moved on cautiously.

At any given time, Garroway had anywhere from five to fifteen of his blood witches on hand. If he were expecting this attack, that number could triple, as he had reserves of men and women tucked in places the rest of us didn't know about. I often suspected he had more than one manor, run by someone he trusted and staffed with a separate coven of witches that never interacted with us here in Salem.

My fears about how many assassins he'd brought was confirmed when we entered the main foyer. Garroway was always a stickler for the angles of the furniture here and the presentation of the valuables he put on display. I couldn't help a grin at how one couch was upended and a handful of artisanal lamps were shattered on the floor alongside the big shards of what'd once been an immaculately polished glass tabletop.

Some of Garroway's assassins pushed the furniture away, making room for the two people who circled amidst a drizzle of embers catching in the ceiling high above. One of the combatants limped, a shiny wing askew as she tracked the familiar form of Garroway. Both wore clothing meant for combat, but hers was already stained with blood, while he seemed cool and in control even now.

We didn't have to say anything—this *definitely* was not part of the plan. Instead of beaming her magic out to cripple Garroway's coven, here she was trying to take on the master who'd taught most of us how to fight the painful way. I doubted the curvy, beautiful cupid could overwhelm a vampire who fed off of emotion, which threw out her magical advantage.

"Shame it had to end like this, Melinda," he said. He spared our group a brief glance before snapping his fingers, causing any nearby assassins to turn on us in a whirl of steel and crimson magic.

"No," she gritted out, flaring her wings behind the onrushing assassins. I staggered from the force of emotion that rolled from her.

Fear dug familiar talons in my gut. The emotion seized me, cold and unrelenting. I'd only ever been afraid of one man this deeply, the red-eyed vampire who drank up every nuance of fear and pain from his witches like they were the finest vintage. He was doing that now, even, while his trained men and women stumbled for a crucial few seconds.

The others rushed forward to meet the assassins while I whipped my head to dislodge the clinging cupid magic. I wasn't really afraid to the extent Aurina made me feel. No longer did I have to fear for my life or cower in front of Garroway, knowing that pain was coming and I was helpless to stop it.

My gaze flashed over the makeshift battlefield, which

had quickly descended into chaos. I spotted Áine sweeping the legs out from under one blood witch while Roe knocked him out with a punch reinforced with stone. Geo had locked his hands around the wrists of a different assassin and held the struggling woman steady as Cress quickly ruined her blood rune with a swipe of her sword.

Garroway whipped a glowing dagger through the air, narrowly missing Aurina's sculpted cheekbones. She was significantly slower than him, and it reaffirmed for me that she was outclassed. She had a sword in hand and a gun at her hip, but she would not be fast enough to hit him with either.

However, he was fighting with only a shard of darkness, the weapon I needed to end my deadline. I tightened my hold on my weapons and stepped forward, ready to come to her defense, when one of his loyal assassins intercepted me.

Flipping a dagger between his fingers like he'd taught me years ago was Seth, his weathered face set in a professional mask. With his salt-and-pepper hair and premature wrinkles, he was the eldest blood witch under Garroway's control. He stood there as calm as ever, even as something in the roof cracked and gave way, releasing a shower of stinging soot and drawing more than one person to cough around us.

"Hello again, Benjamin." Even as he spoke, he slid fluidly into a ready stance. I did the same, mirroring him.

"Step aside now. I don't want to hurt you," I said.

"Nor do I want to hurt you. But it's rather inevitable, don't you think?"

"Bare your blood rune. I can save you from this life." I gestured around me to where the foyer was filling with smoke. We wouldn't be able to stay much longer.

He chuckled and did as I asked, showing the crimson

rune along the right of his ribcage. A thicket of old dead-lines created braided patterns along his chest from it, and at least three of them were red and active. I still lunged without hesitation, blade aimed to cut through his rune, and he caught my wrist with the edge centimeters from his skin.

"It's too late for that," he whispered. His hold on my wrist tightened, and he twisted, forcing me to release the weapon. "Listen to me, Ben. The master has engaged dark forces beyond our understanding."

Blood began to run from his nose and the corner of his lip. "Seth, no," I said, horrified. "Let me—"

"Shh. I've made my decision," he said gently. I could feel the heat from his blood rune from here as it spread through the rest of his body and became a furnace. He'd die a slow, painful death for betraying the master. While he struggled to speak, I leaned in to take in every word so his choice wouldn't be for nothing. "He converses with...what used to be Lucas. He's turned the black dagger on himself. He wants to contain the darkness next..."

Seth coughed blood. His eyes were glassy with fever and an unnatural shimmer of heat lifted from his head, beyond the point of no return. "He has...teleport charm...leave..." he wheezed.

"Thank you," I said.

Heat pricked the corners of my eyes. This man was the closest thing I had to a father, and even now, he was looking out for Lucas and me. His sacrifice meant more than he knew, and all I could do was put my gratitude into those two words before he drew a second dagger, pivoted, and threw both of his weapons.

Seth collapsed, gone in a split second. He'd chosen to go in the only way faster than betrayal of secrets—a direct attack aimed at Garroway. One of his daggers sank to the hilt in the vampire's back, the other opening a nasty gash in his thigh. He turned his blood-hued gaze our way, his lip curling when he realized what'd happened.

"He always was a sentimental fool," he drawled.

My shock and sorrow stoked to an instant inferno, just as hot as the flames that threatened to come down on our heads. "We have some unfinished business, *Garroway*," I said.

I didn't stoop to pick up the weapon I'd dropped, instead switching the other to my dominant hand. I extended my fingertips, pulling at the blood pooling down his pants leg to do what blood witches did best: steal the best attributes and magic of other supernaturals.

I painted runes in his blood up my arm, borrowing his innate vampire agility, strength, and enhanced senses. "Oh, yes, what was it again? You wanted to drag my body outside and dance in my ashes," he mocked.

I lunged, my steel a silvery blur that opened a cut on his arm. He'd stepped back, giving Aurina an opening to thrust her weapon at him. His vampiric blood sprayed when it made an appearance through his shoulder, mere inches from his heart.

Garroway looked down at the wound with an amused tilt to his lips. *Fuck.* I knew that look. He was still several moves ahead of all of us, with something else up his sleeve. That was the only reason he'd be smiling while his manor burned down around him.

"Too bad you won't get the chance," he said, confirming my suspicions as he lifted himself off the sword and disappeared with his enhanced speed.

With the runes I'd painted in his blood, I was able to

track where he'd gone, retreating away from the worst of the fighting. He lifted his hand in a signal.

Another person landed before him from a leap from the second story balcony. Lucas unfolded to his full height, eyes full of white fire and a glowing charm dangling from his fist by a dainty chain.

"Hey, big bro," hissed the Hungering Darkness.

15

CRESS

"He's got a teleport charm!"

Ben's shout drew my attention. I'd been in the process of helping move unconscious blood witches away from the worst of the fighting. Our forces had met up in this foyer, and multiple campus police officials were trying to get us all to leave before the manor collapsed with everyone inside.

There was Ben, standing across from his brother, who stood protectively in front of the man that had to be Garroway. My gaze darted around, looking for Phaeron. I'd held my own, just like I'd been trained, but I knew why I was really invited to this raid. When I finally spotted the dimensional, he'd collapsed to his knees and was clawing at his face, leaving rivulets of fuchsia blood to run down his cheeks like tears. White fire started eating into the shadows that lined his hands.

I touched the mark he'd left upon my wrist, the sign of his protection. Stepping back into a darkened corner, I called out Phaeron's name. His head jerked in my direction, but it wasn't quite like the last time. Ivory flames had already claimed his gaze, which roved over me with obvious hunger.

Quaking with a sudden surge of fear, I jabbed my fingertips into the mark harder. "Phaeron, snap out of it!" I shouted. He paced toward me, licking his lips and the points of his fangs.

"Aren't you hungry, though?" whispered the hissing voice of the Hungering Darkness. Despite being several yards away, I heard it clearly, like it was breathing in my ear. Lucas was looking my way as well, turning his back to Ben.

A huge mistake. Ben moved impossibly fast, leaping onto his back and grappling for something he was holding while thrusting a dagger into his shoulder. "Get out of my brother, you body-snatching freak!" he shouted. With a stumble and snarl, the Hungering Darkness's attention fixed on the young man trying to throw him off balance.

Phaeron shook his head rapidly and paused mid-step, taking a shuddering gasp. He lifted his chin and watched the white flames dancing along his arm rapidly shade back toward their natural color.

"Thank you, bright soul," he said before summoning his full magic. The harsh shadows around us shuddered from the pulse of power that I felt in a wave of goosebumps head to toe.

I'd seen sketches of the shadowborn form Phaeron could take, covered in flickering black shadows that danced like layers of fur in the wind, but this was the first time I saw it in the flesh. Darkness enveloped him head to toe, with features emerging from a ball of shadow that covered his head. First, pointed ears, then a muzzle packed with razor-sharp teeth. He remained upright and looked like a pseudo werewolf with his burning topaz eyes. Shadows covered the length of his ornate swords last, lending them a deadly new edge and several inches of extra reach.

Pivoting, he lifted his weapons horizontally and charged back into the fray, leaping over our friends' heads with one mighty bound and an unearthly, eardrum-shattering sound that could've been a shadowborn's howl. I made to follow, but a mountain of muscle shouldered into my way. Giant, claw-tipped mitts caught my elbows. It was David, showing some of his bear features in the thick of battle.

"We have to get out of here!" he shouted.

"Not yet," I said and coughed. Thick smoke was rolling through the air, suggesting the manor was truly burning. Most of the campus police, and even some of my own team, were already evacuating. I'd barely noticed, but the manor had to be close to full collapse.

I sidestepped David despite the danger, lifting my sword. He growled and grabbed my shoulder, holding me in place. "You can't go back there," he said, his grip impossible to shake off. I accepted this reluctantly, watching the rest of the fighting from a safe distance.

Garroway and Lucas were the only enemies I saw still standing, separated by my allies. Aurina and Bianca were both attempting to strike Garroway, who had barely slowed down despite several bleeding wounds. It was possible his vampiric healing had already sealed over the worst of the damage.

Phaeron had leapt straight for the Hungering Darkness, which relied on Lucas's reflexes to avoid the sweep of shadow-lined swords. It was not fighting well with Ben and Geo also focusing their attention on it. Only one of its arms was coated in white shadow, while the other clutched something to its chest defensively.

For once, I thought we could win—if only we had more time. Sunlight rushed in over the stairs as part of the roof collapsed with a dramatic *crack* and the whoosh of flames finding new, dry carpeting to burn.

The Hungering Darkness attempted to swipe at Geo, just to send up sparks and a distinctive screech like metal shrieking together. Geo flashed his quartz teeth and said something too low for me to understand before launching a spike of stone from his palm.

Instead of hitting Lucas, Geo had aimed for and impaled Garroway through the shoulder. The vampire was mid-taunt toward Aurina as the cupid was mid-swing for another strike that he easily dodged. Turned out, he wasn't expecting the foot-long projectile. He dropped a shard of black stone, releasing a furious snarl.

Ben shouted and scrambled for it, as did Bianca. She caught it first, before Garroway's boot came down upon her wrist. It rolled out of her palm.

Ben grabbed it before the vampire could and touched it to his blood rune. A flash of red and black magic blew his protective vest to the side. It looked like spikes emerged from under Ben's skin, erupting out like shrapnel.

Ben's movements, so fluid and fast with the blood he'd obviously borrowed from Garroway, had slowed and taken on a clumsy edge as he stumbled toward Bianca. She met him halfway, clawing at her clothes to expose her blood rune. He touched it with the weapon and flinched away from the same sharp burst of magic from her rune just in time.

Garroway nailed Ben's jaw with an uppercut, and Ben's eyes rolled upward with the force before he collapsed. The black shard went flying. Peeling away from the fighting, the vampire ducked around Aurina's wing to run after his weapon.

With an irritated hiss, the Hungering Darkness stabbed at Phaeron and took advantage of his flinch, flowing into a wisp of white shadow that formed up again next to Garroway. The bloodied vampire had the shard, and Lucas rested a hand on his shoulder, the other holding a glowing trinket aloft.

David uttered a curse as tendrils of magic swirled around both men before they were gone. His big bear mitt finally released my shoulder.

"What was that?" I asked. Everyone else suddenly cursed a blue streak, even delicate Aurina, who fluffed out her undamaged wing with a sneer up at the burning ceiling. She was the first to turn and run toward the exit.

"They teleported away," David told me before he ran too, probably assuming I was a step behind him. I would've been, but both Bianca and Ben were limping and clutching their sides. They needed help.

That moment of hesitation cost me, and a fiery avalanche came down from the second floor, right over my head. My lips parted to scream when I saw it coming, but a dark blur knocked me out of the way.

Phaeron and I went tumbling, coming to a stop a few feet from the open door, the kiss of cool wind on my uncomfortably hot skin.

"That was a close one," he said. His voice was husky and deeper as a shadowborn, though the magic was receding from the touch of sunlight coming through the threshold.

He'd landed above me, his legs tangled with mine. The shadows dissipated around him, revealing the tracks of scratches down his cheeks and deeper claw marks across his chest.

"That makes us even today, then," I said. A fierce light gleamed in his topaz eyes.

"We are always even, bright soul," he said in a low purr. My heart leapt in surprise when he took a moment to kiss me before standing. With his grip on my hips, he easily placed me back on my feet so I could dash to safety with the memory of his pointed fangs running ever so delicately over my bottom lip.

"Why—" A fit of coughing interrupted me, like the clean air was too much for my abused lungs. Phaeron slowed to match my stumbling pace as we rejoined the dregs of the group escaping to human Salem and safety.

"Because I could see the questions in your eyes, and I'm afraid I don't have any answers," he replied.

My eyes narrowed at the reminder. I did want an explanation from him, but if he truly didn't understand what'd just passed between him and his brother, I at least had a guess. The Hungering Darkness had somehow compelled him and suggested he take a bite of my soul. This was far more serious than I thought. He'd definitely been downplaying the meaning behind the occasional flicker of white in his eyes.

He was quiet when we got back into the van, closing his eyes and holding still when Áine came over to mend his scratches. I moved seats to sit next to Ben, who was one of the last to arrive. I dug into the open kit of supplies on the van floor and started wiping some of the soot off his face with a towel.

"Did it work?" I dared to ask.

"You look. I don't know what I'll do...if it didn't..." He puffed with the effort of speaking, exhibiting all the signs of deep pain like when we'd originally damaged his blood rune. Slowly, he shifted the ragged edges of his shirt to expose it, and I pulled it further to the side to trace his deadline with my gaze.

It'd gone dark, as black as a fresh tattoo. He'd stopped the deadline. He'd live! I told him as much but added with a frown, "You're still hurt." The whole rune was puffy and enflamed, puckering around the scars that marred it to make an ugly, misshapen mass on his skin.

He wet his lips and chuckled. "It hurts more to take out something lodged in you. I'm free from him, Cress." He laced his hand with mine, moving it away from his side to rest over my thigh instead. "But it's not over."

The weight in his words warned me. He sniffed and let me guide his head onto my shoulder; I cupped his cheek and held him while a few tears slipped silently down his cheeks. "He's gone," he whispered.

"I know," I murmured. "But we'll find him again. They've only gotten away from us temporarily."

His brows scrunched before he sighed. "I more mean... you never met him, but..." In hushed tones, he told me a bit about Seth, the father figure who'd just sacrificed his life to warn Ben of Garroway's plans. We could look at what he'd said to Ben at another time, though. I held him until the van stopped and everyone else piled out.

We walked hand in hand to the campus security building to surrender our borrowed equipment and receive any healing we might need and a lecture out the door not to breathe a word of what'd happened to those uninvolved.

"No worries," Ben had answered with a hint of his usual smirk. As soon as we stepped out of earshot, he turned to me. "I'll be passed out in my room until Samhain anyway. Want to join me?"

16

CRESS

ROE CALLED a coven meeting the next afternoon, after all our classes. Six of the seven of us arrived pretty promptly, sprawling around our little room in the Witch's Clubhouse. It felt odd to see Wren, Heath, and Grant again, knowing how much had happened without them present as part of our coven.

The topic of the day was going to be the email we'd all received this morning. It was the talk of the campus, after all. I'd passed whispered conversations several times today, mostly fellow students sharing what they knew about blood barons.

I still had the email up on my phone, knowing it wasn't the triumphant message Aurina wanted to share, with a bolded title like: **ATTN: Curfew Extended**.

Northern Supernatural University
Office of the President

Dear NSU Family,
As Samhain approaches, many of us are looking forward to cele-

brating the lives of our ancestors. It is with regret that I must inform you that the school-wide curfew will continue until the end of the semester. This means our annual Samhain Ball will remain canceled for the safety of everyone gathered on our campus. Students are encouraged to practice their rituals and traditions indoors.

The reason for our caution has been properly identified. A blood baron vampire going by the name Garroway has decided to target our campus and student population. Below is an artist's rendition of Garroway and one of his closest associates. Do not attempt to engage them; these men are very dangerous. Contact the campus police immediately in the case of a sighting.

If you are a blood witch, you will be receiving a separate email with further instructions.

You may notice an increased presence of campus police, who are here for your safety and protection. Thank you for your understanding and patience as we work to bring these men to justice.

Sincerely,

Dr. Melinda Aurina

Attached were artist renditions of both Garroway and Lucas. They had a precise, police-sketch air about them, accurate and colorized. It might've been the first time Garroway's likeness was shared with a large audience. As a vampire, no photo or mirror would show him, and given his line of work, I doubted he had anything but the utmost anonymity until this morning.

Ben sat next to me on the couch, his arm slung casually around my shoulders and fingers playing with the ends of my hair. He'd gone quiet the moment he spotted his brother's likeness right next to Garroway's. "I guess this was overdue," he'd muttered.

They looked so alike, especially when one was just a

drawing, that I worried he'd be mistaken for his brother and reported constantly. I considered scrounging my pennies to buy him a hat or encouraging him to wear a disposable mask to hide his nose and mouth.

Roe was always the last to arrive to coven meetings, and this time, I wondered if that was intentional to bring out the worst in Wren. She was inspecting her perfectly manicured nails with a bored air, flashing an irritated look over her curled fingers when my redheaded friend burst into the room with a boisterous hello.

"Some of us have things to do, Ashbough," Wren muttered.

Roe's expression fell, her brows kitting. "The door's right there," she said, jerking a thumb over her shoulder.

The blonde's nostrils flared. "Excuse me?"

"You're free to leave. I know exactly the witch I want to replace you with, even," Roe answered, looming over Wren with her arms crossed. "I think the university made a mistake, pairing you with the rest of us."

I had a sinking feeling in my chest that this was about to be a messy confrontation. On the way here, I'd asked Ben to keep from mentioning Blaize Starsurge and his alleged role in my life. Without me talking to my mother on Samhain to confirm it, there was still a possibility that there was a different orphan out there who was Luna Darkmore, victimized by Wren's father instead. But I hadn't asked the same of the mother hen of our coven, who was just as likely to get in Wren's face.

"Roe," I said uncertainly.

"Now hold on, you two." Heath sat forward, putting his shoulder between the women. "There's no need for this. Wren's just frustrated that we haven't had a coven meeting in a while, especially with Samhain so close. Right, sweetheart?"

Wren grumbled under her breath. I repeated Roe's name, catching a moment of her attention. When she saw me shaking my head rapidly, she mouthed the word "why?"

"She shouldn't hear about it in a confrontation," I answered aloud. "She doesn't know." As bitchy as she could be, I sincerely doubted she knew the details of her father's illicit dealings. And throwing all of it in her face was the worst way to go about a difficult conversation. Besides, if we judged her for the sins of her parent, what would I need to answer for if I did turn out to be the last Darkmore?

"Are you two talking about me? You better tell me now," Wren snapped.

Ah, shit. I'd walked right into this.

"Could you let go of each other's throats for a minute so we can talk about Samhain?" asked the last person I expected to speak up. I wasn't the only one turning to stare at Grant. Usually, he sat in a corner at meetings like this, staring into space and only answering when asked a question directly. I'd assumed he was usually high, but Lanie's final letter to me had described his condition as "fae trickery."

"I want to know what you're talking about first," Wren demanded.

Grant rolled his eyes. Glaring around at all of us, he seemed to lack any air of a prim fae. "By the Mother Tree, this must be the most annoying coven they could've put me in," he grumbled.

"Are...are you feeling all right?" Roe asked him.

"I'm fine. Let's talk about Samhain," he prompted.

After an uneasy silence from everyone, Roe cleared her throat. Heath held Wren's hand, glaring over at us while she had her mouth twisted with displeasure. Willow was watching everything with wide eyes, her lips moving silently as she repeated something to herself. Next to me, Ben's teeth were practically grinding with how hard he'd set his jaw to remain quiet. I nudged him and smiled, grateful he'd kept himself out of the argument.

"Samhain. Do we want to do anything as a coven? I was thinking perhaps a nature walk or a Dumb Supper. We could have it here, even," Roe said, throwing her arms wide in the narrow space of our clubhouse room. "I've already made an ancestors altar in my dorm. If you don't have one and would like help making one, I wouldn't mind giving some advice or coming over to help set it up."

"Okay, I'll ask it first. What's a Dumb Supper?" Ben said after noticing my puzzlement.

Roe was happy to explain at least, tapping into the same enthusiasm she'd shown for drawing us all together for Mabon. "Dumb" was another word for silent, in this case a silent dinner held with an extra, empty place setting for the dead with an offering of a bit of the food and drink from the meal. After the dinner was finished, the plate and cup were traditionally left outdoors as an offering for the deceased.

"I'm down. My roommate is going to be annoyed that I'm putting it forward, but my place has a big table and more room than in here," Ben said. "You all bring the food. We'll host."

I lifted a brow in his direction. He hadn't once invited me over to see where he was living with Phaeron, but now he wanted to host our whole coven?

"Sounds like fun," Willow ventured quietly.

Wren breathed a heavy sigh. "Why did some vampire

have to ruin our chances to have a Samhain Ball? I had my dress picked out and everything."

Roe spoke over her. "I believe we should set up for Lanie to be the guest of honor. I remember a lot of her favorite foods and things. Would your roommate mind if I came by early to set up?" she asked Ben.

He shrugged. "Yeah, sure."

My throat tightened up. I was so grateful that we'd be doing this ritual to honor the friend who'd given her life for the rest of us. "I'd like to come early, too," I said with a little cough.

"There, that's settled." Roe then turned a baring of her teeth on Wren. "You can go now. Sorry for wasting your time."

For once, the blonde didn't have a catty remark. She seemed more confused than anything as she eased herself to her feet and motioned for Heath to stay. "Could we have a quick chat?" she asked, pointing one of her long nails toward the door.

With a nod, Roe followed her into the hall. The exchange was brief enough that I barely had time to worry before Roe returned and told Heath that Wren was waiting for him. When they were both gone, my redheaded friend blew out a tense breath and leaned against the wall. "Don't worry. I just told her to ask her father about Garroway," she told me. "We'll see if she does."

"I doubt he's going to tell her the truth," I scoffed.

"She'll believe it when SPDI comes knocking. Dr. Aurina wouldn't just keep the list of Garroway's known associates to herself, and Ben named him first," she pointed out.

"You overestimate the police's efficiency." Again, Grant startled us. He was usually the first one out the door, scrubbing away some of the boredom from his face.

An awkward pause hung in the air. Grant wasn't involved in the eventful couple weeks the rest of us had had. He didn't even know what list Roe was referring to.

"Hey, Grant. Where are you from?" Willow asked.

"Just outside of Lowell. Why?" he asked.

She loosed a nervous laugh. "Isn't it super rude for a non-fae to swear to the Mother Tree?"

I raised a brow and glanced back at Grant curiously. Was that true? The only other person I'd heard swear to the Mother Tree was Áine, but if it were forbidden, a verdant witch from a storied line like Grant would know that.

He glanced at his hands and chuckled. "Knew I should've kept my mouth shut. If I show you my secret, it will not leave the lips of those in this room. Understand?"

"Sure," Roe said easily, her eyes narrowed on him.

Willow and I also agreed, but Grant didn't do anything but stare at Ben until he also said yes.

"Thank you for agreeing to my terms. I believe it would benefit us all if you knew a little something about me." He flexed his fingers as he spoke, his voice taking on a soft, lyrical quality that was entirely not human. A transformation rippled over him, and in a few heartbeats, it was a completely different person sitting there and flexing four iridescent wings that wouldn't look out of place in miniature on a dragonfly's back.

Roe sucked in a breath. "Changeling."

Ben stood, dagger in hand. "What did you do with Grant?" he demanded.

The fae now straddling a chair in Grant's place waved a hand dismissively. His skin tone reminded me of the polished pinewood table my mother kept pristine back home, a light brown with striations reminiscent of wood grain. "Off at the Norwood estate with his girlfriend, I presume. His family hid him away in Maine after he struck a deal with me."

"You've been Grant this whole time?" Roe asked. "To think I was worried about you!"

His smile over at her was indulgent. "I rather enjoyed having a beautiful woman's concern. But fear not. I am not broken, just terribly bored with being forced into this coven."

Her face reddened. "Flattery's not going to get you anywhere, changeling. Time for you to go."

"I could leave." He folded his arms around the back of his chair, tilting his head. A braid fell over his shoulder, revealing how his evergreen hair shaded to orange about halfway down. His mischievous, sharp-angled features and unusual amber-brown eyes were quite fae, as was his nonchalance in the face of Roe's anger and Ben's threatening stance. "But you would have a tougher time removing Grant Norwood from your coven than you would, say, Wren, considering you've agreed that my secret does not leave this room. So why don't you hear me out instead? And perhaps put that dagger away?" He glanced Ben's way. "I get that you could gut me about five different ways in as many seconds. I'm a talker, not a fighter."

"I think we should let him speak," I suggested, tugging on the hem of Ben's shirt until he reluctantly sat and rested the weapon across his lap instead.

Roe crossed her arms. "I'll give you five minutes," she muttered.

"Five minutes? Guess I'll speak quickly," he said with playful cheer. "I borrowed a librarian's likeness the other day and saw some of your training sessions in Moongrove Library. You're elbow-deep in something my sponsor would be keen to learn about."

"Who is your sponsor?" Willow asked quietly.

"The less you know, the—"

"Probably the Autumn Queen," Roe interrupted.

"See, you're smart. I knew I liked you. But I don't work for her specifically," he continued on without missing a beat. "I want in on your intelligence. There is a list of Garroway's known associates? There was a confrontation with him and this mysterious young man who looks so much like Ben?"

Ben scowled. "Careful. I could just throw this dagger at you."

"How unfortunate for me! But more so for you. If you share what you know with me, I wouldn't mind putting my skills to use for whatever you need."

"Absolutely no—"

"Ben, wait," I said quickly.

"What's the catch?" Roe asked skeptically.

"Could you help us find Garroway and Lucas again?" I asked, pointing toward Ben. "His brother?"

"I'm sure I *could*," the changeling answered. "Your information in exchange for finding two dangerous criminals. Those would be my terms. Alternatively, we can stop these formalities and be friends instead. I'd do a lot to stop having asinine conversations as Grant."

I opened my mouth but closed it again with a look of warning from Roe. "We'll have an answer for you soon," she said.

"Before our silent meal, I would hope?" He got to his feet, approaching her. Tall and slim, he could look into Roe's eyes without trouble, but I figured if there was a fight, she could knock him out with one good uppercut.

"Sure," she replied.

He flashed his teeth in a smile as he sized himself down

to be human Grant again, leaning up to say close to her ear, "Great. I'll bring the potatoes." He sauntered out of the room, leaving her a little pink around the edges.

She finally selected a chair and sat heavily. "All right, I'll let Áine explain how bad that was."

"MOTHER TREE!" the faun squeaked once we found her as a group and took her to a relatively private location. That ended up being my room, where there was just enough room for the five of us. "You want to hear about the Autumn Court? Why?"

As it turned out, the changeling spy had gotten us to agree to a proper fae bargain. None of us could tell her the true intentions behind the question since she hadn't been in the room when the fake Grant had revealed himself.

"Just a sudden interest in history," Ben grumbled.

"*You* want to know about fae history?" Áine snorted. "I find that hard to believe."

"I could explain the court instead," my handbook said from its position hanging on the ceiling, pages swaying back and forth like a pendulum. "I'm, like, the authority on everything."

"No, no. All right, history lesson," Áine sighed. "The Autumn Court is rather new, in fae years. There are fae courts all over the place, and most are tiny and weak, but the biggest, strongest ones name themselves after concepts like, well, *Fall*. I've told you that NSU and New Salem took over the pocket dimension that used to be the Fall Court, right?

"I skipped telling you the bloody history of this place.

Fall was at war with my home court, Spring, for hundreds of years. The red-haired bitch that leads their court was stealing away fae from everywhere between Salem and the Spring Court, which is located in Florida. By using her captives as sacrifices, she empowered the Fall Court to grow close to the massive pocket dimension it is today."

"For the record, this happened way before any of us were born," Roe put in.

"Yeah. Moongrove Library wasn't even here yet," Áine agreed with a nod. "This was entirely a fae versus fae conflict. Every pocket dimension created by a group of fae and dubbed a court is kept stable by a tree nurtured by the life force of every fae that swears allegiance to the court's ruler. It's the court's Mother Tree. It grows bigger and stronger with the number of fae, which in turn makes the pocket dimension larger and the ruler's magical power level higher.

"What most outsiders don't realize is that the Mother Tree also determines how many fae can be present at one time. There comes a time when the fae cannot have any more children and the Tree does not grow any further. The pocket dimension is complete at that point. The Fall Queen's way around that was not our modern solution—inviting other races to use their own magics to make expansion possible—but instead to force all of her captives to swear allegiance to the Fall Court before slitting their throats with iron at the base of Fall's Mother Tree."

Willow and I both gasped. "Oh, how horrible," she murmured.

"I know," Áine said, frowning. "This caused the Fall Court to grow and grow, supplying the Fall fae with the ability to continue reproducing past the natural numbers a court should reach. We... I mean, the Spring Court only won the war and stopped the sacrifices by doing the unthinkable. A Spring changeling infiltrated their court and burned their original Mother Tree, by then an ugly abomination left to grow with no pruning.

"Big swaths of the pocket dimension collapsed. Thousands of fae simply...ceased to exist." She gave a delicate shudder. "It's the downside of living in a pocket dimension, you know? Fae bend reality to stay apart from humans, but the magic is vulnerable if the Mother Tree is. Because of this, the Fall Court abandoned their remaining land and fled. Many more fell because Spring Court soldiers were waiting for them. Unfortunately for us, several still survived, including the Fall Queen, who rebranded herself the *Autumn* Queen and hid her people away in a new dimension we've never found. Witches took over the remnants of the Fall Court's lands and, over time, rebuilt it to the massive pocket dimension we're in right now.

"Before you go feeling sorry for them, Autumn Court fae have proven to be just as awful as they were when they were trying to eradicate my court. Kidnappings, sacrifices, and trickery abound. They seek to take this pocket dimension back because the new Mother Tree here is nearly as powerful as the one they originally lost. They're banned from returning, as the Autumn Queen has eternally schemed about conquering both NSU and New Salem like it's still the old ages. She wants to have a massive sacrifice session to make a new mega Fall Court. She might reach demigoddess status if allowed to connect to a Mother Tree that powerful."

"Clearly, she can never come here," Roe said, a little louder than conversation volume. She looked between the rest of us meaningfully.

"How is she kept from simply walking in?" I asked. Obviously, her spy hadn't been stopped.

Áine waved vaguely. "Fae magic. Any Autumn Court fae over a certain power level and anyone related by blood to the Autumn Queen are not permitted to cross the barrier unless expressly invited by the fae the new Mother Tree has bonded with."

I exchanged a glance with Ben. His expression was drawn, but he met my eyes and shook his head. "We'll find another way," he said under his breath. I nodded in agreement. Any more deals with an Autumn fae sounded remarkably dangerous.

17
BEN

"COULDN'T you have invited our little friends earlier?" Phaeron asked while we watched Roe transform the front room's plain table into a proper Dumb Supper display. Lanie's cat, Jin, sat in the place of honor for the moment, accepting scratches behind her ears. "For a dinner where we can speak to each other, perhaps?" His tail whisked with some annoyance, but his gaze followed Cress as she went back and forth from the kitchen to retrieve plates and silverware.

"Maybe if they have enough fun, they'll come back," I suggested. I'd known damn well if I'd brought Cress around, he'd try to steal her away for a visit to the master bedroom. When I had a deadline marking the days in a burning path across my chest, I wasn't willing to share. But now that Garroway's unnatural magic was fading to a series of scars, I'd finally felt comfortable enough to invite her here.

He replied with a noncommittal hum. "Entertainment is the last thing on my mind," he said. I hoped he was focusing on the magic he'd have to do this evening to help us commune with the lost.

"Same, honestly. By the way, if Grant shows up, will you take an extra hard peek at his soul?" I asked. He raised a brow in my direction. "You know, just in case?"

"He's a verdant witch with no dark magic tainting his soul," he replied.

I opened my mouth to ask if he was sure about that when the words got stuck in my throat. I coughed into my fist instead. The limitations of the fae agreement I'd stumbled into chafed my nerves. The restrictions reminded me too much of Garroway's influence.

"Hmm. I'll take another look," he said.

Roe passed us on her way to the kitchen with food safety gloves on. "Thanks again for buying all of this on short notice," she said to Phaeron, who put on a charming smile and inclined his head.

The man had gotten a paycheck early due to his "unusual circumstances." The first thing he'd done with the money was buy the best versions of all the ingredients Roe had listed to make two dishes for everyone, a stir fry and beef bulgogi. When Roe had arrived, she'd sliced the meat and prepared the marinade, which had been resting in our fridge for a while now.

I'd made about a dozen recommendations for the rest of his paycheck, which he said he was going to save. Something told me he'd spend the rest of it on Cress if given the chance.

Cress had followed the redhead into the kitchen, quickly becoming a sous chef for everything Roe needed. That left Phaeron and me to welcome everyone that came to the door. The first arrival was little surprise, Áine bouncing into the room with a big plastic container with several layers of sweets in parchment paper.

"They're renewal cakes. My family makes them around this time every year," she explained. I reached over when she popped the top, mouth watering. Each little cake was decorated like tiny succulent gardens, some with fine vines and itty-bitty flowers for pops of color. The faun batted my hand away. "They're *very* sweet."

I smacked my lips. "Fine. I'll wait, just because you asked so nicely."

"The last thing you need right now is a ton of sugar," she said with a roll of her eyes.

Our next arrival was Geo, just starting to transform from gargoyle to man, with a plastic bag in hand. "I got them," he said.

"Is that Geo?" Roe called. "I need those sesame seeds!"

One benefit of not having wings, I guess, is that I didn't get picked to go to New Salem and retrieve the ingredient Phaeron had forgotten. When he went around the corner, he received excited praise from both women for how quick he'd been. I was a little jealous, but I didn't have much time for that as I greeted everyone who followed and got caught in the flow of casual conversation. The sun was high in the sky and we were observing Samhain in the light of day, just as NSU wanted.

"Don't keep us waiting for Wren. She's not coming," Heath said when he arrived.

I tried for an innocent tone as I closed the door behind him. "Trouble at home?"

He set his expression. "She's trying to get transferred to another coven again. I don't really blame her." I shrugged to myself. Roe wanted Bianca to join our coven, but I personally thought we should be removing "Grant" first, not Wren.

And speak of the fae, he came along too, holding a plate covered in tinfoil. "Potatoes, as promised," he said, far too cheerful about his tubers.

"Welcome, Grant," I said, then muttered under my breath, "If that's your real name."

He chuckled. "It's not. And this distrust is really rich, considering who you were."

I bared my teeth in a less than friendly smile. "You know much about that?"

"I've been asking around. By the way, the registrars are concerned that you haven't been by to specify your major and pick up your schedule, so I helped you out."

"You didn't," I practically growled.

"I didn't impersonate you. Who do you take me for?" he put a hand to his chest in offense. "I just told them to reach out to Cress. She's the one who can always find you."

"Thanks," I said with gritted teeth. I stepped aside for him to come in, missing the old, glaze-eyed Grant.

We'd decided that Roe would put this fae back in his place today. We weren't going to feed him information, not when it would get back to the Autumn Queen and endanger us all. But there wasn't much else we could do to chase him off, for now.

He went into the kitchen while the rest of us mingled for a while. Heath and Willow chatted about a couple classes they shared as new oceanic witches. Bianca and Áine were laughing and gossiping together. With Phaeron and Geo in a corner, putting their heads together about something—probably our upcoming visit to the local graveyard, defying every new rule NSU and Dr. Aurina wanted in place—I snuck a peek at the altar Roe had set up at the head of the table.

It was a simple display, with candles and autumn leaves propping up several images of a young woman.

"I wish I'd gotten a chance to meet you," I murmured. My gaze snagged on a picture of her with Cress, the two of them smiling in front of their dorm room full of unpacked boxes.

When Garroway first received information about Cress from Blaize Starsurge, it'd come with several candid photos of her. The only one where she'd been smiling was when she was alongside Lanie, the girl with the dark bob and a penchant for brightly colored clothes in each image here.

I felt...guilty. She must've been a great friend, judging by how much work Cress and Roe had put into honoring her memory. And it had been my brother who ruined that.

No. The Hungering Darkness had, and it was still at large. Still puppeting my little brother and plotting with Garroway. Now that the manor was gone, where were they?

"I think I'm being stupid, Lanie," I said under my breath, turning on my heel to go find Grant. The kitchen was a little too empty, with Cress alone chopping vegetables.

She turned, sniffling and red-eyed from fresh onions. "Have you seen Grant or Roe?" I asked.

She pointed down the hall. "They're having that chat," she said. That's what I figured, so I hoped I wasn't too late.

Roe was the one we'd chosen to turn Grant down since she understood the fae situation the best. The Autumn Queen somehow using us to return to power was obviously awful, but so was my brother's soul succumbing fully to the Hungering Darkness's evil. Every day, we crept closer to the moment it corrupted him or got bored with him and killed him. We needed help... *Lucas* needed help.

We could handle the fae situation another time. But when I found the two standing before the closed door to the master bedroom, they were in the midst of shaking hands.

"I knew you'd see reason," Grant was saying.

"Wait...what?" I looked between the two of them. Grant had his teeth bared in a victorious smile, while Roe's expression was vaguely irritated.

"Meet our new friend," she said, gesturing to him.

The wind whooshed right out of my sails. "You made a deal with him?" But *I* was about to make a deal with him in secret, and she was supposed to turn him down.

"For you, my services are now free." Grant smiled a little wider. "I just ask that you share your juiciest gossip, of course. Right after this meal, I'm off to tail your monsters."

He left Roe and me alone for a moment, and I turned to her for some kind of explanation. "I know," she muttered, refusing to meet my eye. "You're going to find this hard to believe, but I trust him. He swore on his true name that he's working against the Autumn Queen."

That was a pretty big deal, as far as I knew. Fae guarded their full names like treasure. It was a sign of trust and truth to tell someone else their name or to swear on it. "What's the catch?" I asked.

Her lips pressed into little white lines and she shook her head. "I'll share that when I'm good and ready. All you need to know is that I want us to give Grant a chance to be our friend. For all intents and purposes, he's a verdant witch in our coven who can get us any information we might dream of."

I narrowed my eyes, and she lifted her chin stubbornly.

Well, she was entitled to her secrets. "I just hope the price wasn't too high," I said and left it at that.

We went our separate ways until supper was cooked, and we all served ourselves before sitting down. Roe rang a bell to signify the start of the ritual, and from then on, it was silence.

It was interesting to see who was comfortable here. Willow, Grant, and Geo seemed the least bothered, which didn't surprise me too much. Cress kept glancing at the head of the table, where a bit of everything had been served to the empty chair. Her gaze fell back to her plate more slowly each time, as if disappointed Lanie's spirit hadn't taken that seat.

The scrape of cutlery punctuated the meal, which Roe eventually concluded with a second ring of the bell. She exhaled loudly. "Okay, everyone, that's it," she said. Her usual lively voice seemed too loud for a moment, until the table broke into conversation again around her.

"That was good," Cress said, mostly to herself.

Áine passed around her little decorated cakes, which were just as sweet as promised. I admired mine for about half a second before biting it in half, tilting the second part up to save the slow ooze of caramel. "Wow. I'm going to need about ten of these," I said.

"Or the recipe," Cress added.

"That's a secret." The faun puffed her chest with pride. "I'll make them more if you guys want."

There was a circle of yeses around the table. By the time the sun was beginning to set, Áine bounced back to her dorm with an empty container. The rest of our friends trickled out until Cress was convincing Roe that she could handle helping us with the rest of the cleanup. "You've already done so much," she said, patting the redhead's hand. "The ritual was really nice. It was like Lanie was here with us."

"It was, huh." Roe smiled sadly. "Well, if you're sure…"

"See you tomorrow," Cress said, practically pushing her out the front door. They parted ways with a hug. Once the door was shut, she turned back to the three of us who remained.

Phaeron glanced toward the kitchen. "We may as well actually clean up. I need it to be full dark to sneak you off campus with my magic," he said.

She nodded and headed that way. "Tell me how this works again?"

We worked as a team on the simple task: Phaeron at the sink, Cress drying, and me putting various things away. Geo retrieved from the table and back, a thin excuse to let him pace with a troubled expression.

"The veil between the living and dead here on Earth is truly at its thinnest tonight," Phaeron began. "My magic can call to the souls of the recently deceased by asking for them by name. But you should be aware that it is always a *request*, and the dead sometimes do not answer, especially if they're comfortably resting in the next life."

Cress worried her bottom lip between her teeth. "So, there's a chance my maybe birth mother won't answer your call?"

"Indeed. However, if she does not answer, you could sacrifice some of your blood, and we can try again. In theory, I could boost your call to the other world, and if you two are truly related, she will answer. She may be angry to be summoned more forcefully, but it's practically a guarantee she will appear."

His yellow eyes flashed toward me. "The same goes for your mother, Ben."

I swallowed thickly and nodded, momentarily robbed for words. When Phaeron had shared what he was doing for Cress, I'd wanted in as well, if only to apologize to my late mother for believing some of Garroway's many lies for too long.

"Let's go," I said.

Luckily, NSU faculty housing was on the side of campus that wasn't *really* the campus, so we didn't have to climb any of the high walls that'd been erected to separate NSU from the rest of New Salem during the lockdown. They'd been lifted to make checkpoints to screen those coming and going. There was a checkpoint for the faculty and staff, but it was in the opposite direction of where we were heading.

As soon as the sun set, Phaeron shrouded us with his darkness magic, and the four of us walked to a cemetery a few miles away. Discreetly dressed campus police patrolled the outside edges, looking to either stop any trouble or enforce the curfew for any who attempted to follow certain Samhain rituals after dark.

Under the cover of magic, we slipped past a couple of policemen and continued walking. The cemetery was massive, as many supernaturals wanted to be laid to rest with their kin. This also meant the police presence couldn't cover every square inch of the space.

Phaeron led us to a section with headstones worn by time but freshly scrubbed clean for Samhain. "This is the place," he breathed. "Cress, Geo, go keep watch. Ben, you're first."

Geo and Cress conferred for a moment before going to

stand far enough away to give us some privacy. She moved under the shadow of a spindly tree, while his gargoyle form's obsidian stone disappeared into the night except for the hulking outline of his bulky wings.

I turned to the dimensional, swallowing my nerves. "I just need to know her name," he said.

"Marie Evenstar. How long will I have with her?" I asked.

"Half an hour, maybe. It entirely depends on factors beyond our control." He gestured for me to stand back.

I watched from a safe distance as he wove a ball of shadows between his hands and stretched it out into a paper-thin rectangle. He spoke in a foreign tongue, rolling smooth words into a chant. When I started to tune out and let his voice become background noise, he abruptly said my mother's name and reached toward the shadowy shape.

The rectangle glittered like starlight, and he resumed his spell casting. He said her name three more times until there was no hint of shadow in front of him. As gently radiant as the moon, the original rectangle had become a gateway of sorts, and through it stepped a transparent woman with her silhouette outlined in gentle white.

"Is this her?" I asked quietly. The magic faltered for a moment as Phaeron grunted an affirmative. He had his head bowed, lips still moving.

The ghostly woman scrubbed her eyes and looked around in confusion. She was shorter than me, pleasantly rounded around the edges with some extra weight under a modest sweater and dark pants. Her blonde hair was piled up atop her head in a messy bun. I wondered if this was what she'd looked like when she'd passed away.

I could just *ask*, but my tongue felt paralyzed in my

mouth. *How many people would give anything for a moment like this? And here you are, struck dumb,* I chastised myself.

"Um, hello," I said, drawing the ghost's attention. "I'm Ben...Benjamin. Your son."

She stepped closer, tilting her chin up to look at me. I held my breath. Being told about this woman all my life was one thing, but I didn't really know how she'd react seeing me as an adult. I definitely wasn't expecting her to lunge forward and to be embraced by the feeling of icy pins and needles. The sensation moved to the back of my neck, and I bent down just as she wanted.

"Ben!" Her teary, white-lined eyes met mine. "My not-so-little boy! Look at how you've grown. Why, it was just yesterday, you were..."

She released me just as suddenly, her brow crinkling. "You were just a baby. What happened? How...?" Looking down at herself, she inspected her arms and then felt the back of her head. Understanding dawned. "I...I was murdered, wasn't I?"

"Yes," I murmured.

Her shoulders shook with sobs. I reached out and held her as best I could, joining her after a few moments. There was a time where I thought I'd cried my last tear, unable or unwilling to give Garroway another drop of weakness from all the pain he'd inflicted. This was much like reopening an old wound, revisiting the horrors that monster had imposed on my family.

I got myself back together first, however, saying, "We don't have much time."

She wiped her cheeks with her sleeve. "Of course. It's so nice to see you, Ben. Where is Lucas?" she glanced around like she expected him to surprise her from behind the nearest bush.

"Uh. That's a long story," I said. "Did you know a vampire named Garroway?"

"Vampire? More like snake," she muttered.

That was definitely a yes, then. "Did you try to get a loan from him?"

Marie seemed to deflate with the question. "Well...yes. Your father's family left me out to dry because they thought I sabotaged his car for some insurance money. I loved him, Ben. His death was a terrible tragedy that followed the passing of my best friend, Eris Darkmore. She and I were business partners, but without Eris or Liam, your father, I was down a creek without a paddle, so to speak. The debts were piling up, and the bank would've kept your inheritance if I declared bankruptcy, so I sought other options and ended up getting in contact with Garroway."

"He heard you out, then refused to lend you anything, right?" I sighed.

Her lips twisted, and she shook her head. "No, much worse. He offered me millions to buy you and Lucas. Way more than I was asking for as a loan. It was disgusting, and I told him as much and left."

My free hand balled into a fist, the other still resting close to Marie's back. "Then he killed you," I sighed, "and took us anyway."

"What happened next?" she asked with some hesitation.

Aware of Phaeron starting to sweat a few yards away, I kept the recap of my life brief. Marie's anger was understated, her nostrils flared and face reddened by the time I was finished sharing what'd happened with Lucas and why he wasn't here. "I'm glad you're free, I'll say that much. You said you reached out to one of your aunts, though? Which one?"

"Jordan Evenstar. She seemed the most approachable," I said, not mentioning how I'd seen her image. We could be here for days if I needed to explain social media to her.

"Jordan's a good choice. She was still a kid when I passed, but she had a fine head on her shoulders. If she is still an honorable woman, she will be able to give you your inheritance. Now that I know that you're alive and of age, though, I'm going to share some of my power with you. This may hurt," she said.

We'd been so busy theorizing over Cress's ancestral magic that I hadn't considered what'd happen when I inherited mine. "I wasn't very strong in my magic, but my channeling skills were exceptional," she told me. "As a blood witch, you'll have use for it when you take other peoples' magic from their blood. After this, I will try to wake Liam in the next life and have him give you a piece of the Evenstar legacy as well."

"Thanks, Mom," I said, letting her take my hands in hers. Her outline was starting to fade, and I had the feeling our time together was coming to a close. "I'm going to use anything you give me to save Lucas. I'll do everything I can. I promise."

The tingling sensation over my palm faded. Looking down, I spotted a twinkling spark of celestial-yellow magic absorb into my skin. Despite the warning, it didn't hurt for a moment, just felt like another living person had curled their hand around mine.

"What was the inheritance?" I asked like an afterthought. She was fading faster, and I wasn't ready for her voice to become a memory.

"A fine tool," she replied. For a moment, I swear I felt her hand tighten on mine. "Goodbye for now. I will see you in your dreams, and you will know me from my memories. That is the beauty of ancestral magic."

My throat tightened. I didn't want dreams or memories. I wanted her here with me.

"And I have no doubt, Ben, that you will save your brother and bring him here next Samhain. You've grown into a strong young man... I'm so proud of you."

With that, she was gone. Phaeron breathed in a little harder, his eyes opening into two yellow beacons in the dark. I still grasped air, reaching for her like she'd still be there, before turning my face away. I had a new goal now, at least—to bring Lucas here, alive and whole, next year. That way, she'd remain proud of me.

18
PHAERON

"IF THERE'S TIME, there's one more person I'd like to speak to after Cress has her turn," Ben told me before slinking into the shadows to trade places with her.

I released a weary sigh. The process was so much more taxing for bringing back souls that'd been gone for longer than a year. Either that, or I simply didn't remember how difficult it was to use my magic this way.

While witches and most other supernatural creatures relied on reading each other's auras, my kind had always been more attuned to souls. I imagine any confident and powerful dimensional could call to souls like this. Delicious, sweet souls...

With a groan, I shook my head, clearing the stray thought. I called both Geo and Cress back to me. His obsidian expression showed understated dread, and she eyed me with her lower lip between her teeth. My fangs ached to be the one to nibble on that full lip next.

"Geo, you're next. Do I have your permission to speak with Morgana briefly?" I asked.

"You do."

Cress began to turn away. I caught her wrist with my tail while extending a tendril of darkness toward Geo. It took a few moments for it to push past the boundary of his stone skin and wrap around the crystalized heart beating in his chest. Geo simply froze where he stood, all signs of life leaving his quartz eyes.

I released Cress's arm when she tugged herself free. "I want you to hear this conversation, bright soul."

Her brow crinkled. "But...why? Wasn't she your wife?" she asked.

And that reaction was exactly why I'd asked. I worried that when she looked at me, she saw someone still mourning his losses. I wanted to break down another barrier between us. "I think you need to be here," was all I said.

"Well, all right," she mumbled.

I tugged on the tendril of shadow, which had wrapped around Morgana's soul. It flowed free from its cage of crystal and stone, taking shape just like any other soul with white-lined limbs and a transparent form. Unlike Marie Evenstar, though, Morgana was tethered back to Geo by several thick chains made of spell runes wrapped around her. If I severed them, she'd be free to cross to the afterlife, but otherwise, when I released her, she'd go right back to animating Geo.

When Morgana took full form, I struggled with my next breath. She looked just as I remembered her from that fateful day in Moongrove Library. Raven-dark hair back in a strict braid, face free of any cosmetics but still boasting full, kissable lips and a fan of naturally dark lashes around soft brown eyes. She wore what used to be considered a man's clothes, with a tucked-in tunic and tight pants hugging her shapely hips from which hung a librarian's handbook and a sheathed sword.

Even as a ghost, she exuded palpable power. "Hello, my love," she said with a knowing curve to her mouth. "You have freed yourself."

I dipped my chin a fraction. "I was released."

Cress, who'd looked ready to inch away at Morgana's greeting, glanced between the two of us at my chilly tone.

"You must have questions," the ghost said, going nearly as toneless as Geo in gargoyle form.

"That is why I've tried so urgently to speak with you. I lost two hundred years of my life because of your actions, Morgana. I woke to a world changed, with many believing *I* was what Endaeron had become. You abandoned me when you could've saved me." I stepped closer, leaning towards her spectral face. "Why?"

She held her ground, unflinching like she'd been in life. "I did what I had to," she said in a low tone. "I had no time to share that both you and Endaeron were in the stasis room. I painted instructions in my own blood to those who found my body, saying that the room was never to be opened again."

I released a bitter laugh. "Mortals forget a lot in two centuries."

"I thought you were lost." She spoke more gently. "Endaeron left a wound in your back. Do you remember?"

I tried to recall that fight, but the details were like sand, running right between my fingers. Unexplained gaps in my memories and awareness were no longer strange. I'd figured out they were the work of Endaeron but not how they connected us together, giving him some level of control over me. "No, I don't remember that," I answered.

She sighed, her shoulders falling. "After dealing me a

mortal blow, he struck you from behind and sank his teeth either into your back or right above your skin. I've never heard you make such a hideous noise. While I can't see souls like you can…" She cast her gaze away from me. "I knew he must've taken a bite out of yours."

"What?" I breathed out.

"I knew that there was no coming back if he'd damaged your soul, so like I said…I did what I had to. I sealed you in with your brother so you could not transform into a monster too. There was no way I was going to allow any taint into your legacy." She reached out and clasped my hand between hers.

I looked down at her spectral hands leaving cold tingles over my skin. "That explains it all. *Everything*." I looked over my shoulder at my soul, which seemed fine. Someone else would need to study it for any faults. Morgana had saved me from becoming a second Hungering Darkness, but she may have just bought me time. Damage of this sort always allowed Myuna's corruption in.

And my brother, who'd consumed a part of my life force, had power over me because of it. He finally had what he always wanted—a way to drag me down to corruption and depravity with him. There was no way to undo it. We were irrevocably connected.

"You didn't betray me," I said through numb lips.

"In a way, I did, and I see why you would think it. You were the great love of my life, Phaeron. I didn't mean to hurt you."

I leaned back when she reached up for my face. Her huge revelation didn't change how I felt or the fact that she was merely a spirit now. "I know," I murmured. "But that life is over. You chose to become a gargoyle?"

She nodded in understanding and folded her hands

over her middle. "I did." Turning, she admired Geo's frozen form. "Brave, loyal, and protective. Isn't he special?"

"He is," Cress agreed under her breath, catching both of our attentions.

"Who is this, Phaeron?" Morgana asked.

Cress smiled at me uncertainly but looked like she'd rather be anywhere else. Here came the moment I'd been practicing. The grandest gesture I could give her. "A bright soul, a beacon in the night. Cressida Rollins, the woman fate sent to free me." I caught her hand and encouraged her to step closer, face to face with the ghost. "Morgana, I wanted to introduce you before you went back to your rest."

"Your next True Light?" Morgana asked.

I smiled warmly down at the purple-haired woman. "If she will have me."

Cress's sudden blush hid within the blue tones of the deep night with a waning moon overhead. "I...this is unexpected. It's nice to meet you," she said, offering her hand to the ghost to shake, then dropping it after they attempted to make physical contact. "Especially after I've heard so much about you."

"Hopefully none of the more boring events." Morgana laughed. "Phaeron, give me a moment with her, hmm? Go cover your pointy ears over there." She gestured to a patch of darkness.

I narrowed my eyes, but I'd gotten my closure with Morgana. I gave the two of them a moment and let myself brood on the problem of my soul in the meantime.

CRESS

The last thing I expected this night was to meet *the* Morgana Voidbinder, demigoddess and first librarian witch. The soul that gave Geo life was a completely different person than him. Despite the sadness that's shown over her expression when Phaeron treated her with chilly distance, she seemed to come from the gargoyle's heart content and well-rested.

"Is that your handbook?" she asked, pointing to the book I kept on my belt. I had the clasp securely locked to keep it from babbling and flapping around, especially while we were sneaking out here. When I nodded, she asked to see it.

"It's a little special," I warned. Keeping a firm hand on its spine, I unclasped it and held it to my face. "Shhhhhhh."

"Quiet, got it," it said just as loud as always.

"You'll have to hold it steady," Morgana said. She laid her transparent hands on the book's cover, closing her eyes in concentration.

Could souls do magic like this? I watched avidly, seeing her faded purple aura ebb and flow around the book like the flow of the tide. Its pages flickered, and it whispered in my grasp, "That tickles."

"There, I hope that takes. I tried to give it more of what I know," she said, releasing the book.

It immediately started flapping laps around our heads in apparent distress. "So. Much. Knowledge!"

She chuckled. "I don't intend to come out of my gargoyle's body again. I lived my life, and it feels...odd, to say the least, to be myself again. So, while we have this moment, let's talk about Phaeron."

My amusement with the book's antics faded to nerves. "Oh, yeah? What about him?"

He'd looked at me with such longing. *If she will have me.* It was a surprise, but not an unwelcome one.

I might not know what a True Light was, but the context was pretty obvious. I really was fated to three men, and Phaeron was the one I'd tiptoed around the most. This woman was part of the reason—I'd thought he'd need some time to come to terms with her passing.

But the other part, well... Ben had called it. Phaeron was tall, dark, and sometimes scary. What Morgana had revealed about his soul was the most terrifying thing about him, though.

"You are his only hope of surviving what his brother has done to him without succumbing to Myuna's corruption. I don't know the extent of your relationship, other than it seems quite new." Morgana reached out for me, and I flinched at the cold touch of her spectral hand. I turned over the wrist she'd brushed, revealing Phaeron's mark of protection. "Just know that he needs you more than he will ever admit to. You'll have to contend with his princely pride and certain old-fashioned notions of who protects whom in the relationship."

"Can I save him? From what his brother did?" I asked, tracing the outline of the mark. Phaeron stirred from where he stood, glancing back at us. I put my palm up to signal that I wasn't calling to him, and he seemed to nod.

"I don't know, but you should consider it your duty to try. To remind him that he's in control and still the same noble gentleman he's always been." Her determined gaze met mine. "And should he fall, it is then your duty to do what you have to. Can you promise me that you will?"

"I can. I will try, at least," I said.

"Good. Now..." She gestured for me to lean forward and began to whisper in my ear. Cheeks heating, I nodded along, trying to memorize all the naughty secrets she shared about Phaeron. We said our goodbyes when she was done, and I pressed on the mark again, fascinated that I didn't need to do anything else to get his attention.

I walked a few paces away to give them a chance to say goodbye without me there as a third wheel. It wasn't long before he released her from her magic and her form dissolved, melting back into Geo.

I crept back to his side, tempted to run my hand up his tail. Morgana had mentioned that it was sensitive and tended to wrap around things he liked, but I wasn't sure if he'd want an intimate touch right now. He turned his attention toward me, inscrutable in the dark.

"Are you all right?" I murmured.

"I'm not sure how to answer that question, bright soul," he sighed.

So, *no*.

He leaned down, and I caught a better glimpse of his expression. His otherworldly features were colored with longing, his topaz eyes fixed on my lips. Yet when we were nearly touching foreheads, my breath caught in my chest, he paused with the sharp tip of one claw tilting my chin up.

The self-control was masterful. His desire was obvious, yet let me be the one to cup his face, drawing him into a kiss. A proper one, not stolen in a moment of danger. I gasped when he nipped my bottom lip, and he used it as an invitation to deepen the meeting of our mouths. He kissed like a man starved, ravenous for the taste of me. His fingers tunneled into my hair, pulling just right to make my knees weaken.

I was panting for breath when Geo came awake with a

sudden scrape of rock. He startled me off Phaeron, whose pupils narrowed to irritated slits as the gargoyle caught on to what he'd woken to, and turned away with a huff.

"We don't have all night," he said. His voice was as rough as when he'd first awoken, like his vocal cords had something grinding within them. He went to stand guard at his original post.

Phaeron began to chuckle, which turned to full-fledged laughter that he muffled behind a hand. "I swear, we're going to have to share you together at this rate," he snorted.

With him adjusting the bulge in his pants, I had a feeling what kind of *sharing* he was suggesting and nibbled on my bottom lip. I wasn't entirely opposed to the idea.

He turned away from me with a low groan, starting to weave up a coil of shadow magic. "Unfortunately, he's right. You have two souls to visit with. Shall we call Lanie first?"

That effectively dropped a bucket of cold water on my arousal, and I swallowed thickly. "Yeah, her first," I agreed.

I whistled quietly into the gloom, signaling to Jin, who emerged like a shadow and brushed against my ankle. She'd followed us at her own speed from Phaeron and Ben's home. Cats had an uncanny way to notice things that people didn't, so I hadn't been surprised when Jin told my familiars that she wanted to come say goodbye to Lanie too.

We watched him create a doorway with his magic, which turned into a gently glowing portal to the afterlife when he called Lanie's name. She emerged, a petite figure with a dark bob and a navy blue hooded jacket.

"I thought this might happen," she said. Like she'd predicted my reaction too, she opened her arms before I was in motion, and I hugged...cold, static-filled air.

"Lanie. It's really you," I said.

"It is. Thank you for the meal, by the way. I heard everything you all were saying about me. On the other side of the world, my family remembered me too. I've never felt so loved." Her smile crinkled the skin around her eyes, just as kind as I remembered. "If you've called to ask for more advice, I'm afraid I gave you everything I know."

I sniffed, shaking my head. "No, I just wanted to talk to you again. To say thank you for everything you've done. Jin's here, too." I gestured to the black cat who'd moved forward, her silky fur glossy in her former witch's ghostly light.

"Goodness, you're welcome. I would do it again if I had to." Lanie knelt and reached out for Jin, who mewed quietly when she tapped her forehead through the ghost's hand. "Have you accepted Cress as your new witch?"

Jin mrrowed something back.

"It would be okay if you did. I know she will take great care of you. Hasn't she already? I just want you to be happy, Jin, no matter what you choose for yourself. I love you," Lanie said to the cat gently.

With a snort, the cat stood, saying one last thing to Lanie before going back to sitting by my feet. The ghost stood, addressing me again. "I've been resting since...the moment things ended. The next life isn't so bad. You'll see it for yourself one day."

"One day," I echoed. "There's so much I want to tell you. I haven't avenged you yet, but I'm well on the way."

"Answer a question for me first. Are you on the road to happiness?"

"Well...yes, I think so."

I realized that was all she needed to hear. She retreated back a step, toward the doorway where she'd come from. "Then I am content to rest. I am happy for you, Cress, and glad you're not wasting the chance I gave you. It's time you let me go."

A single stinging tear made its way down my cheek. Of course she wanted to sleep, like she'd earned. I couldn't just bring her back to listen to all my problems and deliver keen advice. "You're right, I'm sorry. I just wanted to make sure you knew how much I appreciate what you did."

She nodded. "I know. Of course I know. I saw greatness in your future, by the side of three men who adore you. Just consider it this way—I'm keeping your spot in the afterlife warm for when you're old and weary. Don't come any sooner than that, okay?"

"Okay," I said, fighting the emotions that wanted me to start bawling. I'd gotten more than most, a chance to say a proper goodbye.

"Bye for now. Share my love with Roe and the rest. Oh! And don't forget you have my mother's number if you ever need real help," she said. She soon faded, and the doorway closed.

Phaeron's chanting ceased. For a moment, his eyelids lifted halfway, fatigue weighing his bearing. "I can see that was hard, bright soul," he murmured. "Would you like a break, or shall I start trying to call your mother?"

"Maybe birth mother," I corrected. "I...I should be okay." He really needed to call Eris Darkmore before I lost my nerve or let my doubts sink in. How would a spirit know I was her daughter or not anyway?

With a grounding sigh, Phaeron began his chant again and made a new doorway. This one remained dark, no matter how much he spoke to it. He stopped and crooked his finger at me, which turned into a talon of shadowy darkness. "She does not answer my call. Let's see if your blood will help."

I offered my non-dominant hand and flinched as his claw turned toward my skin. "How much of that are you going to need?" I asked.

He pricked the pad of my middle finger, squeezing a few drops on the ground around the darkened portal. "About that much. Repeat after me so you are the one calling to her," he said.

Presumably, he translated his dimensional language into Latin, as I recognized some of the words to the spell now. If this worked, it would be the most telltale sign that I really was related to this woman. I'd repeated the spell three times before the doorway started to twinkle with magic.

"She's coming," he said with a low hiss. "Keep your distance." That was easy to do when he was holding my hips, taking up the chant in his old home's language when the portal seemed to tremble with the incoming arrival.

Eris didn't so much emerge as explode through the barrier between worlds with a scattering of golden rays and a roar of power about her. "Who dares disturb my slumber?" she full-lung shouted.

I winced. The campus police were definitely going to come running at such a loud disturbance. "I do!" I practically felt timid under the steely stare of this ghost. My mother, summoned by my blood and call.

She smoothed the sides of her dress, an elegant black evening gown with a low shimmer from her ghostly outline. "Well, what do you want?" she prompted.

I cleared my throat, standing a little straighter. I didn't want to make an even worse impression on my birth mother. Gently pulling Phaeron's hands off me, I stepped forward to get a better look at her. She'd apparently died right before attending a function of some sort, as she wore a full face of makeup that gave her honey-colored eyes a sultry angle. Her hair, the same shade of dark brown as mine without the dye, was styled into a full head of ringlets draped carefully around her shoulders.

A soft voice squeaked somewhere around my feet, but I paid it little mind.

"You're my mother," was about all I said before Ben's shouts tipped me off to a disturbance. I reached for my sword, drawing it and casting Lux to make it glow in one practiced movement.

Phaeron's attention shifted, his chanting fading alongside the image of my mother and the otherworldly portal behind her. He stumbled, panting with fatigue.

Leaping over Ben was a white figure, but not a ghost. The Hungering Darkness howled as it swung its foot-long talons down to strike at my chest. I caught those talons with the edge of my sword, sending blood everywhere when it cut into its hand. The monster flinched away from me.

"Such a delicious feast of souls you've called tonight. Did you do that for me?" It tilted its head.

"Oh, fuck," I whispered.

Lucas's features were swallowed up by white shadow, replaced by a wolf's maw lined with jagged canines and topped by two forward-facing horns. It traced a healing rune in his blood over its split hand before looking over my shoulder.

"I *told* you," that soft voice said. I glanced down in disbelief for a split second at Jin arching her back and hissing. Otherwise occupied, I hadn't felt the familiar bond slide into place between us, but Jin had taken Lanie's blessing to heart.

Behind me, I heard Phaeron drop to the ground, his

unsheathed swords clattering away from him. *Fuck!* I imagined him clawing at his face but couldn't take my gaze away from his brother.

I reached out to the one trick I had up my sleeve, Jin, asking to borrow from her. I needed her reflexes, but that wasn't what filled me a split second later. My hand clenched around the sword, and I jabbed and slashed at the Hungering Darkness, taking it by surprise with a sudden burst of ferocity courtesy of the witch's cat it had wronged. I slashed its shirt and dug the point of my blade in its side while sidestepping a couple swipes of its claws, feeling invincible for the few seconds my connection with Jin was active.

The moment it faded, I moved my sword in a new pattern and shifted to a defensive posture, casting Refracto with the spell word under my breath. Phaeron himself had taught me that only baby witches shouted their spells like Roe and I had done in our last fight with the Hungering Darkness. The shield Refracto produced would stay in place while I had my sword held at the right angle.

A silver blur flashed in the dark and caught the Hungering Darkness with a jerk and howl. "Hey, ugly!" Ben shouted.

"I'll deal with you in a minute," the monster said. Its next strike caught my shield, but unlike its weaker cousin spell, Repello, this barrier pushed back hard, throwing its arm wide and taking its balance with it.

I felt the impact through my sword, vibrating through my arm, but managed to keep it upright. I just had to bide my time, and my three men would help me fight him on more equal grounds.

"New tricks, little witch? How qua—"

A quartz spike grazed his forehead, exposing bone as it

also blew off the shadowy mask over its puppet's face. I couldn't help a shocked shout at the grotesque sight. Had Geo aimed a little to the right, he would've ended Lucas's life right there.

While he stumbled backward, I risked letting down my shield and turning to Phaeron. The tendons stood out on his neck as he resisted the white fire starting to claim the shadows over his arm. I touched my fingertips to his mark of protection, calling his name. Clarity returned to his expression, which dropped to horror as my body jerked.

I looked down at the points of three white talons emerging from my torso. It didn't hurt until he ripped them back out the way they came.

19

GEO

Cress hit the ground, her body rolling with her momentum. There was no movement for a moment, like we all held our breath. My gaze flashed from her to the Hungering Darkness, who started to grin in apparent victory and…I saw red.

Even within my gargoyle form, my stone heated with my mounting fury. That creature had hurt Cress, and for that, it would pay with its very existence. Any quartz I still had in my body was rerouted to form a club that I removed from my palm and the hollow pocket within my arm.

"Stand back," I barked at Ben, who stood in my way. His brother's face turned my way, half of it stained with blood and gore from my initial strike. The monster within him put up its fists. Sidestepping the heavy swing of my weapon, he hammered my chest with punches.

I didn't feel them at all. No matter how augmented with shadows, no matter how quickly it healed the fractures it had to be giving its host's finger bones, I was beyond any kind of pain. I'd drag its sorry shred of a soul back to Moongrove Library myself and stand guard over its stasis room for eternity.

First, I'd tenderize its chosen body until it couldn't continue to regenerate from every blow. My next swing caught its shoulder, knocking it to the ground. It barely rolled away from the overhand strike of my club.

"She's not dead yet, Morgana. If you act quickly, you might still save her," it taunted as it stood. Extending its blood-soaked talons, it lunged at me.

There was a pulse from within my chest, my recently stirred patron's soul speaking with me. "I am not Morgana, I am Geo, animated and given new life from her death." I caught its talons with my club, which began to crack from the pressure of being between us. "Killing you would bring her soul great pleasure, however."

"Hah! That's impossible," it said, baring crimson-stained teeth in a rictus grin. "You cannot kill that which has no body."

Ben attacked it from behind again, this time reaching around and burying a dagger to the hilt in its lung. "Shut the fuck up," he said. He hooked an arm around its neck and arched its spine while I jabbed its solar plexus, shattering my weapon in the process. "Quick, bind his wrists!"

I had no more quartz to form manacles, so I grabbed it with my stone hands instead. The Hungering Darkness caught its breath and snarled, struggling between the two of us. "If you value your brother's life, you would let me go," it hissed once it caught its breath.

Ben froze, paling. It was the opening it needed to slam its skull into his chin and knock him off its back. Thrashing out of my hold, it reduced to a white wisp before either of us could grab it again.

Ben picked up the dagger that'd dropped when the

Hungering Darkness went incorporeal and slammed it into the ground point-first with a vicious curse. I busied myself picking up the pieces of my quartz, absorbing them back into my body, and looking around for Cress. The only sign of her was a patch of bloodied grass where she'd fallen.

"Phaeron said he was taking her to Moongrove Library," Ben explained.

I touched my fingertips to my forehead, snarling like an animal. "There's a perfectly good medical center where you were seen—"

"He said he was taking her to the powercore. Do you know where that is?" he interrupted.

"Yes."

"Let's go, Geo."

Were I in my human form, I might marvel over how this may be the first time I'd seen Ben fully serious. Maybe I would later, when I had Cress back in my arms. I didn't want to consider what would happen if Phaeron made the wrong judgment call and took her to bleed out on an unforgiving stone floor.

Ben startled more than me when the glare of flashlights approached. One focused directly on his face. "NSU campus police! Freeze!" a man shouted.

"Wow, they are truly worthless," Ben muttered.

Definitely. We could call the dead and fight a dimensional monster without them finding us. Now that all the danger had passed, of course they arrived.

"Geo? A lift? Any time now."

I didn't feel it, but Ben had grabbed one of my stone wings and rattled it. I shook him off and folded my arms around him. When I'd flown Cress, it'd been intimate to have her pressed flush against me, but that same sensation was uncomfortable for both of us as I surged into the air with Ben in tow.

"I didn't realize you could fly so well," Ben commented once I got up to speed, taking him on a relatively smooth ride straight toward Moongrove Library.

"Guess I'm full of surprises," I rumbled.

"No more of those tonight. Cress had better be all right, or I'll burn the library down."

Another thing we agreed on. I took on speed to get us there as quickly as possible.

CRESS

The darkness moved in to sweep me away on feather-soft wings. I hung there, suspended and wondering if I'd slid into the afterlife to rest despite my promise to Lanie. It was my fault; I'd broken one of the first rules of combat. *Never turn your back to an enemy.*

Phaeron would be so disappointed in me. We'd drilled the basics over and over until I could slip into basic combat stances and recite his rules in my sleep.

The first thing I became aware of was his voice, panicked. "Braza!"

I cracked my eyes open, boneless and woozy. A familiar ceiling swam into focus as I thought, *That's not my name.* The purple glow of the library's powercore washed over everything except for the ethereal white glow of the ghost suddenly standing beside my head.

"Look at me, Luna," Eris commanded. I tilted my head toward her shiny heels, recognizing that could've been my name in another life. "You cannot die. Do you understand me?"

A laugh bubbled in my throat, along with a stream of blood that escaped the side of my lips. I was definitely dying to be hallucinating my mother's ghost. Gentle hands started to lift me.

"Stay with me, bright soul. Just a little more," Phaeron soothed. He supported me against his strong chest, my limp body swaying in his hold with each step we took upward toward the luminescent powercore.

Then he leapt straight into it. The tingles from touching its surface were all over my body, probing my injury, surging into the gaps. Needles of pain erupted over each inch of my skin, and I knew no more.

I KNEW the passing of time by the voices that came and went.

Phaeron was always there, as was a woman's voice that seemed like one I should know. Ben and Geo were around, too, but never too close. Strangely, my birth mother's presence also seemed steady. They blended to a blur, no words distinct amongst a melody of fear, pain, and anger.

I came to full awareness with the gentle pressure of a cool washcloth passing over my hot forehead. "She's not ready for that kind of power." Phaeron's smooth tone was soft, like he was cautious of waking me.

"It is her birthright. She will be receiving it soon anyway," my mother answered.

"She took the librarian affinity. Have you considered

what will happen to her if you blast her with the might of your celestial magic?"

"She can handle it!"

"No, Eris, she cannot," said a third presence, the one that felt familiar. "She is still an inexperienced witch with her chosen affinity. Her soul blazes with the potential of the Darkmore line, but she will be unable to express any celestial magic from her body. The two magics are incompatible."

"Well, what do you suggest?" Eris demanded. "The Darkmore line stretches back centuries, and she is the sole recipient of the whole bloodline's pure celestial hereditary magic. Why was she ever permitted to take the librarian affinity in the first place?"

"It was her choice," the other woman replied.

"Can you not take it back?"

"It would bring her soul needless trauma. She would never be the same. Affinities are considered lifelong choices for a reason."

"She's awake," Phaeron said. He helped me sit upright, propping up my back with what felt like several pillows. I peeled my eyelids open slowly to a blurry world, my other senses slow to return.

I'd been moved into a bed of some sort. Everything was shaded with purple and black, and when I tipped my head up, I realized the dome of the powercore shimmered overhead. We were *inside* it, which I hadn't known was possible.

Phaeron pressed the cool lip of a glass into my lips, feeding me slow sips of water. "How are you feeling?" he murmured.

"Confused," I replied, coughing from a scratchy throat. He gave me more water, raising a brow slightly at my answer.

I peeled back an amethyst-toned sheet, revealing the clothes I'd been attacked in sporting three new rips. The skin underneath was puckered with new, pink scars.

"You are fortunate, brightest of souls. Phaeron got you here just in time."

I turned my head to pinpoint the speaker. There was a couch a few feet away on this stone platform, and on it sat the ghost of my mother and a dimensional woman formed of the same purple and black magic as the powercore.

I shifted my attention back to Phaeron, my expression begging for some kind of explanation. He sighed and helped me sit back, his fingertips drawing some of the hair out of my face. I recognized the feeling on my skin. How long had he been here? The ghost of his touch lingered in my memory. His roughened fingertips had cupped my face what must've been dozens of times, his concerned tones registering in my mind where his words did not.

He was also still dressed in the same clothes as he'd been wearing on Samhain, and purplish shadows lingered in the hollows of his eyes. It looked like he hadn't left my side. "Braza healed you from the inside out with a surge of magic. You were punctured in some vital places and bleeding internally—had I taken you anywhere else, the outcome would've been much different," he said.

"Who?" I asked weakly.

"Me, dear girl," the other dimensional said in that too-familiar voice. "The powercore of Moongrove Library."

My mind flooded with dozens of questions. Well, Phaeron had referred to the powercore as a person, as a *she*, before but hadn't elaborated. "I didn't realize you were a person," I mumbled.

She laughed to herself. "*Was* a person. I'm only a bit

more alive than your mother here. I'll let Phaeron explain the whole story some other time. We have other news."

Phaeron cleared his throat, shaking his head slightly.

"I'm glad you're okay, Luna," Eris said. "Now we can talk about your magic."

"I think that can wait," Phaeron put in pointedly.

She threw her hands up in frustration. "First you strand me here, and now you won't let me fulfill my purpose."

"Again, I apologize for the timing. I will attempt to reopen a portal back to the afterlife for you as soon as—"

"Oh no, it is far too late for that. Not after everything I've learned," Eris burst in, waving a delicate wrist. "My daughter obviously needs my guidance. More than I could've given her with a brief visit on Samhain night. I think I'll stay."

"Great, now we're haunted," he said under his breath.

I squeezed his hand, finding it nestled in the covers over my hip, and laced our fingers together, hoping to ground him at least a little like how he was keeping me steady in this surreal situation. "Let's start over, shall we?" I suggested. "Hello, uh, Mother. I'm Cressida Rollins, your daughter."

"Hello...Cressida." She made a face like she'd had to swallow something bitter with the name. "Let me tell you a little about myself. I am Eris Darkmore, formerly a celestial witch of renown and a contender for the fourth seat of the Crown Coven. By day, I was a professor in the Mystic Collegium, where witches and other supernaturals of all kinds go to study magic for their masters and doctorate degrees. In my spare time, I helped my best friend run a successful business reading star charts for newborns."

It felt a little like she was reading a resume to me, but I understood. This was awkward. What did a ghostly mother say to her grown child who'd never really known her? "Did you have any hobbies?" I ventured.

Finally, her ruby red lips lifted into a subdued smile. "I enjoyed making art."

I seized that, learning that she was something of a painter in her free time, which she had very little of. Phaeron excused himself to let us talk, and Braza left by transferring herself into the sphere of magic that surrounded my mother and me.

I got the impression that my birth mother was something of a career workaholic with a long list of accomplishments. The Mystic Collegium was a blip in my mind, a place that existed but one I had never aspired to go to before. Eris not only had a doctorate in celestial witchery, she'd outcompeted hundreds to become a professor there. No wonder she'd told me about that first. She'd been highly proud of it.

I told her about my life. How I'd been adopted by a kind nurse who'd been Mom in her place, and a little about Carly, as close as a sister. I felt a twist of sadness—I hadn't spoken with either of them in ages. I'd need to fix that. Once I was finished, I asked, "Are you aware of how it all ended?"

Eris frowned. "I remember being taken by surprise in my own home by a blood witch. And flames."

I took a deep breath. "That was an assassin. Blaize Starsurge paid to have all of us killed that night." I wasn't expecting the surge of power from her ghost. Her aura blinded me with rays of light, leaving me to blink rapidly to clear away the spots in my vision.

"That lowlife snake in the grass." She bared her teeth in a disgusted sneer.

"That's not all," I sighed. I shared the rest, that he'd

prompted Garroway to send another assassin after me when he became aware that I'd survived the tragedy. As I recapped, I noticed Braza taking form against the edge of the platform, waiting with her hands folded over her middle.

"Hate to interrupt," Braza interjected. "But I've had my librarians do a bit of research, and I think I know how you should proceed with the transfer of hereditary power."

Eris jumped to her feet. "Tell me! My daughter has a man to smite."

The powercore leaned away from the force of her shout. "Ah, indeed. It's not quite as effective as her inheriting her family line's magic directly," she said in a tone of warning.

When she held out her hand, my handbook came flying over, its spine landing in her palm. It strained against the clasp over its pages, making, "Mmf!" noises as it struggled to put in its two cents.

"I suggest you augment her librarian witch's handbook. It is bound to serve her for life." Braza stroked down its spine to make it relax in her hold. "With suitable channeling ability, she will be able to tap into the magic you and the rest of your ancestors have left for her."

Eris looked skeptical. "Do you know your power level yet?" she asked me.

I shook my head. I was too new of a witch for anyone to put me through the tests to see what my power level was out of fear of hurting me.

"I think it sounds like a good idea, if it's possible," I said.

"It should be. The book is connected to you by magic, thus a viable object to turn into an artifact. There's one downside, though. This basically restarts the Darkmore bloodline," Braza said. Eris's expression twisted with distaste. "It cannot be undone, and any children of yours will have nothing to inherit until you pass the book along. You also won't have any dreams made from memories of your ancestors."

I turned to my mother, hoping she'd understand. "It's better than the alternative. This way, I can actually use what you give me."

"If that's your wish," she sighed. "Before I start the process—and lose the energy to be semi-corporeal to you—about Blaize Starsurge. You said you have an idea of how to ruin him?"

I wet my lips to keep from grinning. She cackled as I outlined what I was thinking, giving pointers along the way. Since she understood the system better than me, she explained and adjusted a few parts to a more realistic course. With her help, Crown Starsurge would be on trial by December break.

20

CRESS

The Librarian Witch's *Handbook* flew in drunken zigzags just above my head. Granted, I wasn't doing much better. My mother's ghost had disappeared for now, all the power she'd gone on about condensed into the brilliant star of magic she'd shoved into my book.

After exiting Braza's glowing chamber with her assistance, I'd nearly acquainted myself with the ground at the bottom step of the powercore's pedestal. It was a good thing Geo stood there, waiting in his human form. He lunged and caught me in the nick of time.

"Cress," he said with a long sigh and pulled me to his strong chest. He rested his chin atop my crown, rocking gently with me in his arms. "I was so worried."

"Sorry."

"Don't be. You're okay now?" He didn't move to look for himself.

For someone recovering from at least three punctures through the chest, I felt remarkably well, actually. "Just a little weak."

He shook his head. "You've been unconscious for three

days after losing a great deal of blood. It's amazing you're on your feet at all."

"Wow," I said before reality really set in. "My friends! And classes."

Geo cleared his throat, withdrawing my phone from his pocket. "Ben and I have made sure they know what's going on." At this point, the device was basically his, but I was grateful he'd kept everyone from panicking. "The college also tried to contact you."

An icy feeling doused its way down my spine. "What do you mean?"

"Mmm. Don't worry about it right now," he said, handing over my phone. He also offered a bundle of fabric he'd been holding in his other hand. One of my shirts.

I pulled off the ruined one before he had a chance to turn around. His quicksilver eyes widened. Though I was hardly at my best right now, I still lifted my chest as I practically felt his gaze trace a path over my cleavage. It was like my new scars were invisible for as little attention he paid them.

"You can touch if you want." I crooked a finger to invite him closer. Any new wobbliness in my knees could be attributed to the desire that twisted his expression. He didn't hesitate to cup my chest with his broad palms, exploring the silkiness of my bra and the soft squish of my breasts with an experimental squeeze.

I didn't know when it happened, but Geo was all man, no sign of his cool stone façade now. He freed a boob from its confines to roll in his hand, thumb circling the hardening nub and giving it an experimental pull. I stumbled forward into him from the sudden shock of pleasure, and he caught me for a second time.

"Perhaps we can continue this another time," he said, eyeing me with concern.

"Soon," I replied, meaning it.

With that agreed upon, he helped me into the clean shirt. The next thing I knew, he'd swept me up bridal style and was carrying me to the elevators despite my laughing protests.

He took me straight to one of the overnight rooms, where Ben, Phaeron, and Grant were chatting. The conversation died abruptly as their heads turned my way.

Ben stood, rushing over. "Cress!" He kissed me with relief, helping steady me after Geo finally put me down.

"Hey, Ben. Sorry for giving you a scare," I said, though I leaned past him to the changeling sitting in full view of all three of the men as his actual fae self. Now that was weird.

Grant waved enthusiastically. "Glad you're not dead."

"What's going on?" I asked, wary.

"I decided to reveal myself to your men. They're under the same agreement about my identity that you are," Grant said.

"I figured out that he was a changeling," Phaeron put in. "He hid it well."

"Yeah, that too. Now I get to tell the big guy the juiciest details." The changeling pointed to Phaeron. "He's basically your leader, you know."

"So, what are these 'juicy' details?" I asked with air quotes. I let Ben guide me to a chair and closed my eyes for a few moments to ward off a dizzy spell.

When I opened them again, I realized the men were staring at each other. "Fine, I'll tell her," Ben said, rolling his eyes. "Spy extraordinaire here thinks he's found evidence of Garroway. Meaning, he hasn't found the vampire, just linked a number of sudden kidnappings back to him."

"He's stealing more witch kids?" I asked, feeling sick at the idea of anyone else being put through the same childhood that Ben had to endure.

"No," Grant put in. "Adult witches. The fae courts and other supernatural cities are all on high alert because his people haven't struck in the same place twice. Any abductions caught on camera end with the abductees being taken away by teleport charm. And those are *very* pricy."

My hands curled into fists. "So he's building an army."

"I was just saying, Garroway carves the blood runes into his witches at age eleven. There has to be a reason for that," Ben said. He flipped a pen between his fingers with some agitation.

"Is this the moment I make it worse by telling you it's not just blood witches he's stealing?" Grant put in. "Assuming they can handle the blood rune, he's taking any witch with an affinity good in a fight. Mostly blood witches, but also guardians and a few witches who've already made a name for themselves with their weapons, like a trio of librarians and an augury witch known for being undefeated in the dueling circuits of the Night Court."

Anxiety made me want to scratch my skin all over. "But there's no sign of Garroway himself?"

"Not a single one. Don't you worry, though. I'm on the job." Grant winked. "By the way, you're in huge trouble with the college for breaking curfew and summoning spirits. Maybe you should use all this information to sweeten the pot with Dr. Aurina when she inevitably calls you in to yell at you."

That really wasn't helping my headspace right now.

Geo and Phaeron shot him looks of censure. "Well, there goes my chance to ask her for a favor," I sighed.

"Oh, what might a freshman librarian witch want from the University President?" By the glimmer in the fae's orange eyes, I'd intrigued him.

"Don't worry about it yet." I got to my feet slowly. "I'm going to go shower. We won't get anything done by sitting around talking anyway."

IF I THOUGHT I was walking to my dorm room without all three of my men coming along, I was quite mistaken. Phaeron held my hand and also used his tail to help my balance if I ever faltered, while Ben lingered at my other side, and Geo walked behind us protectively. With them all supporting me, it was easy to think of them as "my men," even if the claim felt a little premature.

When we arrived at my dorm and I patted my pockets for my key, it was Ben who handed it over. "I fed your cats," he said.

"Thanks." I felt some tension between them, though. Glances were exchanged as I moved toward my destination. I'd only ever had them up here one at a time, after all. "Hey, guys. I appreciate you walking me this far, but I need some alone time." And honestly, I needed to figure a few things out on my own.

"I'll be here," Geo replied.

Ben shrugged, fitting his hands in his pockets. "Guess I'll keep trying to convince Phaeron to spend his money on some cool stuff." The dimensional rolled his eyes. I had the feeling this was an ongoing conversation. "See you for dinner?"

I confirmed it and took the stairs up to my dorm room slowly, breathing a sigh of relief when I was safely inside and greeting my familiars. Milo and Bella crowded the end of my bed, while Jin sat in a cat loaf in the center of the mattress on the far end of the dorm.

"I heard you were so brave," Milo said.

"And strong!" Bella pitched in.

"And a monster attacked you from behind." The boy cat sounded indignant.

"That's about right," I confirmed, giving them rubs at the same time before I went over and scooped up Jin.

She made a soft "hey now" in protest but settled in my lap when I sat cross-legged on my bed and put her there. I realized that was just her voice, a demure hush compared to Bella's squeak or Milo's purr.

"What you should also know is that Jin helped me a lot and let me borrow from her when I needed it most," I said.

She started to purr a bit. "It was nothing."

"What's wrong with the book?" Bella asked. While both of my other familiars seemed impressed for a moment, their attention had bounced up toward the ceiling, where my handbook was flying drunken zigzags in uncharacteristic silence.

I shrugged. "I'll check in with it in a minute." Until then, I had some messages to read. Dozens had been sent from my phone on my behalf, and I could tell from the texting style that the ones as short and to the point as possible were from Geo, while the ones sent in bursts of individual thoughts were Ben.

They'd comforted my friends individually, letting them know I was okay and spending some time in the library. Roe and Áine had the longest message logs to read, as they wanted to know why they weren't invited to participate and help guard. They'd been told the truth—we'd thought the Hungering Darkness was far away, like Garroway. How wrong we'd been.

"If I'd known it was possible, I'd want to say my final goodbyes to Lanie too." My heart hurt to read that from Roe. Phaeron had wanted to keep the group small, predicting that everyone would have a spirit they'd want to chat with, but I still owed Roe an apology.

There was also a new group chat, started by Roe. "Hey everyone, two things: 1—We need a coven name. We've been putting this off too long. And 2—The Ashbough family always hosts a giant Thanksgiving celebration, and I wanted to invite you all to come. We're going to be in the Crystal Court, which is in Tennessee. Portal service available!"

Ben had made it clear that he was texting from my phone and said he'd go if I went. Presumably, he'd also saved the numbers of Grant, Wren, and Heath, as their names appeared with their messages over the course of the chat.

I read the resulting argument over our coven name with a relieved smile, glad I wasn't a part of it. From silly to serious to far too edgy, none of the names put forward had much agreement. We had to come up with something that didn't overlap with the name of another registered coven as well, which added to the complication. Roe had to shelve the discussion and asked for us to think on it.

When I saw who was, and who wasn't, going to this Thanksgiving get together, I tapped the message bubble and sent, "This is Cress now. Are ordinary people allowed?" My adopted mother and sister knew about supernaturals because of me. I'd love to see them again over the week-long break coming up, and if they could meet my friends too, all the better.

I'd questioned whether or not witches celebrated Thanksgiving, especially after experiencing Mabon. The week off was built into the college schedule no matter what, and it seemed Roe couldn't resist any event that brought us together.

Jin's ear tilted back lazily as my phone buzzed with several incoming messages. Roe responded in the chat but also messaged me directly asking if I was all right. While I was halfway through a reply, both an apology and an explanation of why I wanted to take my human family to her Thanksgiving get-together, Wren's name and part of a message flashed across the top of the screen.

My thumbs halted. That was a direct text, not one to the group chat. I backed out of my current text to see what she wanted.

It was the first message between us. "I have something important to ask you. Can you take a call right now?" she'd texted.

My heart flipped within my chest at the question. I never expected Wren of all people would want to talk to me over the phone, but when I texted back a yes, my device started ringing nearly immediately.

"Hi, Wren," I answered.

"Hey." Her sigh breezed over the receiver. I heard her muffled voice whispering to someone else, and then the steadier blowing of wind before she must've cupped her hand over her phone outside. "Okay, I'm alone."

"What did you want to ask?" Though it sounded like her claws were sheathed right now, that could change in a heartbeat.

"Um, yeah. How to even start... I feel like I'm missing something and maybe you know what it is."

Oh, she had no idea how big of a "something" she was missing. I petted Jin idly and waited for her to get her words straight.

"I know we're not on, like, the best of terms. But it sounded like Roe was going to tell me something the last time our coven met, and you stopped her. She then told me to ask my father about the vampire who got the Samhain Ball canceled..." She drifted off uncertainly.

"Well, did you?" I asked.

"Yeah. He, like, freaked out and asked how I knew the guy's name and if he'd reached out to me. He didn't know there was an email sent out with his name and picture, and when I told him, he seemed embarrassed and ended the call real quick," she explained, sounding uneasy. "It was really weird. But he's been weird in general lately. Remember our affinity test?"

"Yeah. Of course."

"He wanted me to film you getting tested. Like, just you."

I distinctly remembered that. It'd been really uncomfortable to turn around to see a stranger with her phone camera pointed straight at me.

"I can tell you why," I said carefully. While I was glad I was getting the chance to tell her myself, I wished she were here in front of me so I could see her expression.

"Please. I think he's the reason we were placed in the same coven. He's asked a few times about my coven but seems rather interested in you, and that makes, like, no sense. He doesn't know you."

"Okay, hear me out." I spoke a little slower than usual, afraid I was going to lose her once the shock of this revelation wore off. "About twenty years ago, he was running for an open position on the Crown Coven. His closest rival for it was a woman named Eris Darkmore."

"Oh, stars. He's told me this story so many times," she burst in. "She was a shoo-in for the job; all the polls said so. But she died when her house burned down a few weeks before the election. My father won and dedicated part of his victory speech and his first year ruling on the Crown Coven to her, blah blah blah."

I gripped my phone hard enough to hear the case's plastic flex in protest. That fucking bastard, to offer my birth mother such tokens after having her murdered. "Okay, so you know about all that," I said, working my jaw to loosen it. "Do you know what a blood baron does?"

"I think everyone knows by now," she huffed.

"Well, consider this. Your dad acted weird when you asked about Garroway because not only is he incredibly dangerous, but he knows just how dangerous. He's hired Garroway before."

Silence buzzed along the line, punctuated only by her breathing. "I find that really hard to believe. He's not a dirty politician," she said finally.

I bit my lip hard to contain a laugh. "What the rest of us know is from one of Garroway's former assassins. Not only has your father worked with Garroway before, he paid big bucks to have Eris Darkmore and her family murdered. You said it yourself; he didn't have a chance at the Crown Coven with her as his rival."

"No, that couldn't—"

I didn't let her interrupt me for long, wanting to get it all in before she hung up on me. "And we know this because your father went back to Garroway a few months ago with pictures of *me*, Wren. Eris had a baby girl who everyone thought perished in the fire, but she survived and was adopted by a human family. He wanted a loose end tied before the Darkmore hereditary power was passed on and the memories of the murder—"

"What the f—"

"—And I can confirm it to you. I'm that survivor."

I thought she hung up, but her hitched breathing registered after a few moments. "You're lying," she accused in a watery tone. "My father would *never* do that. Where's your proof?"

"It's here with me." My gaze lingered on the book flying a little more steadily along my ceiling.

"Aren't you worried I'll go tell him everything you've just said?"

Of course I was. But more importantly, I wanted to be the one to plant the seed of doubt within her. Perhaps mistakenly, I assumed the coincidences would line up in my favor and she'd see the truth. "Go ahead. Let him know just how fucked he is," I replied, calling her bluff. "See for yourself how he responds."

"Maybe I will!" *Click.*

I glanced at the screen and the call disconnected message with a smile. The first piece of the plan I'd concocted with my birth mother was now in place.

21

GEO

Cress's color was returning by dinnertime. I forced myself to consume a full meal, despite not being hungry. As Marl had told me, it took time after shifting out of gargoyle form for all the human functions to return, like hunger and the full vibrancy of emotion.

I sat by Cress's side with my full plates. We'd gotten a booth in one of the dining halls with Ben and Phaeron across from us. I'd noticed we all greeted her a little differently. While I was satisfied with the warmth of a drawn-out embrace, Ben gave her a quick hug and a kiss on the lips, while Phaeron folded his tail around her hips and rested a chaste brush of his lips over her forehead. I wondered which one she preferred and made a mental note to ask.

"Okay, we have to talk about something," Cress said once we were settled. "How come none of you mentioned the fact that we have a disciplinary hearing to attend this weekend?"

"Verrrr-eee rude," the book flapping just above her shoulder put in. It looked like it was struggling to stay aloft.

Ben smirked, and Phaeron crooked a finger, catching

the book with a lasso of shadows to drag it over and inspect it.

"Well, let's put it this way," Ben said. "I'm not a student, Geo's an agent of the library duty-bound to hunt the Hunger no matter what time it is, and Phaeron does whatever he wants. We're going to whip up a different story to sell Aurina and her people. You weren't there. You were just out of town or skipping or something."

"I'm going to go alone to the hearing," Phaeron said, sounding distracted. "Aurina is unlikely to challenge my word."

"That means I missed nearly a whole week of class," she protested.

"Well, you know you have an A in at least one class, bright soul," Phaeron responded in his effortless purr. A touch of pink dusted Cress's cheeks.

"You're helping me catch up with the rest," she said, waving her fork in his direction. "And by that, I mean my fashion classes."

His smile widened to show some fang. "Does that mean I get to model for you? Might I suggest—"

"Okay, we're not doing this right now," Ben interjected.

"I wanted to hear what his suggestion was," Cress said.

"C'mon, you know what he was going to say."

"You're making it weird, Ben."

Phaeron calmed his grin with another bite of his dinner. Once he swallowed, he said, "I was just going to say I look best in dark colors."

Ben rolled his eyes. "Sure you were."

I turned to Cress and said earnestly, "I will wear anything you make proudly, regardless of color."

"Thank you, Geo. That's sweet of you to say." Her smile

and the brush of her hand on mine left me feeling warm. I felt a bit of my appetite return.

It wasn't long before Phaeron released his hold on the book, which fluttered slowly to Cress and perched its spine on her shoulder. "Its handling the influx of power and knowledge it was given well, all things considered," he said. "The wispfly within the book is still adjusting."

"I'm plenty well-adjusted," it replied before tumbling shut and landing in Cress's lap.

She picked it up with both palms. After a few moments, she gave it a little shake. "Uh, book?" No reply. She looked up at Phaeron. "Are you sure the wispfly didn't just die?"

"Cressie," the book whispered. "Come closer. I have some final words." She lifted it up to her ear.

"It's fine. Just dramatic," Phaeron sighed.

"Wispflies don't die. They just fade away. And should I fade, I want you to know..." It rattled off a string of Latin at twice the volume, causing her to jump. "That celestial witch spell summons light! You're good at that!"

"Okay, I think I need a break from you," she said, closing the clasp over its pages and tucking it against the wall. "Maybe if it's quiet and still for a few days, it'll figure itself out."

"Mmf! Cwess!" Despite the volume it tried to speak at, it could barely flex its pages and was greatly muffled.

"Well, mostly quiet," she added.

We ate the rest of our dinner in relative peace, conversation turning to the coming Thanksgiving break. Cress intended to invite her human family to go to the Ashbough family's event since they already knew about the supernatural.

"I will go if you do," I said, echoing what the other men had to say about it.

Her safety was of utmost importance, after all. And...I looked forward to accompanying her to something more relaxed like a big feast for friends and family. For a moment, I imagined her on my arm in a couple weeks, seeing the Crystal Court's namesake together. It sounded like we'd be going to a lesser known, subterranean fae court. I could pull out my understanding of minerals, something in every gargoyle's baseline knowledge. Since I'd lost some of my quartz by this point, I could also take the opportunity to look for more with the fae's blessing.

Once the meal was over, we lingered to chat a little longer. I don't think I was the only one feeling a flutter of anticipation when Cress was finally ready to leave. Her brown gaze took the three of us in before she walked slowly for the exit.

Would she invite one of us to accompany her into her dorm this time? Her promise earlier lingered in my ears, the breathy "soon" she'd uttered.

Yet I couldn't forget how she'd been tangled up in Phaeron's arms Samhain night or how often she'd dragged an eager Ben through the dorm's back door with her. She had two more men to take her pick from, both more experienced and charming than me.

She turned toward them as we stepped into the evening air. "Thanks for dinner, gentlemen. I think Geo can see me home from here."

The unearthly light behind Phaeron's yellow eyes flared brighter for a moment. "Very well. See you for class tomorrow," he said and winked.

"Actually, same," Ben said. "It'll be Friday."

"Not a student, huh," she teased.

He laughed. "I am for exactly one class!"

They waved a quick goodbye, going the opposite direction. Cress drew the zipper of her jacket up with a shiver and shifted closer to me. It felt like a hint, so I put my arm around her waist, and she slid into my side. "Oh, Geo. You're warm this evening," she said.

Think charming. Don't just comment on the weather, I told myself.

I was feeling more human than ever, actually, with her soft curves nestled against me like she belonged there. It wasn't so difficult to think of something more clever than usual to say. "Enough to warm your bed as well?"

She covered a surprised giggle with her hand. Well, I thought it was clever, at least. "Is that where you want to be?" she asked. Her full lips pursed as she considered me. The light from a passing streetlamp lent her gaze a playful glint. "Is that what you feel, Geo?"

"What I feel hasn't changed," I rumbled. "I feel that you are mine and that I haven't had a chance to show that I was made for you."

She was quiet for a while, until her dorm was close. "Haven't you?" she finally asked. I took her to the door, and she unlocked it, extending a hand to me in clear invitation. I curled my fingers around hers.

Giddiness bubbled in my chest as she led *me* up to her room. Not Ben, not Phaeron, but her guardian gargoyle. Yet when the door closed behind us, a bundle of nerves knotted lower in my belly. Her body was a temple and a mystery to me. How would I please her best so she wouldn't regret her invitation?

I'd seen snippets of sex online. It was inevitable, really, with how much regular people loved the act. At first, my adventures down the pocket dimension that was the Internet led to me turning off and browsing away from such things, too distanced from the rest of the world to see why watching two people get intimate was desirable.

Lately, though, I'd avoided it out of respect for Cress. Her naked body was the first one I wanted to see, the only one I wanted to be aroused by. But it left me in a pit of inexperience, and now I could kick myself for not at least learning the basics.

She sat at the foot of her bed and patted the space next to it. "Relax. We don't have to do anything you're not ready for," she said.

I sat as she indicated, not sure how to reply to that. I felt ready…but also conflicted with other emotions I still had little grasp of. I worked through listing them in my head, finding that they were all negative ones: doubt, indecision, and fear of disappointing her.

Her palm traced a path down my chest. "I don't suppose they program gargoyles with anatomy lessons."

"No." I cleared my throat, correcting myself. "I mean, unfortunately not."

"How about this? We'll go slow. You'll tell me if you get overwhelmed, okay?" she offered. With her fingers slowly tracing patterns lower on my abdomen, I would've agreed to anything she said.

"Yes."

She breathed a little laugh. "All right, Geo."

I sucked in a breath at the sensation of her fingertips slipping under the hem of my shirt and stroking over my skin directly. Each touch was faintly electric. I didn't want her to stop—I only needed more, so I was the one to lift the fabric off and toss it to the side.

"I still wish I could thank your sculptor," she said, tracing the lines of my muscles with her hands. I lifted my shoulders, proud of my physique simply because she liked it so much.

Her thumbs rubbed over the tight buds on my chest. My moan came out throaty, and my manhood twitched, hardening in my pants for her and the sensual sway of her body as she lifted herself and sat astride my hips.

"Cress." I practically moaned her name too, begging her for more.

"Touch me," she said, guiding my hands to her body. I obeyed eagerly, shifting my hold from her waist down to her hips. She took off her shirt for me and unclasped her bra, setting both aside and letting me look my fill.

I was never more aware of how large my hands were compared to her body or how fragile she seemed with skin like silky satin. My fingers followed the trails my eyes had set, worshiping her delicate body from the planes of her belly to the weight of her breasts, which were enough to fill my palms. I rolled them like I'd wanted to earlier, plucking at her nipples again and smiling when that drew a breathy sound from her. Anything she liked, I would do a hundred times more, given the chance.

She cupped my nape, drawing me into a slow kiss to match the pace of my roaming hands. I mapped every inch of her exposed skin and listened to the hitch of her breath when I found the most sensitive places, committing each to memory. The kissable curve of her neck, the curve of her shoulder, those breasts that weighed soft and full without the support of clothes or my hands.

My hands inevitably found the top of her jeans last, and I hesitated for a moment. There was more of her to view and explore, and I wanted to experience all of her. I tunneled my hands under the layer of fabric, giving her ass a squeeze. A shudder went through her form.

With a roll of her hips, she rubbed the heat of her core over my cock, which strained against the fabric of my pants, begging to be released. The starburst of sensation spread like an explosion, and again I understood why my fellow gargoyles would abandon their duty for this.

Time and again, I'd judged my peers for setting aside their services and the reason for their creation to pursue women. But I was the one who'd been mistaken, who'd jumped to conclusions too soon, and denied myself for too long. As I held Cress against me for more, to *feel* more, I recognized this as the point where I transitioned.

I was no longer a statue in the service of Moongrove Library. I was a man, here to serve my woman.

My fingers trembled as I undid the button on her jeans, and she helped me get them off of her, discarding the slip of her panties as well. "C'mon up here," she said, lifting off of me and moving further up her bed.

Sitting upright, she spread her legs, and it was all I could do to keep myself in my pants as she beckoned for me to look at the folds of her sex. "Couple pointers," she said, taking my wrist and guiding my hand between her thighs. "This is the clit. Most men can't find it, but I bet gargoyles can." With a wink, she pressed my thumb to a nub of flesh at the apex of her folds.

I rubbed it, getting an electric thrill to see the pleasure that flushed her. "Doesn't seem so hard to find," I rumbled.

She smiled at that and guided me by touch through the rest of her slick sex, which opened like the petals of a glistening flower. I pressed one of my fingers into her channel and watched her legs draw up. "Ooh," she breathed.

Fitting a second one in with the first, I felt the strong muscles within her stretch around the digits...and I knew what she needed from me and why she was already reaching out to take it, freeing my cock at last and shoving my pants away.

"Lie back for me," she ordered. I kicked my clothes the rest of the way off and did so, propping up my back on her pillows while she went rummaging in her bedside table.

"Condom. Very important." She showed me the package and how to apply one.

Properly protected, I throbbed in the open air for her, my breath coming short at the sight of her beautiful bare form. She straddled my waist, too far up, so that I nestled in the cradle of her ass while she rested her weight atop me and let me draw her in for another, fiercer meeting of our mouths.

"Geo," she whispered between kisses. "Are you sure?"

Pulling away, her gaze searched mine while I cupped her neck, thumb grazing her cheek. Had there been a more stunning sight than her with kiss-swollen lips, her lidded eyes full of intimate promise? "I'm sure. I was made to be yours," I said.

"I love when you say things like that." She kissed my neck and jaw, rolling her hips again to tease my throbbing length. Just as my grip tightened with a thread of impatience, she guided herself back and took my cock in hand.

I bit my bottom lip as she lowered herself inch by inch. To be sheathed within her was bliss. She took it slow for my sake, bracing on my chest. Each bounce of her body had her breasts jiggling, a feast for my eyes alone. Her full lips parted, panting and moaning as she took her pleasure from me.

We fit together perfectly, just as I knew we would, and the rest came from the fleshy instincts I hardly knew I had. With a grasp on her hips, I met her halfway, rewarded by the delight that flashed over her face.

"That's right. Take me," she invited. I hardly needed encouragement when her expression was flush with pleasure.

I rolled us, still inside her, rocking the creaking joints of her tired bedframe. For once, I just felt. I just *was*. Her moans and cries, the way she curled her legs around me, inviting me deeper, it was my purpose fulfilled. I shuddered with bliss as she came, soaking in the smell and the feel of her, the flush of her skin.

She was *mine*. But more importantly, I was *hers*. My stone heart beat for her alone, a realization I had after I came and nearly collapsed atop her. I shifted onto my side, holding her to me with both arms.

"I feel like I adore you," I said. And that, truly, was an understatement.

"Sure that's not the sex talking?" she whispered.

I shook my head, stroking her silky purple hair. The shift in the bedrock of my emotional state was something I could self-analyze at a later time, but I knew it was permanent. My duty was answered only in her pleasure.

"Do you have another condom?" I asked.

"Mmm. Plenty." She rested with her eyes closed. "Aren't you tired, though?"

In answer, I pressed my erection, still rock hard, against her thigh. "Some of the rumors about gargoyles are true."

22

CRESS

I SPENT the following weekend with my books, missing work, and laptop spread out over Ben and Phaeron's table, nearly despairing at how much there was to do. Keeping me out of trouble with the university was a double-edged sword: though I wouldn't have a blemish on my educational record for breaking curfew, I wouldn't get any forgiveness or extra time for the work I'd missed.

I wasn't alone for any of it, at least. Phaeron was around early Saturday to help with Latin, but he disappeared for the rest of the weekend after that. Presumably, he attended the disciplinary hearing for us, but he didn't return. Geo and Ben helped where they could, the latter going so far as to forge my handwriting and finish some assignments for me.

Roe and Willow visited separately to help as well. "Any luck on mastering your mer magic?" I asked Willow while we puzzled over some of the Introduction to Witchcraft work together.

My shy friend scrubbed at her cheeks, as if she could rub away a sudden blush. "One of my professors looked into it. He thinks I need to visit one of the mer kingdoms because that side of me is dormant right now. Maybe if I was around the people and their energy, it'd help."

I took her in for a moment before asking, "Did he offer to take you himself?"

"No, but one of his assistants did."

"Is he cute?" I laughed.

"Cress!" she protested.

I tilted my head and gave her a look until she sighed and nodded. "I guess you could call him that. He's going to take me on a day trip to Neptris—a mer city in the Atlantic Ocean—sometime soon. I really hope it works." She traced the wood grain on the table with a sigh. "I'm tired of sitting out all the dangerous things you and the others are doing because I can't control my magic."

"It's really overrated, trust me. You get behind on your work," I tried to joke, gesturing to the piles of books on the table. She gave me a skeptical look. "Danger or not, I hope you get in touch with your mer side soon."

Maybe it would help her self-confidence, which was always low when the rest of us were able to use our magic without trouble. I'd seen Willow's troubles. She was still the Goldilocks of oceanic witches, either summoning too much or too little of her water-based magic for a given task. Having access to this mysterious other half of her abilities could be the balance she needed to get it just right.

She left to enjoy her weekend, and Roe came by Sunday afternoon with a bag full of snacks and soda to share around. "I looked into petitioning the Crown Coven for you," she said with little preamble, having a seat at the table across from Ben. Both of us perked up.

"Can a coven of baby witches do it?" I asked.

She wrinkled her freckled nose. "Yeah, but we need

endorsements from two established covens in good standing with enough clout to get our case heard. It'd be easier to take it to the supernatural court system."

"Crown Starsurge is rich enough to rub elbows with a blood baron," Ben put in. "He'd just hire a bunch of lawyers to legally fight us on his behalf."

As Eris had explained, there were two different systems I could use to go after Blaize Starsurge. The courts were for supernaturals of all kinds, while the Crown Coven only involved itself in witch affairs. It was particularly ballsy to petition the Crown Coven to air a grievance against one of its members, but it was also my only chance to stay out of a prolonged court battle I didn't have the money to fight.

"That's true. My mother and her coven can be one of our endorsements, but we need another," she said. "And, you know, an ironclad presentation with proof of Cress's claims."

I sighed, glancing upward. My handbook was still acting erratically, but it'd let me sift through the newest knowledge left within it this morning. Its pages had liter-ally quivered with the power forced into them, making it difficult to read for long. "Still working on that. All the memories my ancestors wanted to pass down are in the book, but I'm not sure how to share them."

"You have time," Roe sighed. "It takes up to a year for the Crown Coven to decide whether or not to hear a case. It really depends on who you have behind the petition, though."

The Crown Coven was a lot like a combination of the Senate and the Supreme Court, able to pick and choose who they spent their time listening to. Appointment to one of the seats was for life, and they alone made new witch laws for the whole continent of North America. There were six more covens like it across the world. It showed me how limited the witch population truly was for a handful of covens to be able to run the show that way.

And, also, how powerful and corrupt Blaize Starsurge had to be. Despite my bluster at Wren and the limited guidance I'd received so far from Eris, I was still just a mouse taunting a venomous snake.

"We do have an ace up our sleeves, though." Roe raised a brow. "As long as you've made sure that's true?"

Well, no. I still had Hana Graygazer's business card somewhere on my desk. I wanted calling Lanie's mother to be the very last step of our plan, which was foolishness Roe wanted to address head-on.

The seventh seat on the Crown Coven was currently filled by the venerated Kwan Graygazer, according to a well-hidden website. His short biography confirmed that he was from the famed family of augury witches.

"Cress," Roe grumbled. "Didn't Lanie even tell you to contact her mom if you needed help?"

"Uh, yeah." Shame warmed my cheeks. "Sorry again."

She waved my apology away, as she'd been doing from the moment I was healthy enough to text her. She wasn't hung up on not being able to talk to Lanie directly, especially after hearing how brief the conversation was and how much our friend wanted her rest.

The sticking point was that I hadn't brought her along to watch my back. I could only promise to be better in that regard. I'd never had such a loyal friend and needed to do better by her.

"Call her soon, okay? Maybe she can convince her coven to be our second endorsement. Imagine if she could just pick up the phone and have the ear of Crown Graygazer," she reasoned.

"You're right, that would be amazing. I will call her, promise," I said.

"One more thing for now—you're aware that if you go this route, Crown Starsurge will know exactly why you're appearing ahead of time? Petitions are read out, and a majority vote within the coven is what decides whether or not they're heard," Roe said.

I bit my lip. "Yeah. My birth mother mentioned that too." I wished Eris were here to lend some advice. After passing the Darkmore hereditary magic into my handbook, she'd vanished and hadn't reappeared yet. "I have to have a damn good case."

"*We* do have a damn good case," Roe said. "You're not doing this alone—the whole coven will be behind you, one way or another. If we have to bring Bianca instead of Wren, we totally will."

I smiled at last. "Thanks, Roe. I'm thankful this is a whole-coven affair. Maybe we'll even decide on a name soon."

"Well, yeah! We can't submit a petition without an official coven name. I'll text everyone about it again."

She shot off a group message, and we sat there chatting and laughing as this kicked off a second argument over the group chat about what the name should be. She showed me where to access a database online where we could type in prospective names and see if they were taken or not. Many otherwise good names were, and she didn't want to add a numeral to the name we decided on. What a headache.

THE BUSINESS CARD had a couple dented edges and was buried under a few assignments I'd felt were important enough to keep. "Graygazer Augury Services" stood out in big, black letters, along with a phone number and email address. I flipped it back and forth, working up my nerve.

"Just do it," Jin sighed from my lap. "They're nice people."

At first, I'd put off the call because it was dinnertime, but I couldn't be sure where Lanie's mother was right now. The Graygazers were known to move around, using their power of future sight to slightly alter the path of fate, saving lives simply by being in the right place at the right time. Lanie had believed strongly in this calling because it was her parents' lifestyle.

"You're right. I should get a hold of myself," I said.

"Yes, you should," the little black cat agreed without sympathy.

Well, maybe Hana wouldn't pick up. I dialed the number listed on the card and put the phone to my ear, counting the rings.

But it barely rang. "Hello, Cress," a woman answered.

"Err, hello, Missus Graygazer. Have I reached you at a good time?"

"I've been waiting for you to call for some time now," she said. I felt my cheeks heat, but she sounded kindly over the speaker. "Do you seek advice about your future?"

"Yes. And help in the present. I have so much to tell you." I recognized I echoed what I'd said to her daughter's spirit and cleared my throat. "How much time do you have?"

"I have time. Tell me everything."

I watched the light of evening shade to full night as I ended up doing just that. Jin left my lap to sleep on the spare bed in my dorm, while Milo and Bella came and went for pets and to take turns in my lap when I wasn't pacing the length of the room.

Hana listened quietly, occasionally confirming that she was still on the line. The faint sound of typing signaled that she was taking notes as I spoke. When I was done, she said, "You should have called sooner. This is no simple gaze into the gray, but a convoluted puzzle with multiple dangerous angles."

"Sorry, ma'am."

"Don't apologize, I'm happy to help."

"Would you be able to convince your coven to endorse our petition?" I asked, holding my breath while she considered.

"Hmm. I will discuss the possibility with my coven mates and Madigan."

My lips pursed to ask who that was when she answered in the next breath. "Your friend Roe's mother. I'm positive this will lead to my husband and me attending her Thanksgiving celebration, so I will see you there with a list of possible futures."

"That sounds amazing," I burst out.

"Let's discuss your immediate future, though. You've been entrusted with the Darkmore hereditary magic in a way that makes your librarian book a powerful enchanted item. With enough practice, you will be able to cast basic celestial witch spells. This means you will need to find a mentor who will be willing to teach you how to use the magic. I suggest you get a hold of a woman named Jordan Evenstar, who, as we speak, is trying to verify whether a letter she received in the mail is truly from a nephew she thought was dead."

"I think Ben gave her my number," I said.

"He must've. I see her reaching out after Thanksgiving and acting quite skeptical when you answer the phone. You will need to convince her to come meet Ben in person. What else... The monster that attacked you has returned to its master. They've burrowed far under cover." Her voice took on a dreamlike quality as she spoke. "The best thing you can do right now is train and improve yourself, because the next confrontation with it will decide the fate of its host's life."

I grimaced, imagining the panic Ben would have when he heard that news. We hadn't even come close to freeing Lucas of the Hungering Darkness up until now. "What about Garroway carving a blood rune on himself?"

Ben had finally shared what his mentor and father figure had died to tell him. "That is quite concerning, to think anyone would willingly take that monster into their body," Hana answered. She sounded like she was coming back to herself. "However, my magic encounters a fog any time he is involved in one of your futures."

"Is it because he's a vampire?" I asked.

"That could be part of it. More likely, he is wearing some sort of enchantment to be untraceable."

I put a finger over the receiver. "Shit. Fuck."

"However, when you've done this as long as I have, this kind of fog on your timelines suggests whether a decision leads you into danger. I will have more for you soon," she promised. "Is there anything else you'd like help with right now?"

"Can I ask for someone else? My friend Willow just learned that she's half-mer, and she's trying to access that side of her magic."

"I will speak with her when I see you all for Thanksgiving. Anything else for you?" she prompted.

"Got it," I said, running my hand through my hair as I mentally crossed off concerns too small to ask her about. "Do you know when I'll see Phaeron again? He's been missing almost all weekend." I was starting to miss him, even if I had spent most of my time with my other two men. I just didn't quite feel complete without the third around.

She answered after a couple minutes of silence. "Monday if you find where he hides in Moongrove Library. Wednesday if you wait for him to come to you after he resolves what troubles him."

"Is there something wrong?" I asked, instantly worried.

"I will let him explain," she answered with a chuckle. If she was laughing about it, I figured it wasn't so serious and relaxed.

"Okay, last question. Will my birth mother's spirit be returning?"

"Oh, a good one," she murmured. She was quiet as she read the future again. "Yes. If you spill your own blood and call to her ghost, it will come to you for a short time. She is much diminished but still present on the mortal plane out of sheer stubbornness. I see her being an excellent ally and source of knowledge when you need her most."

I breathed a sigh of relief. "Thank you. I feel so much better."

"Find your peace, but don't be complacent. I will see you soon," she said.

We said our goodbyes, and I glanced at the time with a sigh. I'd need a lot of coffee to get through tomorrow's classes.

23
CRESS

"B*RAZA*?" I said in a quiet corner of the library's lobby, hoping to get the powercore's attention the next morning.

I wasn't willing to wait until Wednesday to see Phaeron again, and if he was hiding in the library for some reason, there was one being that would be able to tell me where—the powercore herself. I was usually marked present for my class in the library, regardless of whether or not Mr. Eriksson saw me that day, so I took my chances on not appearing for one more session.

A feeling like static had the little hairs on the back of my neck lifting. *"Good morning, brightest of souls,"* Braza answered promptly.

"Good morning. Do you know where Phaeron is?" I asked quietly, hoping none of the people studying a few tables overheard me whispering to myself.

"Floor negative fourteen."

"Thanks." That was nearly painless. I headed for the elevators.

"I'll tell you which containment room he's entered if you chat with me," she said. She followed that up by teaching me

how to talk to her silently...since she could skim the most dominant thoughts in my head. A side effect of holding on to some of her power to fuel my librarian witch spells.

"Is there something wrong?" I asked her.

"Oh, no, I'm just horribly bored. Phaeron won't talk to me right now, and nothing's happening in the library out of the ordinary," she sighed.

Well, that did sound boring. As I took my elevator trip down to floor negative fourteen, she told me a little about her existence. There was no such thing as sleep for a power-core, but she preferred her constant vigilance over the certainty of death she'd been left with long ago.

I tried to lighten her mood with a quick story, picking up pretty quickly that she wanted someone to gossip with. I stepped off the elevator and leaned against the wall until the conversation was finished.

"Okay, chat later? He's in the room at the very end of the left wing," she eventually told me.

"Sure. Thanks again," I thought to her. Her static-filled presence faded as I walked down the left hallway, which had only a few doorways on either side, signifying the rooms here were quite large. The last door was shut, and no one answered when I knocked.

With a shrug, I tried the knob. It was unlocked. Braza hadn't given any warnings about this room, but I still peeked inside and blinked owlishly as I received a nose full of night air.

The "room" was like a pocket dimension from the moment I closed the door behind me and shut out the hallway's artificial lighting. Springy, grass-like plants cushioned my feet as I stepped further inside and took my handbook off my belt. *"The Librarian Witch's Handbook,* scan for any hostile entities," I instructed it quietly.

"Aye aye, captain!" it answered at full volume, fluttering off into the underbrush.

Logic dictated that no door in Moongrove Library was left unlocked if there was something hostile inside, but I just wanted to be sure, considering the size of the space I'd entered. I didn't feel like there were any walls here, just an open stretch of forest with the sound of rushing water somewhere close. The sky was a beautiful spread of stars, with a slivered crescent moon lending dim light that my eyes eventually adjusted to.

I didn't recognize any of the trees, with their sharp, irregularly shaped leaves and deep ruby hue. Everything around me was one shade off from black, severely desaturated from normal.

I took a few steps forward, calling, "Phaeron?"

"Over here," he answered. I shifted toward the sound of his voice, finding a trail through the underbrush. The sound of water became a louder rush by the time I spotted him sitting on the rocky edge of a cliff hanging above a slow, small waterfall of violet water.

He turned to look at me, his eyes twin lamps, but didn't move to stand. "Stay right there," he said. "Did Braza tell you where to find me?"

My feet stilled, and I paused, uncertain. There was a certain husky quality to his voice, but I couldn't make out his expression from here. "She did. I haven't seen you in a few days... Why are you hiding out here?"

"It beats several alternatives," he said in a near growl.

"What's wrong, Phaeron?"

"Nothing. You should go."

I took a step closer. He definitely growled at me this time. "I'm finding that hard to believe," I said.

His hand passed over his eyes, muting their light as he

released a tense sigh. "Fine, but I did warn you. I am not in full control of myself."

"Is it the soul hunger again?" I asked, feeling a flutter of nerves in my belly. Usually, that was accompanied by the presence of his monstrous brother.

"Partially. Aurina used her magic on me again. I could kill her for it," he snarled, snapping his tail. "She asked me to join her mating circle."

A surge of anger hit me too, but also an intensifying of my nerves. "What do you mean, she used her magic on you again?" I asked. It was clear her request had pissed him off.

He stood, stalking over until his features were bathed in pale starlight. His face was taut with desire, and his otherworldly eyes practically blazed with feverish intensity. "She filled the air with lust," he answered. "And I made it clear that I would rather drag you to her office and fuck you right in front of her than be forced to become her mate. I've been here ever since, waiting for my desire to cool, and *it hasn't*, not even by a fraction."

"That's not her asking. That's coercion," I said, pissed for him. Yet my face was flaming. He nodded and edged closer, leaning toward me. My gaze snagged on the rather impressive bulge in his pants. "Do you want some help with that?" I offered, reaching for him.

He moved away at the last moment with a frustrated snarl. "No. There's...there's more." He balled his clawed hands into fists. "I've fantasized about you joining me here, wet and eager. I could take you against a tree or out on the grass where it's softest. A hundred times, in a hundred different ways. I could have you naked and screaming for me in minutes."

My knees went weak. *Yes, please!*

"But I also lust to sink my teeth into your pretty soul

just as much. I could bite your neck and leave my mating mark or simply tear into your soul. Would it be as sweet as you are?" He gave his head a vicious shake.

"Hey, Cressie!" exclaimed my book as it flapped over to us. "There you are. Everything's clear—"

With an irritated swipe of Phaeron's hand, a coil of shadow snapped the handbook shut and secured its clasp. It thumped to the ground and rocked indignantly.

"You need to go," he growled at me. His familiar, other-worldly power pulsed in the air around us, hanging there like humidity.

I worked my jaw, struck nearly speechless. After all that, he wanted me to leave? I don't know who that would hurt more. While he was so worked up and trying to warn me, I couldn't find an ounce of fear.

"I can't just leave you like this," I said. He narrowed his eyes, tail undulating behind him. "If you weren't in control, you wouldn't have the words to tell me all that. You'd have just acted."

"Don't tempt me, bright soul." He slid a little closer, but I didn't back away.

"I don't think you will hurt me," I answered. We were nearly nose to nose. Heat rolled from his body in waves, and he breathed shallowly, staring at the full curve of my lips. And there was the truth of his intentions, his eyes on what he wanted, not what he was afraid he would damage.

"Cress," he said roughly. It had the sound of a final warning.

The man just needed a little relief, and I knew the way to give him some without his fangs anywhere near my soul. My coy smile was my only answer, and it frayed the last threads of his self-control. His mouth met mine with bruising intensity, our tongues and teeth clashing. My eyes widened, recognizing he'd snapped the powerful leash that kept both his lust and power in check. Tendrils of shadow took form around us, trailing off him like smoky fur and wrapping around my curves.

He lifted me effortlessly by the hips, lips still locked with mine. Roughened bark met my back, and he pinned me there with his erection grinding against my core. He tugged my hair and smoothed a hand up my waist, his claws hooking over the band of my jeans. It took me a few feverish moments to realize he'd lifted and supported my hips with the solid muscle of his tail, and the flexible tip was wrapped around one of my thighs, keeping that leg spread.

When we parted for breath, he trailed sharp-edged kisses down my neck, hesitating at the curve of skin where he'd tugged my shirt aside, exposing my shoulder. "I won't mark you today. Not like this," he murmured. I moaned from a firm thrust of his hips. "But one day, you will carry my mating mark. You'll beg for it."

"I will," I agreed breathlessly. I could already tell that I'd beg him to take me in all ways with the same fierce, animal desire that he wore openly on his expression.

But for right now, I pushed his shoulders. It was like trying to move a wall. "Second thoughts, bright soul?" He began to disentangle us, unable to hide the disappointment the thought gave him.

Even in the grasp of a lust spell, he had the control to stop. I would compliment him on it—later. The moment he stepped back, he gave me an opening to drop to my knees and pull open his pants. I felt his reaction in the squeeze on my thigh from his tail and watched a desire-filled grin erase his doubts.

"Naughty witch," he practically purred.

I freed his cock, pleasantly surprised as it bobbed free. I didn't know what to expect, but he was shaped and proportioned like a human man. With how dark it was around us, I felt him for any surprises, and he throbbed in my palm. His shaft was designed for pleasure, with a few extra nodules that seemed well-placed to rub a partner intimately. I wanted to feel it for myself.

I cupped his balls and licked a trail down his length, trying to contain my eager smile so I could fold my lips over my teeth. The pressure of his tail was shifting up my thigh, and I only noticed it when it snaked around my waist, the tip hooking into my waistband.

Magic leaked from Phaeron's fingertips, hard to detect until I felt his shadows like tiny fingers plucking at the button of my jeans. I had the crown of his shaft between my lips when one last nudge had my jeans coming undone and unzipped. He tugged with his tail, exposing my bare ass to the night air.

My gaze flashed up to his face as I took the rest of him into my mouth. I wasn't the only naughty one here, it seemed, as his tail felt a lot like a third hand as it brushed over my skin and through the lips of my slick pussy. He threaded his fingers through my hair, guiding my head while he rolled his hips at a slow pace to start.

I loved the look of relief in his expression, all of his attention and focus on me. The thin tip of his tail searched for and flicked my clit, sending a starburst of pleasure through me. I jolted in his hold, fingers digging into his thighs.

"Spread your legs more," he ordered. He had me tilt my hips back, and I did so with a thrill of anticipation as his tail stroked and teased.

Was he going to fuck me with that tail? I sure hoped so

as I wiggled my hips, shivering from the cool breeze touching my wet lips. It nudged my pussy, and his grip on the back of my head tightened. He'd looped the thinnest part of his tail around itself, creating a knobby ride that he thrust into me like a cock. The drive of his hips matched its pace.

For a moment, I wondered how exactly I'd gotten into this situation. I'd come to the university a blushing virgin, and within a few months, I'd become an anam cara for a blood witch, awakened the emotions within a gargoyle, and was now getting tail fucked by this demonic man who'd never worn his emotions so openly on his expression as now.

His desire was no longer buried under decades of poise and princely dignity. I was proud to help him strip it away to the honest, raw core of who he was. He looked at me like the wolf his shadowborn form resembled, hungry and passionate.

It was a shame I could only give him my mouth until he figured himself out, because I wanted to feel him in the hundred different ways he promised he'd fantasized about. It was the truth that had my pussy growing slicker for his tail. I'd become far too aware of the pleasure my three men could give, that we could share.

"Cress," he breathed raggedly. I shuddered in echo to the naked pleasure he spoke into my name. With one last throb, he came, flooding my mouth with the taste of him.

I'd barely swallowed all his come when he took a knee, still pumping his tail into me. Cupping my cheek, he kissed me without shame for the taste of him that remained on my tongue. The pad of his thumb circled my clit, pressing, demanding I find completion too.

He was soon swallowing my moan as I came apart,

slowing the frenzy of his kiss and helping me down from that sharp peak with a slower, more gentle touch. I didn't miss that he gathered my slick with a touch down my folds and licked it from his thumb with an expression I could only label as both vicious and victorious.

I lay a little limp on his shoulder, panting. "Better?" I asked.

"Much." His voice was back to its smooth warmth, and the feverish intensity in his eyes was fading. I knew all he needed was a good release. There was no talk of souls or biting or tearing, just his reverent touch over my cheek, combing through my hair. He held me against him as we both caught our breath. "Thank you, bright soul. I think I can return to polite society now. What time is it?"

I fumbled with the jeans tangled around my knees until I withdrew my phone. "About lunch time." I'd completely missed the time block for Library Science 101, but I'd had a hell of a lot more fun here in... "What is the room, by the way?"

Phaeron sighed, casually using tendrils of shadow to fix his clothes back on and offering a hand up once I'd done the same. "My sanctuary. I was a little surprised it was still here, to be frank." He guided me back to the ridge where I'd originally found him, the two of us sitting with our legs dangling over the trickle of the small waterfall. He put a casual arm around my waist as I leaned against him. "It's mostly an illusion."

I blinked away the afterimages of my phone's screen. We could see a valley of dark plant life stretching far into the distance, with the spires of buildings even further. "I made it with my magic and memories. This was one of my favorite places to stop and think back in Soiluire. Of course, there was more life back then. The call of animals, the slow creep of mushrooms, and the turn of seasons," he continued, glancing toward the sky. "I gave it Earth's stars as well."

"It's beautiful." But so was this moment, with the continuing glimpse of him so relaxed and open.

"I agree."

"You must miss it."

The back of a claw traced up my waist as he considered. "Sometimes, I do. But there's no going back, so there's also little sense in yearning for the impossible." He turned a fanged grin my way. "Besides, I've never had a complaint about Earth's women."

PHAERON and I went separate ways until that evening, when I showed up in our usual spot in workout gear and my sword. Neither of us mentioned the moonlit tryst, yet things had changed between us all the same. Thus began the game Morgana had warned me about.

"He'll drive you mad with little touches and whispers in your ear. He'll pretend he has no idea what he's doing to you, but he knows and is waiting for you to snap and tear his clothes off."

I saw Phaeron nightly for training from then on as the days counted down to Thanksgiving break and the moment I'd need to explain my relationships to Mom and Carly. There was no hiding it now, not with my time divided between my three men.

Mornings and midday were for Ben, grabbing coffee and flirting before and between classes. Late afternoons went to Phaeron, who continued to drill me on sword skills, magic, and, with a *tisk* after hearing me butcher some Latin homework, proper pronunciation of various Latin words. He snuck little touches in between sessions, sweet kisses on my neck and nibbles on the shell of my ear. Inevitably, I took his teasing and unleashed the results on Geo, who turned out to be rather insatiable since he hadn't shifted back to gargoyle form during this time. He slept in my bed instead.

Things were oddly peaceful, a portent of a storm to come. I felt it looming as I worked with Roe to fill out a template petition to the Crown Coven, leaving it saved on my computer for now. All we needed was a coven name and for me to get more than a few meager sparks of light from the celestial power locked inside my handbook.

For once, I was confident. I was becoming strong and capable. It was only a matter of time before Blaize Starsurge paid dearly for what he'd done to my family.

24

BEN

"I DON'T NEED A FAMILIAR," I said one sunny afternoon as Cress tugged me along by the hand. I was hopeless to resist, even if she was taking me toward a familiar fair to meet up with the rest of our coven.

"Nonsense. Every witch needs a companion," she said.

"But *you're* my companion."

She wiggled her brow at me over her shoulder. "Yeah. But not that kind of companion. My familiars feel more like built-in best friends. They never judge me."

"They're literally cats. That's what they do," I pointed out.

"Okay, Jin judges a bit."

"See?"

"That just means a cat probably isn't for you. But there's a company bringing in potential familiars of all kinds. There's going to be something for you, promise," she said. And from her excitement, I figured she was looking forward to meeting them, despite her three familiars trailing us at their own paces.

We slowed as we spotted a series of multicolored tents

set up around one of the university's fields, this one criss-crossed by sidewalks and featuring a few fountains. "There's Roe," I said, pointing out the distinctive redhead a moment before she noticed us and waved.

When the fair had rolled in, we'd learned that Cress and Wren were the only witches in our coven who'd already bonded with familiars. My babe had her cats, while apparently, the queen bee had a finicky hawk that preferred to keep to itself. Heath was texting for her in the group chat now, and we were told not to expect either of them to come with us today.

Her loss. Roe, Willow, and a bored-looking Grant were already there waiting. "Why are you here?" I asked him as Cress let me go to greet her friends.

Grant shrugged. "I have to keep up appearances."

"What appearance?" Bianca found us in that moment, smirking his way.

"Some discretion would be lovely," he answered dryly.

At this point, I'd lost track of who he'd revealed his changeling form to. It seemed like everyone who regularly came in contact with our coven except for Áine—for obvious reasons—plus Heath and Wren since they'd become so standoffish.

"Aren't you cold?" I asked Bianca. She was dressed in a tank that left much of her trim midriff exposed and the tiniest of shorts. All the better to show off the new piercing on her belly button, which was a silver stud until it healed naturally.

"Haven't you gotten the memo?" she countered. "I do what I want now."

"And this is different from normal, how?"

She punched my shoulder, drawing a laugh from me. She was too easy to bait sometimes.

Roe cleared her throat. "Now that we are gathered here today, let's decide on a coven name." She showed her phone screen around, which displayed the official registry of witch covens.

I tapped my forehead. "Using the familiar fair to rope us into this again. Smart."

She rolled her eyes at me. "Thanks, Ben. If we can't agree on something, I'll stop being stubborn about adding a number to our coven name. We could just be NSU Coven Number Fifty-seven if it means it's done. There's always a way to submit a coven name change later, or we're allowed to shuffle around at the end of the year if anyone wants to do that."

Cress pulled out her phone and brought up the same website Roe was on. "Okay, I'm ready," she said.

"Witchy Ways?" Bianca ventured.

"We already looked up that one," Roe said, but she typed it in anyway. "Fifteen versions of that name."

Roe and Cress alternated looking up potential names and telling us how many of those were in use. "Ben is Awesome Coven?" I put in eventually.

"No," Roe answered.

"Oddly enough, there is one of those," Cress said a few moments later.

We kept trying. When no two registered covens could be named the same thing, we just had to agree on something and add a number to it. "Try A Little Wicked," Grant suggested.

Roe did and leaned back in surprise. "It's available," she said. I exchanged a glance with Cress, whose face had lit up. "Guys! There are several covens with that name, but the one without a number disbanded...four days ago."

"Better lock that in," Grant murmured.

Willow scuffed her foot. "Are we really wicked enough for a name like that, though?"

"A little bit." Cress shrugged. "I mean, doesn't the name suggest that we're just a bit that way?"

"Don't question it," Roe said, holding her phone closer to her face as she tapped its screen rapidly. "We're taking it. You guys enjoy the fair. I'll be right behind you, okay?"

The rest of us left her to submit the name application and crossed over to the tents. Most of the animals were out of their cages, the hum of conversation everywhere as college-aged witches conversed with the handlers, most of whom were fae. Certain types of fae could talk to any animal they wanted to, and it seemed they had, as we passed by a fully grown tiger lounging on its own stretch of grass like a striped king. He paid us little mind.

"What kind of familiar do you guys want?" Cress asked.

"Something fierce. Maybe that big kitty or a wolf," Bianca answered.

Willow shrugged, her head on a swivel. "I'll need an aquatic familiar, but I don't see any."

"It's not like there's a body of water around," I pointed out. "Unless you count the fountain."

The soft-spoken girl cracked a little smile. "You haven't been around many oceanic witches, have you? There's magic that can put a floating bubble of water around anything that can't breathe air. They basically swim behind their witch on land. One of my classmates has a dolphin and has a charm to shrink it down to teddy-bear size!"

"That doesn't hurt it?" Cress asked.

"Not at all." Willow clasped her hands with a little happy shrug. "It's so cute! I want one of my own."

A witch wearing a shirt with the familiar company's green logo approached us. "Hello, have you all been helped?" She faced Bianca with a trained customer service smile as the young woman tickled the tiger's massive back paws. It flicked its tail in annoyance but didn't lift a claw to bat her away yet.

The worker led us on a tour through the tents, showing off everything from lizards and snakes lazing under heated lamps, to a flock of various birds perching on specialized bars set up under one tent. I found it interesting that the fae bird keeper had managed to enforce harmony with eagles sitting next to sparrows or, in some cases, tiny birds twittering playfully as they hid in the wing fluff of their much larger cousins.

There were also a *ton* of critters that were more popular pets. Cats and dogs made up a good third of the animals we saw, and there was a sizable population of other small mammals too. At some point, we lost Grant, who snuck away after stopping to pet a couple of the dogs. Bianca stopped to ruffle a wolf's thick pelt.

The next thing I knew, Willow and I were the only ones still on the tour. I turned to say something to Cress, but she was a few yards away, talking to Phaeron, who had a hand resting on her hip and was whispering something in her ear that brought about a distinctive blush. *Sneaky fucker,* I thought. I'd been the one to clue him in about the familiar fair earlier by complaining that Cress was making me go.

"Our aquatic pets should be along shortly. They'll have to be walked here from the marina," the worker was telling Willow when I tuned back in to what she was saying.

"I'll just wait here, then," Willow answered. With a nod, the worker slipped away to help some other newcomers.

Since I wasn't all that keen to see any animals, or interrupt Cress and Phaeron's moment, I turned to my coven mate. "Sooo...how exactly do the swimming familiars get to NSU? Isn't the marina a lake?"

Willow had that amused look again. "There's an ocean gate at the bottom of the marina. It's like a standing portal that only activates if you have a magical key, but it links up to a couple locations in the Atlantic."

"Those finned folk have their own technology, huh," I said.

"It's like a whole different world." Her eyes suddenly widened at something she spotted over my shoulder. Her mouth popped open in a wowed O.

I turned to see what it was and stifled a laugh. A merman in his land form strode our way, followed by a fleet of fish and other aquatic creatures swimming in their own personal water bubbles, just as Willow had described. Two oceanic witches in damp wetsuits flanked the animals. They both carried gleaming tridents, creating a nearly invisible tide of water midair to wash their charges along faster.

It was definitely the merman she was staring at. He wore nothing but a pair of shorts, cerulean scales glimmering on his broad shoulders and sculpted cheeks. The man had abs for days; if I wasn't happily taken, I'd stare too. Instead, I turned a smirk Willow's way. "You wanna go talk to him?"

She ducked her head shyly. "Who?"

I elbowed her. "C'mon, you know who. Let's go."

Though she made a sound of protest, she followed a step behind me as I approached and waved to the merman. "Hey, man. Are these for the familiar fair?"

He skimmed over me with disinterest. "They are," he grunted. His gaze landed on Willow next, and he stood a little straighter. "We ran into some trouble along the way from Deeptide. A hungry kraken thought to get a familiar snack, but I put a stop to it."

"Oh, wow," Willow said quietly.

She startled when I nudged her forward with a hand on her shoulder. "Willow here is in the market for a familiar or two," I said.

"Is that so?" the merman asked, flashing a perfect white smile.

She bobbed her head. "Yeah."

"Well, you're in luck." He offered her his elbow like an old-fashioned gentleman, escorting her back to the fair. "We have many interesting and powerful potential familiars for a discerning oceanic witch."

I watched them go for a few moments, proud of how well that went. I drifted back to the tents with my hands in my pockets, a little lost with all my friends now spread out. Usually, I had someone around to distract my thoughts, but alone, one threaded in to take over my headspace.

Lucas would love to be here right now.

He was definitely the animal lover between the two of us. I imagined he'd be thrilled to pet a real wolf and debate the merits of the various types of familiars. Here I was, enjoying a few moments of peace while he was still out there somewhere in serious trouble. What kind of brother did that make me?

Cress was sure we'd have another chance to properly fight the Hungering Darkness and pry it from Lucas. When we did, I'd take him to three familiar fairs to make up for him missing this one.

"Are you just going to brood, or try to find a familiar?" Cress asked, startling me from my thoughts.

"I wasn't brooding," I protested. "I'm just...overwhelmed. Where do I start?"

Phaeron had followed her like a shadow, the two of them flanking me now. "Have you tried over there?" he asked, pointing to the tent overflowing with tiny furry bodies. I shrugged and headed that way, standing a good foot away from the animals.

A cotton-white blur jumped on me anyway, clinging to my shirt. It was an albino mouse, tiny and cute with beady red eyes. I scooped it into my palm and smiled awkwardly to the fae woman watching. This section had a number of rodent-adjacent creatures. I'd have been offended if I didn't realize they were having the equivalent of a mini party, playing within assembled plastic gyms of pipes both big and small and chasing each other. It looked like a good time for a small creature.

"How, exactly, do I know I've found a familiar?" I asked the fae just so she'd stop waiting for me to do something other than pet down the mouse's silky fur with just my index finger.

"You'll feel a kind of draw to an animal you're compatible with. They choose you as much as you choose them. If an animal speaks to you in a way you understand, you know you've been adopted," she answered happily.

I held the mouse closer to my ear, only hearing squeaks. I placed it back on the table, just for it to jump and cling to my shirt again. "Okay, okay. You could sit on me for a minute?" I asked it like it understood, lifting it to sit on my shoulder. To my surprise, it stayed.

Cress watched this with a giggle. "Try a ferret, Ben. I think one would be perfect for you." She knelt down and offered her hands to the opening of one of the tubes big enough for the energetic things, coming back up with a wiggly ferret.

"What's that supposed to mean?" I asked in a teasing

tone, taking it from her and looking into its face. "Do I seem like a mischievous, masked thief to you?"

It had a darker stripe across its eyes, like a bandit mask. When I asked the question, though, it tilted its head thoughtfully and sniffed my arm more closely. "Kind of," it said, clear as day.

In shock, I dropped the poor thing. "Hey!" it protested in a small, boyish voice. He scampered his way up my jeans and back into my hands.

Cress leaned in, smiling wide. "Did it talk to you?"

"It...he, I think. He did," I answered. I didn't feel all that different, but the ferret must've picked me, because I was vaguely aware of him laughing at me even if he showed no signs of it, simply sitting stretched between my palms.

"Nice to meetcha," he said. "I'm Flit. Are you fun?"

"Am I fun?" I echoed to Cress with a little smirk.

"Sometimes," she giggled.

"C'mon, I'm trying to impress a ferret here."

"Very," she amended. "*Very* fun."

That seemed to satisfy Flit. Before we could leave, the fae woman started to talk about an adoption fee and produced pamphlets and a starter kit for caring for him. Cress and I both turned to Phaeron, who lifted a brow. "What?"

"You got money, Big P?" I asked.

"Oh." He rolled his eyes, taking a wallet out of his back pocket. "How much is it?"

I cringed when she named the sum, but he didn't flinch.

"And the mouse?" the fae asked.

"Yes, the mouse too," he sighed before I could say anything. It was looking right at him from my shoulder with a piteous expression. It only added twenty bucks to the total, at least.

"Well, they made off like real bandits with that one," I murmured as we rejoined our coven mates, most of whom had a new companion.

"Good one!" Flit exclaimed. I think I liked the little guy already.

Bianca had her arms crossed. "Really, a mouse?" she asked.

I looked around her in an exaggerated fashion. "Where's yours?" I asked in the same judgy tone.

"Not here, I guess," she sighed.

"Well, I have a ferret now, actually. His name's Flit," I said, letting her take him off my hands for the moment. She scratched between his ears and nearly fumbled him when he went boneless.

Cress was kneeling before the dog that sat obediently by Roe's side. "Yeah, he's a retired police dog. They said the gray on his muzzle should fade pretty fast along with his aches and pains since he'll live as long as I do," the redhead was saying.

I took a closer look at the dog, recognizing his markings as a purebred. He was a unit of a Belgian Malinois with tan fur and a darker muzzle, alert despite a few signs of old age. "Going to chase down bad guys together?" I asked.

She grinned. "Sure are. Right, Tank?" The dog woofed in agreement.

That was a good match, I thought. I would be about a thousand percent not surprised if she got a job with SPDI enforcing supernatural law once she graduated.

I turned to Willow, who held a bubble of water with a squid-like creature within. "Well, did you get it?" I asked.

"Yeah, this is my familiar now. She's a cuttlefish," she told me. I leaned forward and squinted, and the animal within the bubble shifted colors to be harder to see. Just as shy as her witch, apparently.

"Cool, but that's not what I meant," I said. "Did you get his number?"

The question was a magnet, drawing the attention of the other three women. "Whose number?" Bianca followed up with.

"Who was it?" Roe asked.

Willow's shoulders lifted, a red tinge spreading across her cheeks. "Uh, yeah, I got his number."

Grinning, I stole a high five before our friends converged on her for details. I took that moment to coax the mouse from my shoulder. "Hey, you. Sure you want to come with me?" I asked it. It bobbed its whole body like a nod. "You want to be my familiar too or something?" It made a sound like it was sucking on its teeth, regarding me with little red eyes. After a few moments to consider the question, it bobbed another yes.

"All right. Welcome to the crew." I chuckled, setting it back on my shoulder. With our new menagerie and name, it felt like we were finally becoming a proper coven.

25

CRESS

I FIDGETED with my sleeves a few days later as I waited on a sidewalk in human Salem for an old sedan to roll down the road. We were around the place where Mom and Carly had to drop me off so I could pass into NSU without them.

The rules about ordinary people visiting the university were loosened slightly around vacations. Witches having human family members was not unheard of, and they were permitted to use portal services like the couple of companies that'd set up on campus to send students home the fast way for their vacation.

I bubbled with an overflowing mix of nerves and excitement. So much had happened since Carly and I had dyed our hair different bright colors and had a tearful goodbye last summer. Mom had taken a rare extended break from work to come for the whole vacation week, too. They expected to see a lot of me...

But that also meant they'd be meeting all three of my guys. Since one of them was always around, I'd asked Ben to be there with me as we waited. He was the most approachable of the three when it came to meeting a super-natural.

I had a *lot* to explain because I'd saved the serious topics to talk to them about in person. I was seriously hoping my three men could play it cool until I had an opportunity to sit down and chat with Mom and Carly.

"Relax, babe," Ben said, for once the less fidgety of the two of us as I jittered in place with my thoughts.

"You try explaining to your regular human family about supernaturals taking multiple mates," I muttered.

"Oh." He grinned, tapping the side of his chin. "Want me to do it?"

"Noooo. I don't want anyone to, frankly."

"They're going to notice that Geo, Big P, and I follow you around like lost dogs," he pointed out.

I sighed and nodded. They definitely were, and Carly would be the one to ask, loudly, if I had three boyfriends. "What happened to 'tall, dark, and terrifying'?" I put up air quotes. Now that I thought about it, he hadn't called Geo anything but his regular name in a while too.

He shrugged. "Too big a mouthful."

Seemed more like he was maturing and trying to get along to me. I was really proud of his progress, and some of my fondness must've leaked onto my expression, as he smiled back and said, "What? It is."

"You're a good man, Ben Evenstar," I said.

He put a hand to his chest, smacking his lips in mock offense. Any sassy response was lost when someone leaned on a car horn for two honks. My heart jolted, and I leaned past him to see Mom's old junker rolling to a stop a couple feet away.

Mom cut the engine, and Carly half-fell out of the passenger's side, rushing over with a big grin and her arms open. The corners of my eyes pricked as we hugged for a few prolonged moments. She was petite and fair, just like Mom, and the electric blue dye she'd put in her hair was faded to a greenish shade with exposed blonde roots.

"How'd you get yours to stay so nice?" she asked, fluffing my still-purple locks.

"Magic," I whispered behind my hand. Verdant witches sold potions that changed hair colors, and I was waiting to give her a couple as a gift later.

Mom came over for her hug next, a briefer embrace. "Hi, baby," she said. "Let me get a look at you."

As a nurse and the woman who raised me, she had the uncanny ability to sense if anything was amiss. She could practically tell me when a cold was coming on when the symptoms were barely showing themselves. "Hmm, you're practically glowing. Who is this young man with you?"

"Mom, Carly, this is Ben, my boyfriend," I said. He'd stepped back to wait but came over for a round of hand-shakes with his usual charming smile.

Carly pointed to his back while he chatted with Mom briefly. She flashed two thumbs-up, a rare double approval, and I mirrored the gesture. We giggled together.

"Well, we'd better get ourselves to NSU. How will this work, exactly?" Mom asked.

We piled into the car, with Ben and me sitting in the back. I offered her a plastic sign to hang off her mirror, with the university's "normal" name, Northern State University, spelled down its side. "Just keep driving down this road. This will activate the entrance to the pocket dimension, and the scenery will change in a blink."

The engine gave a labored start, but Mom still got a feeble *vroom* from the old car after we rolled into motion. She had the same look of excited anticipation I remember first entering NSU with. It was like going into one of the story worlds I loved to read about, and I'd gotten my love of books from Mom.

I heard more than saw my family's wonder as we passed onto the roadway that led in two directions. Left for the NSU campus, and right for New Salem. The sky had shifted from overcast to bright and sunny in a blink, and the roadside plants had a vibrancy that came entirely from it being late fall in the former Fall Court.

I guided Mom around campus, parking in a lot on the outskirts of campus. We wouldn't see much of NSU, as the company of celestial witches creating the portals today were set up not far from here to catch most of the non-supernatural visitors before they wandered far. Ben helped carry some of the luggage my family had brought for their extended stay, leaving Mom and Carly with rolling bags and the chance to look their fill at our surroundings.

"Just try not to stare. I know it's hard," I told my sister.

The Ashboughs had bought us tickets with the biggest portal company, which had a large crowd amassed for their turns. I could practically feel Carly's giddiness as we slid around the side of the gathering, looking for my coven and friends.

"Is that a mermaid?" she whispered, inclining her head toward a woman standing with a tower of bags, greenish scales glimmering on her cheeks and her black hair giving off an emerald sheen in the sunlight.

"Yeah, in her land form," I said just as quietly. "There are several mer in the Fashion Design program. They're gorgeous, especially in the water."

The question made me think of Willow, who'd been disappointed following her trip to one of the underwater mer cities. She was as human as ever, with no sign of her latent mer side emerging. The professor she'd been conferring with about the problem suspected her magic would rise to the occasion if she were ever in serious trouble, but none of us were keen to push her into danger to give it a try.

"Over here!" Roe's shout and wave drew us to her. She'd watched our things while Ben and I had gone to get my family, the two of us only having a bag each. I'd brought my laptop too, for entertainment and to check on the status of my petition, which was still open for sponsoring covens and minor changes before it was sent off.

Roe was happy to lead introductions, sharing names and affinities of those coming. Áine waved shyly as the immediate center of my sister's attention. Not everyone had taken up Roe's offer to feast with her family and spend their break in the Crystal Court, but Willow and, to my surprise, Bianca had decided to come along.

Our newly expanded group of familiars were tagging along too. Bella and Milo chirped hellos to my family from where they snuggled up to Tank, Roe's retired police dog, who was already looking a little more spry. Ben's shoulder mouse had found him again, climbing up to its usual spot and observing the world from its safe perch.

Geo stood at the back of the group, offering a stoic nod when introduced. He'd been in human form long enough that his eyes had darkened from an uncanny silver-white into a gray that was warm and looked more natural against his dark complexion.

The least human-seeming of us was the last to arrive in a wisp of smoke, taking form next to the gargoyle with a single bag of his own. "Glad I'm not too late," Phaeron said.

"Whoa," Carly breathed.

In the middle of introductions, he came over to kiss Mom's fingertips. "A pleasure," he said smoothly. His gaze flashed to me, and I knew this was the moment my secret came out. "Your daughter is a delight."

Mom turned toward me, a thoughtful frown tugging at her lips. "She...certainly is."

Roe observed the interaction and said, "Something you should be aware of, Mama Rollins, is that supernatural families can be rather nontraditional. Powerful men or women usually take multiple mates. My mother's a legend, and as such, she has three men she calls husband. You're about to meet them when we reach the Crystal Court."

This effectively distracted her from what Phaeron had said. I gave silent thanks yet again for a friend like Roe. "That does sound unusual, I must admit," Mom said.

"It's pretty normal if you grow up with it." Roe smiled and shrugged. "Just means there's a lot more family around for big gatherings like Thanksgiving!"

We moved up in line, and I fell in step with Roe, pushing some of our luggage along with us. "I didn't realize you had three dads," I said in an aside.

"Well, surprise." She clapped me on the shoulder. "Seven younger siblings, too! My mama only retired for a little bit to have all of us. Now she's back in action."

Wow, that was a *huge* family. No wonder she was always trying to draw the coven together for rituals and meet-ups.

"To save you from another big surprise, one of my dads is a prince of the Crystal Court. My family owns about a third of the caves, which is why my mama always hosts big groups there. You'll have your own hotel room for yourself or...well, you know." She lifted both shoulders in an exaggerated shrug.

"No way—why didn't you mention that before?" I asked with a disbelieving laugh.

"I'm not the one who's a big deal here, so it's not like I'm going to brag about what my family owns," she said. "All I can do is point at my mama and remind people that I'm related to her."

I nodded in understanding. There were times I'd done the same with my adopted mother, proud of the lives she'd impacted and even saved in her line of work.

We weren't waiting too much longer before Roe's name was announced as having the next portal up. I went ahead, eager to see how this worked. If Eris were here right now, she'd be reminding me that I could've done this magic myself someday, but thankfully, she was resting instead of making subtle jabs at my choice to be a librarian witch. That gave me a chance to see the process in peace.

A pair of celestial witches were working with a loop of metal engraved with flowing runes around its edges. A third man moved heavy brackets along its side as they calculated together the exact place we were heading from details on a printed piece of paper. It took fifteen minutes before they were satisfied. They touched the tip of their magical staves into the sides of the metal loop. Sparkles of buttery yellow, like sunlight, flowed from the staves. They circled midair at ever-increasing speeds, expanding and stretching until the loop contained a sheet of magic with the thickness and consistency of a soap bubble.

"Let's go home," Roe said. She went through with a bounce to her step, making the portal wobble as she disappeared inside of it.

The celestial witches gestured me on impatiently, so I swallowed my nerves at trying this unfamiliar magic and stepped through with my luggage. It was like taking a long blink, except when I emerged in the Crystal Court, there was a dizzying whiplash from the change of scenery and abrupt yank of appearing in a completely different place.

I held my head with a groan. Roe pulled my elbow gently to clear the area for the next person arriving. "Don't worry, the feeling passes fast. I can't wait for you to see everything," she said.

I cracked my eyes open as the rest of our friends and family piled through. The wall behind us was one of the exits to the court's pocket dimension, according to Roe. It looked like a blank granite surface, no sign of a doorway or anything else to walk through.

The Crystal Court was nothing like I was expecting. When I'd heard "subterranean," I'd imagined low ceilings, tight corridors, and the distant *plink* of water falling from eternally growing stalactites. Instead, the nearest ceiling was ten feet up in this entranceway, and it transitioned smoothly to a cavern with a dome of earth overhead three stories high. A generous seam in the rock let in fresh air and light, which hit clusters of spiky crystals lining the walls that gleamed in every shade of blue I could imagine.

"Each section of the Crystal Court is big enough for a village," Roe told me. "There are paths between the formations and signs to guide you. You're actually staying here... over there." She pointed to a structure leaning against one of the cavern's walls. The windows suggested it was three floors high, with a roof that could brush the ceiling. It looked a lot like a hotel, if one could build with gleaming crystal blocks rather than bricks. In fact, most of the buildings along the way were also made of different shades of gleaming stone, like they'd grown there over the long weathering of centuries.

"It's so beautiful," I said, turning to her in awe. "You grew up here?"

Her smile was wistful. "Part of the time. We also have a house topside, with enough of a backyard for us to run around. My family took over the red cavern for our house and the business—there's no exit out that way, and it's mostly twisty, sharp corridors. It's a great place to stow and protect valuables."

Geo caught up with us and tugged the bag out of my hands. "Let me carry that for you," he said.

"Thanks." I lifted my chin so we could share a quick kiss.

"Do you think I could take some of the crystals here?" he asked.

Roe eyed a particularly large and jagged shard that'd grown partway over the path we took toward the hotel. "I'll ask my fae dad, but I don't see why not. They sell shards at the tourist shop." She grinned and cupped a hand over her mouth, whispering in my ear, "You should take one of your guys to the singing caverns. Folks come from all over to see them."

I nodded, already thinking of who I wanted to ask. I hoped the hotel had a map to point the way and a list of everything there was to do like any other hotel I'd stayed at. In the meantime, I fell back to chat with my family, who seemed both impressed and overwhelmed by everything at once.

The hotel had a short staircase out front, but the fae had roughed the top texture of the crystal bricks so shoes wouldn't slide around. Its entranceway was built for giants, spanning eight feet tall. An intricately carved statue of a fae man propped one of the crystal doors open, which I was thankful for since they seemed heavy.

The fae of this court had imported wood and other materials from somewhere, as the main foyer was far more familiar, with wood floors and a marble countertop. A pair of women stood below a chandelier dripping with teardrop-shaped pearlescent crystals. "There they are, just as you said!" the larger of the two exclaimed before sweeping up Roe in a huge hug.

"Hey, mama," Roe said.

My eyes widened. Roe's mom was practically a giantess, well over six feet tall, with obvious muscle in the flex of her arms. She wore clothes that molded closely to the lines of her body, with a big circular pendent of multicolored crystal hanging from her neck. Her wavy orange hair was slicked back in a puffy tail, bouncing behind her. Roe was her smaller, less fit double, which was crazy when I knew how much my friend dedicated her time and effort to physical fitness.

"And you brought your college friends," she was saying with a big smile. "I can't wait to meet you all! For now, get yourselves checked in. Your rooms here are free of charge."

She waited at the end of the line with Roe as we assembled a line to do as she said. I glanced past the two to make eye contact with the woman who'd been speaking with Roe's mom, waving shyly to Hana Graygazer as she stood a few yards apart from this gathering. Her gaze was faraway, and when I checked her aura, it pulsed with the gray-tinged magic that suggested she was glancing into the future.

After I received my room key, it was my turn to meet Madigan, who introduced herself and asked permission a moment before she squished me in a hug. "Roe's told me so much about you," she laughed.

"Good things, I hope," I squeaked, taking a deep breath when she released me.

"Of course." She rested a hand on my shoulder. "I'm

sorry to hear what happened with your family. Hana and I were just discussing the circumstances of your petition."

I was quite aware of my adopted family behind me, listening. "Would you be willing to sponsor it?" I asked.

"My dear." She sounded indulgent. "Sponsor it? First, we're going to get you a date before the Crown Coven as soon as possible. Then, my coven and I will be there with you all. I'll wear my old armor, as long as it fits." She patted her flat stomach.

"Really?" Roe's eyes glimmered as she looked up at her mom. "You're going to pull Mad Ash out of retirement?"

"You know it, kiddo. Don't worry, Cress. Stick around here long enough, and you'll hear all kinds of stories about me in my prime." She didn't sound like she was bragging, either. I glanced toward Roe in curiosity, who just mouthed "later."

I stepped aside for Madigan to meet Willow, nearly bumping into Carly. "Hey," she said, lowering her voice. "Um, did you know the guy with the white dreads is totally into you?"

I hazarded a glance toward Geo, who was still carrying my bag for me. He smiled warmly from where he was still waiting in line.

Could my sister be a *little* less perceptive? I leaned in and whispered back, "Yeah...I can explain. Later. In private."

There was intrigue in the curve of her lips. "Okay. It better be soon," she said.

26

CRESS

Carly took the news well. I mean, she kind of shrieked, but at least she helped me talk to Mom when the three of us eventually ended up in her hotel room together. Each suite was twice the size of my dorm, with full room service, so we sprawled out on the couch and loveseat with snacks. More friends and family of the Ashboughs were expected later to fill the whole hotel, but we were amongst the first arrivals and situated on the ground floor.

"So, uh, that's not all of my news," I said once Mom got some of her color back.

She held up a hand. "Wait. You just want to skip over the fact you just told me you're dating three men?"

Uh, yeah, I definitely did. "It's not, like, as unusual as—"

"Cressida Ann," she interrupted sternly. I sat a little straighter. "*What* have you gotten yourself into since we dropped you off at NSU?"

Carly leaned in, hands under her chin. She was definitely ready for the gossip and romance side of things.

I breathed a sigh. "We're going to be here a while. I

actually have a ton to tell you, but maybe it'll explain why I haven't been calling home as much as I should."

We ran out of snacks by the time I was done. I told them nearly everything, filling in their understanding of events from the details I'd told them here and there over the phone but editing the edges around events like me almost dying on Samhain night. The whole tale showed how I was connected and drawn to my three men, which delighted Carly, but Mom had a troubled frown while I mentioned Eris, Garroway, and the petition I was about to put in to appear before the Crown Coven.

"I never expected any of this when I adopted you," Mom said finally. "Forget about the men for a second. To think you're from a secret, powerful witch family and confirmed it by summoning a *ghost*. If you are truly going forward with this petition, then I want to be there to support you. Tell me the when and where, and I will speak to the authorities about the circumstances in which you came into my care as a baby."

"Okay," I said quietly. If she could come with me to appear before the Crown Coven, I'd love to have her there for support. "Thanks, Mom. I know it's a lot." I hesitated but knew I needed to bring up one more thing rather than blindside her with it. "Witch families and their bloodlines are a big deal. So much so that when I first enrolled and was tested for my magic, the NSU officials wanted me to take a new last name to start my bloodline. I was a nobody to them as Cressida Rollins."

Realization crossed Mom's face, but I continued before she could take it the wrong way. "I would have more respect in the supernatural community if I took the Dark-more name, but I want to honor where I came from and everything you've done for me. I was thinking of being Cressida Rollins Darkmore."

She dipped her chin in a short nod. "What about 'Luna'?"

"That's not what my mom named me," I said, getting a little misty when she did. Mom wasn't much of a hugger, not like my college friends, but when she reached out and squeezed my hand, I knew she approved.

"Whatever works best for you, baby," she said. "Never say no to opportunity."

My lips curved at the familiar advice. "You're right, Mom. I won't."

"Now, you'd better reintroduce me properly to your... boyfriends," she added. "Especially the demon."

"Dimensional," I rushed to correct. "He's from another planet, not Hell." Even though his descriptions of what became of Soiluire definitely qualified his old world for hellish status.

I stood and checked my phone for the time. "I'm sure you'll get the chance to talk to him at dinner. Looks like we have some time." Madigan had wanted to see us at seven for a meal downstairs.

I left to take some quiet time in my room, tending to my familiars for as little as they needed it. They'd found food and water downstairs, plus plenty of scratches from the fae staff. I put some of my stuff away and rested on the couch, surfing the Internet and reading my messages with Bella napping on my lap.

There were a few emails waiting for me. Two covens had signed on to sponsor my petition, and the online portal asked whether I wanted to submit it yet. Madigan had sent me a message over the system, telling me not to. I assumed her coven was Mad Ash Coven, but the second one was a mystery, Inevitable Defeat Coven.

As I read all my emails, another popped up. "Guardian Alliance 3 Coven has signed your petition as a sponsor."

"Whoa," I said under my breath, containing an excited wiggle so I didn't wake Bella. Roe's mom must've been pulling some strings at that very moment.

I put my phone away rather than refresh a hole in the screen hoping to see more sponsors. I'd snagged a map of the Crystal Court and a few pamphlets downstairs and leafed through them instead. There was plenty to do down here if one liked hiking and pretty vistas, enough to fill nearly a week's stay with the Ashbough family's hospitality.

I must've dozed off, because the next thing I knew, I opened my eyes to a knock on the door. The angle of light through the windows had changed to reflect coming evening. I fell off the couch in a clumsy moment, and Bella went launching off me with her fur all puffed out.

"Cress?" There was a note of concern in Phaeron's muffled voice on the other side of the door.

"Coming!" I called. I checked the time and muttered "shit" when I saw how close to seven it was. Instead of going to the door, I rushed to the en suite bathroom and checked my reflection. My makeup was all smudged on one side, and I could do with a change of clothes.

I rifled through the chest of drawers at the foot of the bed as Phaeron knocked again. "Is everything all right?" he asked.

"Yeah, just...just come in," I said, taking a moment to catch my breath after I found where I stowed my shirts. With that invitation, he turned into shadows and curled under the door, solidifying in a moment wearing a comfortable gray sweater and pants. "Have I seen you wearing this before?" I gestured to his whole ensemble.

He glanced down. "Probably not? But I assure you, I look better without them," he replied.

Oh, he was still playing this game, I see. Two could do that. "I agree. Clothes should be optional." I ditched my current shirt and felt a shift in the air. Phaeron only touched me with his gaze, burning brighter as he took in my exposed skin and little lacy bra.

"Take off much more, and we'll miss dinner." There was an edge of a growl in his tone.

"Oh, I don't intend to do that. Madigan wants to see us all, so we'll be there," I said, putting on my next shirt and heading into the bathroom to do something about my makeup.

I saw him join me in the mirror as I cleaned off what I was wearing and started putting on a simpler look so we wouldn't be late. "You're lovely without all that," he said. He tested the steadiness of my arm as he traced his claws up my sides, pressing featherlight kisses up the side of my neck.

"A lady never goes to an event without makeup," I answered, struggling to give my lids appropriately small wings. I nearly dropped the brush when he nipped me with those fangs of his. Okay, no wings. I tried to have even eyeliner instead.

"You *just* said you don't want to miss dinner," he pointed out while his lips traveled to my ear for more kisses.

I paused to take in the sight of him in the mirror, the dark and deadly prince, his fingers moving slowly over my hips and sides. Even if he was just teasing, his attention was fully on me, eyes dipped to watch my reactions to him. As much as I wanted more from him, I didn't mind the anticipation that had my thighs pressing together more firmly.

"I did. You know what I think?" I drew out the moment by applying mascara.

"I'd be thrilled to know," he said in my ear, his warm breath drawing a shiver down my spine.

Turning in his hold, I reached up to kiss him. "You'll be my date to dinner," I said.

I knew he'd find a way to tease me throughout the meal, but that meant he'd be coming back here with me afterward. If he wanted *me* to rip *his* clothes off, he'd have his wish.

I felt more than heard his soft laughter. "Very well, bright soul. I'll get you safely there and back. If you're ready?"

"I just need my lipstick—"

He interrupted with another kiss. "No lipstick. I'd rather not wear it later."

I had a shiver of anticipation, but I was the one that eased away, reluctant to break the simple contact between us. *Tonight*, I promised myself. It would be better for all the soft touches and gentle kisses, the whispers in my ear when no one else was looking. "So, is this the night you finally seduce me, or are we still just playing?" I asked, closing the lipstick tube and putting it aside.

He stilled, pulling his hands away from me. "Bright soul." The sigh in his tone was telling.

That'd been the wrong question to ask right before we'd have to go be social. The sinking feeling in my chest was my feelings taking a tumble to the ground, slipping through my fingers from putting myself out there so boldly to this man.

He stood there with his lips parted, gaze darting. "I...It was not my intention to..." Breathing another sigh, he shook his head. "No, that is a lie. I've wanted more of you from the moment you rescued me from Aurina's magic."

Some of the tension in my spine relaxed. I had a feeling I knew where this confession was going, with the obvious *but* hanging at the end of his statement.

"But I am still not sure I can trust my desire when it comes to you. I've been testing myself." He brushed the back of his fingertips across my cheek, his expression a mix of yearning and the deepest frustration. "Hoping that, with some familiarity of desire for you, the foulness of my lingering hunger will fade."

"And it hasn't," I said.

"No. If I am to claim you as my mate, then I must be in full control." His touch fell away from my face, fingers curling to fists.

I nibbled on my bottom lip. "Have you considered that it doesn't have to be that serious?"

His eyebrows creased. "Ah, but I am not human, Cress. I think and reason much like you do, but get me naked, and the instincts come out to play."

I nodded, as I'd definitely seen the animal in him before, the wolfish shadowborn side he usually kept under firm control. He slid closer, mere inches between us as he bent down and placed his lips on the smooth curve of my shoulder. I felt the pressure of his fangs through my shirt.

"I would mark you here. As you are not a dimensional, I would take care of making it a mating bite."

I tilted my head, breathing shallowly. "What makes that special?"

His warm breath washed over the curve of my neck. He nuzzled my sensitive skin, like those instincts were coming to bear as he imagined it. "A mating bite is not just a mark. Not like this." The tip of a claw circled the mark of protection he'd left on my wrist. "It's an exchange of essence. A near-instant swap of a tiny piece of our souls to bind us closer together. You may see now why it is too risky?"

"I know you won't hurt me," I said.

He hugged me around the hips, and I rested my palms on his solid chest. A stream of velvety, unknown syllables slipped from his lips as he pressed our foreheads together. I closed my eyes, enjoying the tender moment for what it was—as far as we could go, for now.

"What did you say?" I murmured.

He stirred with a slow breath, replacing the warmth of his touch with a fleeting kiss. "Roughly translated: my heart grows more enamored with you hourly, True Light, and I am helpless to resist."

I drew in to reply, dangerously close to using the L word in return. *Love.* I'd been flirting with the concept, sure that my affections could not be cut into three even pieces for each of my men. But...I'd never been so sure I loved princely Phaeron, just like I loved loyal Geo and playful Ben. It just seemed too soon to say it and risk him withdrawing from me more.

A harsh rap of knuckles on the door interrupted me. While I startled, Phaeron breathed a low growl. "Cress?" called Ben from the other side.

"It's time for dinner," Geo added a moment later.

"We almost missed it after all." Phaeron offered his arm. "Don't forget, *I'm* your date tonight."

I took his arm, not missing the glances exchanged between all three men when I emerged from the room on Phaeron's arm. Ben shrugged first, but Geo's lips tightened in reaction. No one said much until we arrived and took what seats remained open at a banquet table in a large conference room. Rich red and gold wallpaper and several hanging fixtures of multicolored crystal made for a warm, cozy atmosphere.

Madigan sat at the head of the table, with three unfamiliar men alongside her. Geo ended up seated next to the fae to her left, while I sat between Phaeron and Roe further down, across from Ben. "That's my fae dad. And those are my witch dads," Roe told me. The men in question turned their attention toward us as she did introductions.

The fae, Prince Orthus of the Crystal Court, was immediately eye-catching, with granite-colored skin that held a faint sheen and growths of jagged crystals that forced him to tailor his shirt to be sleeveless. They poked out a few inches around the side of his shoulders and trailed down his arms to form sharp, exaggerated elbows and hooked stone claws. Despite how inhuman it made him, they were pretty and polished, a pure emerald green like his eyes. He had the sharp elfin features typical of a fae and short-cropped hair a shade darker than his crystals.

Madigan's witch husbands, Aaron and Ajax, were twins and nearly indistinguishable except for their clothing choices. Aaron wore an eclectic, colorful ensemble, while Ajax preferred a suit. But their features were similar—short brown hair, neatly trimmed beards, and easygoing smiles. They were also guardians, with strong auras to match built, muscled physiques.

More of the Ashbough family were here, seated further down the table. Of Roe's massive roster of siblings, the four eldest were sitting politely as we awaited dinner, while the three younger kids were under the tablecloth, emitting the occasional giggle. As soup, salad, and drinks were served, Madigan glanced down. "Josie, please," she said.

A fluffy black and white border collie went trotting around the table, tongue lolling cheerfully. With a few authority-filled barks, she herded the kids back to their places, even helping the smallest climb back into his seat.

"What a beautiful dog," Mom said.

"Josie's been an Ashbough longer than anyone else in this room," Madigan shared. "She was my grandmother's familiar and helped keep me in line, too, when I was smaller." The dog had also disappeared on the other side of the table, except when her nose popped back up to accept a few table scraps.

Dinner was pleasant, the food a far step up from what I'd been getting in the dorms. Madigan made a point to ask all of Roe's friends about themselves, but the person she chatted with most was Mom, connecting over a show they'd both watched recently.

Geo and Orthus talked at length about rocks and crystals, using scientific names. Under the cover of conversation, Ben circled his fork toward Aaron and Ajax. "Which one's your dad?" he asked Roe quietly.

"All three of them," she answered.

"You know what I mean."

She exaggerated a shrug. "I dunno what else to tell you. I have three dads."

"You've never been, like, curious?" he asked.

"Ben," I said, raising an eyebrow his way. I wasn't exactly sure if it was different in supernatural families, but I thought pushing for an answer was a little rude.

"We get this question all the time," said Aaron, picking up on the conversation. "Our official tally is Orthus with three, me with five, and Ajax with one."

Ajax pulled an annoyed face. "That is *not* true."

"Hey, it could be," Aaron replied, grinning. His brother punched his arm. "Okay, it's not. Truth is, we don't test it. If you want to live in harmony in a family like ours, things like this can't be a contest."

"Even though those two are the most competitive men I know, it's still good advice," Orthus added. His voice had a ring of fae power, soft but deep. He was looking directly at me, so I nodded. I'd already seen how difficult it was to bring together my own three men, and there were still lingering tensions.

One day, I wanted a family that looked like theirs. Maybe with less kids, though. Just the thought of more than one made my belly suck in. No, I just wanted the tender looks like the ones Madigan's husbands gave her despite them being married and together for quite some time. An easygoing, tight unit.

I knew my men and I could have this, too. It would take time and hard work, but I wanted this to be a glimpse of our future.

27

CRESS

Thanksgiving was a communal event in the Crystal Court. My Thursday began when sunlight started to peek through the cracks in the cave's ceiling, helping a small army of people, both fae and witch, prepare a massive feast.

The cavern where we were staying, named the Sapphire Cove for its blue crystals, was too small to host what felt like the entire Crystal Court, the Ashbough family, and friends and other visitors. We spent time carrying over food and setting up tables two caverns over to the Diamond Square. Ringed in crystals formations both clear and cloudy white, it was a space kept for a few shops and restaurants, with an empty field ready for blankets, picnic tables, and fryers.

Mom had insisted we help, as the least we could do for our hosts. We weren't the only ones, by far. The cooking took up the kitchens of three restaurants in Diamond Square, and I saw friends and hotel neighbors alike helping prep and cook. It'd felt right, like we'd come together to assemble a community for this one meal. As Mom said, it was "the spirit of Thanksgiving."

Between tasks, I looked for Hana. She'd been exceptionally elusive during the last few days, though I'd caught glimpses of her in serious discussion with Madigan or sharing hushed whispers with other older, trained witches. I had the sinking feeling something was happening, or *about* to happen, and it wasn't being shared with me or my friends.

When I finally caught sight of her, she was sitting at a picnic table, drinking from a steaming mug across from Madigan herself. The matriarch of the Ashbough family was rarely still or quiet, always meeting with someone or doing something. But right now, she was quietly rubbing the ring of her mug, turning to face me a moment after Hana did.

"Ah, Cress!" The redhead looked happy to see me. "Have a seat."

In a moment straight out of an old film, Hana gestured to the space beside her and said, "We've been expecting you."

"Oh, you have?" I released a nervous chuckle and slid onto the bench where she'd indicated. It seemed they'd decided the time for secrecy was over the moment I did.

"The future is set," Hana replied as serious as ever. "Every route from this moment ends in the clouds that shroud your blood baron enemy from my sight."

I sucked in a breath. "When? I mean...when does he appear again?"

"We're going straight into the unknown, young woman," Madigan said for her.

Hana's softer voice behind hers reminded me keenly of another time, seated at a merfolk restaurant with Roe and Lanie. My friends took so much after their mothers. "Your upcoming petition to the Crown Court is where the timelines grow shrouded. Sometimes, you disappear in that fog. But there are no other options except to go forward," Hana said. "You should have several allied covens sponsoring your petition by now. It's going to be heard."

"I haven't submitted it yet," I said, turning to Madigan.

The redheaded woman dipped her chin. "Hana has suggested we keep it open until you make friends with some celestial witch."

"Jordan Evenstar?" I guessed.

"Yeah, her. You'll set the date, and we'll all be there."

"We will go prepared for combat. You should do the same," Hana added.

I nodded slowly. Ever since word had returned that Garroway was raising a new army of unwilling witches, I'd known the only way this ended was more bloodshed. But I hadn't expected it to be focused around the time of my audience with the Crown Coven.

"We'll be ready," I said. If Hana thought there was no other choice, then I believed her.

"I don't believe anyone is truly ready for the future, even a Graygazer," Hana replied.

Madigan slapped the table with a hearty laugh. "But we have a head start on destiny, and I give thanks to the goddess for that. A feast awaits, ladies! Let's not get dragged down by what will be." She was up and off with her mug the next moment, calling after one of her younger kids, who was creeping behind a crystalline fae who carried a still-steaming pie.

My gaze fell to the roughened wood grain of the table. I thought it was wise to be a little "dragged down" by what Hana had said. "Will we be able to save Lucas, Ben's brother?" I asked her.

"There is a chance. But he is caught up in the section of

the future I have not been able to gaze into," she replied with a vague circling of her hand.

Well, that was frustrating. Ben, in particular, was taking this more peaceful time hard, knowing his brother wasn't nearly as safe or happy.

She contemplated the dregs in her mug with a sigh. "Things are falling into place, and that's all you really need to know right now. Let's go enjoy Thanksgiving." It was obvious she didn't want to dwell here, so I did not push her.

Nodding, I stood and went back to meal prep, so deep in thought that I appreciated the repetitive tasks of peeling and slicing and a near-endless parade of pots and pans to scrub and rinse to be used again.

Dinner was ready before I knew it, and by the time I emerged from the kitchen, I'd decided not to share what I'd learned with my friends and men today. Instead, I looked around as I joined a parade of chefs, bearing a jumbo bowl of stuffing to the longest table, set up with a cheery cloth covered in cartoon turkeys and cornucopias.

The fae had brought out a kind of projector and fastened a matte sheet of crystal much bigger than any wide-screen television to one of the walls. It looked like they'd used their magic to warp the naturally growing geodes to clutch it on all four corners. As I passed by, there was a zone I walked through where I could clearly hear the football game that was being projected on the screen.

Ben was seated up front, a bowl of popcorn between him and Geo. He threw up his hands. "Did you *see* that?" he exclaimed.

"I fail to notice anything particularly significant," Geo answered.

Ben gesticulated wildly as he explained whatever foul

the referees hadn't flagged. I smiled to myself, glad to see them trying to spend some time together.

"Would you keep it down?" a pregnant fae called to him. I blinked rapidly as I continued walking and the sports commentators faded out of my ears. From another angle, the screen was playing an animated kids' movie, and I stepped into a zone where I could hear the sound effects, but also Ben's excitement over his football game.

"Sorry!" he called back.

A cluster of kids, under the watchful eye of Madigan's border collie familiar, were gathered around. Actually, an assortment of familiars were here, including Bella, who was slow blinking up at a young girl who snuggled her in both arms, and Ben's ferret, Flit, who was stretched to his maximum length and sleeping with his head poking out of a blanket fort.

Heads turned all around as the food was set up, and by the time everything was in place and straining the table, a line was forming. "Chefs, helpers, and kids first," Madigan's fae husband, Orthus, was saying, opening a space at the front of the line for us.

I wasn't sure who the man who carved the turkeys and hams was, but judging by his crystal-encrusted shoulders and the simple diadem he wore, he could've easily been the Crystal King, Orthus's father. If so, he made no fanfare of himself, other than making sure we all got our protein. I was glad he wasn't as ostentatious and grand as I assumed most fae rulers were.

When I had a plate piled high from the feast, I looked around at the picnic tables like it was a high school cafeteria, unsure of where to sit. Some folks filtered around me until someone closed their fingers around my hip with familiar pressure.

"Hi, Phaeron," I said without turning around.

"Hello. I believe our friends claimed that table," he said, pointing with his tail. We both headed that way, soon joined by Roe, Mom, and Carly.

"I wish I was a supernatural," Carly told me as she sat down. She had taken the hair potion I'd given her a couple days ago, so now she twirled a lock of candy-blue hair between her fingers with a wistful sigh.

"I know," I said with sympathy. It was hard not to want that when surrounded by the merriment of fae and whimsy of casual magic usage. No one here had to hide what they were.

Phaeron eyed her with a soft hum. I glanced his way, and he met my gaze, shaking his head briefly. Pure human, then, just like Mom.

"You can come back here any time you like, though. Open invitation," Roe said.

Mom caught the glowing look in Carly's face and added, "But if you want to live here, you'll wait until *after* you graduate college, young lady."

I started quizzing Carly on the colleges she'd applied for to distract her as Willow, Ben, and Geo eventually came by with their own portions of the feast. "How's your game going?" I asked Ben with a playful smile.

"Fuuu—effing awful," he amended quickly with a glance toward Mom.

"He is quite displeased that his team is losing," Geo reported.

"*Our* team, Geo. You're in this with me."

"I thought you wanted to watch the other side of the screen after this," the gargoyle said.

"Well, yeah. I'd rather watch animated ogres than whatever the heck our team is doing," Ben grumbled.

"I was thinking we could go for a walk after dinner," I said. I could've gotten whiplash from how fast Ben agreed to do that instead. "All of us could go, maybe? We still haven't seen the singing caverns."

Carly pulled back from her initial interest for the idea, leaving my three men the ones nodding. I'd hoped the singing caverns would be less crowded right after everyone stuffed themselves. I definitely needed some time to digest first after eating everything I'd taken, plus a slice of still-warm pumpkin pie. For a while, I lingered with my table, chatting, but followed the lead of others who wandered from table to table, talking and hanging out. I felt I'd made a few new friends here, especially amongst the Crystal Court fae, who were mostly quite friendly.

It'd be hard to return to NSU this weekend, but I'd enjoy the time we still had here. When my belly was more settled, I gathered up my men and followed the signs out of the Diamond Square, leaving behind the waves of sound from multiple voices speaking at the same time. Geo breathed a soft sound of relief.

The corridors between major caves here were wide enough to be a two-lane street, though there were no cars here. "So, the singing caverns are supposed to be like a maze," I said.

"And the walls, like, ring when you touch them or something?" Ben asked.

"The formations you'll see are a different kind of mineral than those in the other caves," Geo said. "They're grown from exposure to fae magic and resonate when exposed to sunlight. The people here make their weapons and armor from them."

I glanced his way curiously. Orthus had agreed to give

him some new crystals, I knew, to replace much of the quartz he used in his gargoyle form. "Armor? Wouldn't armor made of crystals just shatter?"

He smiled back at me. "That's why they're grown from magic. They crack from excessive force rather than dent, which a Crystal Court fae, guardian witch, or gargoyle could fix. I'm fortunate. Prince Orthus gave me a tempered shield of it for free. Usually, it's incredibly expensive."

And the fae here had a whole cavern full of it, wow. My awe only grew when we turned down the proper path toward the singing caverns and I started to hear their namesake. We passed a building labeled the gift shop and emerged into a narrow cave with several small slits in the ceiling to let in patches of light.

The crystals here were definitely different, lining a maintained path that went up, down, and around this space and led to a hole in the farthest wall that looked like a tunnel. Instead of growing in giant, jagged shapes, the fae-grown minerals were like clusters of slim stalagmites, reaching up to hip height.

I started forward eagerly, inspecting the first couple formations. They were opalescent under direct sunlight, emitting a sound similar to the ringing that followed when someone rubbed the rim of a glass half full of water. I tapped one formation, delighted when it made a resonant *piiiing* and sparkling dust seemed to ripple within it.

"Different crystal sizes and colors make different sounds," Geo said, escorting me up the path to another patch of sunlight. It seemed these minerals came in all shades of the rainbow, too, some obviously growing back after being harvested at around the halfway point of their maximum height.

"How do you know all this?" I asked. He'd found a slim, silvery formation that made a higher-pitched *biiiiing* when tapped. "Wait, that's a dumb question. You're made of rock sometimes."

He flashed his teeth with a grin, which sparkled even amongst all the beauty around us. I paused, captivated by the easygoing display. Geo had come so far, and I think it was all the time he'd spent in human form. "One might say I have a passion for such things," he said.

"It's in the name," Ben joked. He'd roamed ahead of us, poking formations that were currently in shade. No sound came from them.

We kept climbing in relative silence, coming across the occasional diminutive fae lingering amongst the patches of sunlight. The first one I spotted went very still, like he was trying to become one with the formations. Others were spider-like, with many spiky legs, watching us with eight sparkling eyes as we passed by. They must live here, I thought, not wanting to disturb them.

I stopped to admire a disc of crystal that'd been fused of many different colored minerals and placed in the path about halfway in. It glittered half in sunlight, rippling from within around my shoes with each step. I walked into Geo's arms and relaxed there as we overlooked much of this cave and its singing geodes.

I met Geo's eyes, a bit like crystals themselves, and leaned up to kiss him. He pulled me closer, sure to give the native fae critters a show as he squeezed my ass. I'd forgotten about the other two until I picked up the smooth murmur of Phaeron's voice. I opened my eyes, spotting him nudge Ben.

"I'll keep watch," the dimensional said a little louder. I felt the heat of his gaze as much as Ben's clever hands brushing up my belly and his kisses on my neck. Both men had me sandwiched between them and the growing hardness of their arousals.

My hands fisted in the fabric of Geo's shirt. We were doing this...*now*? Here? There were still fae around, the shy kind, and the chance we'd get caught by others seeking a post-Thanksgiving walk.

Ben palmed my breasts, making me reconsider complaining. Our hotel rooms were a several-mile walk from here—talk about a mood killer.

"Did you guys plan this?" I asked when Geo and I parted for a breath.

Ben tweaked my nipples, his laugh husky. "Who plans things?"

"I just wanted my beautiful woman in this pretty place," Geo said. He loosened the button on my jeans, sliding the zipper down.

Ben opened the clasp of my bra through my shirt and then tunneled his hands underneath the hem, his callused fingertips teasing my skin. "And so do I. So we might as well share. Right, Geo?"

Geo's answering grunt was less enthusiastic, but he still helped push down my jeans, my panties following shortly after. I couldn't complain, not with him caressing my thighs and helping keep me upright as having both of them touch and tease had me feeling weak in the knees.

"All right, but..." My gaze sought the blaze of Phaeron's otherworldly gaze. He watched me moan and arch into Geo's touch as his thick fingers explored up my leg to gather some of the slick from my pussy lips. The dimensional's jaw was so tight he might've grinded off the tips of his fangs.

If I thought this was the moment he'd let go of his

control and join us, I was mistaken. Cool disappointment made goosebumps up my arms when he turned away to focus on his post and keep watch for anyone coming while he cupped his obvious arousal.

Ben and Geo more than filled the space between us, though, chasing away any chill I felt. Ben edged around my shoulder, kissing me deeply and swallowing my sharper cry when Geo finished sampling my slick from his fingers and delved between my thighs to collect more with his lips and tongue.

I was panting and out of breath, grinding on Geo's face, when Ben lifted his head to ask, "Hey, Geo, you bring any protection?"

Geo's muffled response sounded a bit like "no." He held my knees open to him, eating me out like a man starved. I trembled and held fast to Ben to keep me upright.

With an eager grin, Ben flashed a condom at me, plucked from his back pocket. "I know exactly how we'll share you, babe," he said.

"Oh?" I asked with a breathy whine. Geo had me on the edge of oblivion already, and that was where he stopped, leaving me slick and needy. If they hadn't told me this was unplanned, I wouldn't have believed it. Ben guided me down onto my hands and knees and hurriedly freed his cock.

The face of the crystal disc below us was pleasantly warm, rippling with pearlescent patterns around my body. I reached for Geo, helping him withdraw his own arousal from where it strained the front of his pants. As the pressure in my belly slowly eased, I glanced over my shoulder at Ben.

I didn't need to ask when I saw him getting onto his

knees too and rolling the condom over his length. They'd take me between them, like how this surreal event had started, with Geo's mouth on mine. I beckoned the gargoyle closer and licked my swollen lips, dipping my gaze to his throbbing cock with obvious intent. His fingers threaded through my hair, guiding my head down to lap at the bead of precome welling up for me.

I gripped the base of his shaft, sinking him into my mouth until my jaw ached. He held me there while Ben grasped and positioned my hips, his length teasing through the cleft of my body. "You're ours, babe," he said before sinking home within me.

Usually, I responded to him saying, "You're mine, babe," with a simple, "Yours." But I simply moaned and swayed with his claim. They took it easier on me than usual, my body rocking from their rhythm. The slow roll of Geo's hips gave me momentum back into Ben's thrusts and vice versa.

They shared me beautifully, I thought through a haze of bliss. Like they were meant to. They'd put aside their differences for the moment, for this. And I had no complaints but one. Phaeron stroked himself as he stole glances at us yet made no move to join in. I wanted him too...to share in this moment.

It was obvious he wouldn't, though, so I kept my attention on the two who'd made me the center of theirs. Geo's stoic features were slack, and he tightened his fist in my hair while he chased the pleasure of my mouth. Ben's usual teasing was absent until I heard him ask Geo in the same tone he reserved in the bedroom with me, "Know what she really loves?"

"Many things," Geo rumbled back.

"This might be a new one," he replied. I shivered with

anticipation as he spread my legs further, his thumb coming down to tease the rosette hiding between the globes of my ass. I came like a sudden detonation, as I had the first time he'd tried it a week ago, shocking the hell out of both of us.

Geo's eyes widened. His thick flesh absorbed my sudden cries, and he throbbed on my tongue. His laugh was deep, and his grin eager. "That'll help us share her more." I think he finished just from that thought, filling my mouth with liquid heat.

I liked the sound of it, too, fantasizing about doing this again, pinned between their solid bodies. The moment Geo withdrew, Ben quickened his pace to follow after us, and I saw stars by the time he came with a harsh breath and ground his hips into mine.

"That was amazing," I said. Now that I was full of both food and pleasure, though, I figured they'd need to carry me back to my room. I stood unsteadily with them, the three of us helping each other fix our clothes.

"Of course, because you were here." Ben threaded an arm around my hips, guiding me back the way we'd come. Once we were done, Phaeron had disappeared into a curl of smoke—avoiding temptation, or just avoiding us, I thought. But he was a fleeting thought as Ben and I kissed, and he said, "I fucking love you, babe."

I released a surprised laugh. The blurted admission was so like him. "I love you, too." After a moment, I turned my smile toward Geo. "Both of you."

The gargoyle seemed startled, his eyebrows raising. He mumbled something about duty as he took his place walking just a few paces behind us. "C'mon, you can say it too," Ben encouraged.

Geo cleared his throat. "I...I love you as well," he said. "And it's still not the sex talking."

Well, the sex had certainly opened up some talking, as the two of them bantered all the way down the slope until we had to tiptoe past the remnants of the Thanksgiving party back to our hotel.

28

CRESS

The next day, I was packing to leave when my phone started ringing. An unfamiliar number flashed on the face of the screen and my belly twisted with nerves as I swiped and put the device to my ear. "Hello?"

"Ah, hello there. Do you know a man named Benjamin Evenstar? He left me this number to call," a woman replied.

My heartbeat became a staccato pulse. "You must be Jordan. We've got a lot to talk about."

Ben's aunt teleported herself to the Crystal Court within an hour, after I convinced her that she'd received a legitimate letter from her long-lost nephew and then put my phone into the hand of said man. He and I awaited Jordan's arrival at the same cave wall where we'd first come in, and he tried to mute his twitchy energy by shoving his hands in his pockets.

I had my arms around him, feeling how he shook with

nerves as the air thrummed with the movement of magic. It became visible in golden tendrils, forming a circle through which Jordan stepped through, holding a staff that glimmered with gold plating. She was tall and elegant in a gown with a slit up the side that showed a glimpse of her thigh.

I expected her to be wearing obvious signs of wealth, but she had no jewelry on, not even a wedding ring. Her brunette hair was down in simple waves around her shoulders. She placed the staff on the ground and said, "Ben? Is that you?"

"Hi, Aunt Jordan," he replied with a stiff wave.

I let him go so he could approach with his hand extended, but she went for a full hug. "Oh, goddess. It's been ages. I was still a kid when you were born," she said, releasing him except to hold his shoulders to take him in. "Liam let me hold you when you were a baby, and we all nearly regretted it. I remember you were the last baby I held, even."

"It's okay, Aunt Jordan." He repeated her name like he barely believed this was happening. "My friends will tell you I act like I was dropped on my head a few times."

"Hmm, I doubt that." Her smile started to fade. "That was the last time I saw you. I see that you have a blood witch aura. Everything you wrote—it was true?"

"Unfortunately," he sighed.

"In that case, there's something for you here. I just need to find—well, her." Jordan brushed past him. We both turned to see her hugging Madigan as the redheaded woman approached with Hana by her side.

"Jordan! A certain augur saw you coming," Madigan exclaimed. "You'll be wanting access to the vault, right?"

Ben and I exchanged a glance. "Does it feel like

everyone knows everyone in the witch community?" I asked.

"I think Madigan does, at least," he replied.

"This way, then!" The redhead in question was saying.

I'd learned that the Ashbough family home was at the very end of the Crystal Court, a few miles' walk from here. They'd claimed a back wall of sorts for their business, a line of caves terraformed with only one entrance and exit. Madigan's business, the one Roe didn't particularly want to inherit, guarded those caves, which were filled with other witches' valuables. Ashbough Protective Services also offered escorts for valuables and bodyguards for events, and I'd heard they had a hundred percent success rate in keeping both important items and people safe.

Jordan claimed Ben's arm, keeping him talking about his life and preferences on the way to the vault. When he introduced me as his anam cara, her eyes shone with unshed tears. "Oh, you're Eris's girl, aren't you?" she asked. "Marie read the star charts and was sure you two were destined."

"She was right," I said, a little surprised she remembered that detail.

"Eris was practically another sister, with how often Marie would bring her around. Marie convinced her to take it easier so she could have you," she told me. "I'm glad you survived, too. It just breaks my heart to know how much love you two were born into but barely got to know."

"Us as well," Madigan said, glancing over her shoulder. "But we're going to fix what we can. Has she told you about the petition?"

She dropped her voice and told Jordan of the petition I'd written to appear before the Crown Coven. We stepped into the narrow cavern that held the Ashbough's vault, this one lined with jagged red and orange crystals and a ceiling that sloped lower after we passed their sizable house.

The door to the vault was obvious, a disc of polished fae crystal with no obvious handle. It rolled to the side at Madigan's touch. "That's as far as you two go until you have something to store in here," she told Ben and me.

Madigan, Jordan, and Hana continued chatting in quiet voices, the latter sharing something when she was just out of earshot. I sighed and turned to Ben, squeezing his hand. "How are you feeling?" I asked.

He turned a conflicted look my way. "I mean, she seems nice. Just, it's weird to have someone who remembers all these things about me and the family I never got to meet. I think...Lucas would've loved to be here. I wish he was." He pressed his lips together until they were a tight, white line.

"He'll meet her too. We're going to save him, Ben," I said. "Then we'll get to catch him up on everything he's missed."

"I hope you're right. I just don't want my aunt to think I'm a shitty person because I'm here while he's not," he muttered.

I put my arms around him, and he rested his head on my shoulder. "You're not. You're doing what you can so the next time we see Lucas is the last time there's a monster within him. We haven't been able to free him when fighting as a team, so you know you can't just...go off on your own and try to do something."

"I know that you're right. It just doesn't stop my guilt, though," he sighed.

I didn't think anything would until he had Lucas safe and healed. I simply held him until approaching footsteps suggested that Jordan had found what she wanted from the vault already. She carried a long leather-bound case, which she set before Ben. "What's this?" he asked.

"Your inheritance," she answered. He sucked in a sharp breath. "Your father's staff. I know about ten relatives who're chomping at the bit to have it, but no one's been able to unlock the box."

She knelt and gestured to the clasps, which were overlaid with glowing blue runes. "We should've known you and Lucas were still alive. If you are truly Liam's son, you should be able to open the box without effort."

Ben swallowed audibly before bending down to give it a try. Madigan and Hana inched forward, looking over Jordan's shoulder. There was a click of metal unlatching and the sound of glass shattering as the runes popped off the box without trouble. He lifted the latch with shaking fingers, washing the room in silvery light as an ornate staff was uncovered, lying in a custom velvet mold.

"Wow," Jordan breathed. "Just like I remember it. Its name is Evening Guidance, Ben, one of a set of five that have been in the family for generations. Now it's yours."

Ben picked it up carefully, setting it upright. A few delicate chains clinked as they met gravity for the first time in nearly two decades, linked to dozens of slim pieces of paper etched with celestial witch runes. They hung down from the centerpiece of the staff, which was a silver-plated crescent moon wrapped in the tails of several falling stars. It was how their magic worked—each represented a spell pre-prepared and stored on the staff, awaiting use. Jordan's staff only had three, by comparison.

He turned and offered it to me. "You'll find more use for this than I will," he said.

Even though I took it, I immediately opened my mouth to protest. There was no way I'd accept Evening Guidance from him, not when it was such a valuable link to his family. I didn't voice those thoughts yet when its solid weight filled my palms and I found the smooth grooves where I was supposed to hold it properly.

It was heavier than I expected, wobbling awkwardly as I manipulated it. I figured, by its height and balance, it was made for a man. Yet it pulsed with power that felt familiar, reminding me strongly of Eris when we'd first summoned her ghost and the taste of power that was locked deep in my handbook.

"It's beautiful," I said, inspecting the intricate pattern of silver stars and falling trails painted into the dark varnish of the wood. I simply *knew* it was an expensive tool, not truly meant for Ben or me to have. Yet I passed it back to him, and he set it reverently back into its case.

"It is," he agreed. "Thank you, Aunt Jordan, for giving it to me. I imagine there are family members that just wanted to break into the case and steal it."

"Plenty of them. But it belongs to you by right," she said with a nod.

There was a pause where aunt and nephew simply looked at one another for a while. "Do...you want to stick around for a while? There's something I was hoping you could do for us," Ben finally asked.

"Anything you need," Jordan answered.

She meant it, as evidenced by her presence in NSU after we said our goodbyes to the Crystal Court, Madigan, and Hana. I hugged Mom and Carly long and hard, feeling the pain of parting from them again as keenly as our original goodbye when I went off to college. They *all* promised that I'd see them again by the time my petition was heard by the Crown Coven.

I'd finally sent it off with an incredible sixty-three covens sponsoring it. The Ashbough, Graygazer, and Evenstar families had gathered friends and allies and backed me with the kind of force that *had* to be heard by our governing council of witches. So it would be, December nineteenth, a day before the Crown Council rested for the holidays and New Year.

That gave me three good weeks to finish up my first college semester with decent grades, rehearse what I'd say in front of the Crown Coven, and continue advancing my magic. Training with Phaeron fell to the wayside with Jordan around, as she'd taken an extended leave from her job and moved into an apartment in New Salem. Ben's big ask was getting her to teach me how to use my family line's celestial magic, which she'd agreed to.

I spent my evenings with her in the combat practice room, splitting my attention between her and Eris's spirit. Unfortunately, I was the only one who could see Eris, and she had...opinions.

If I had a dollar for every time she said, "She's teaching you wrong," I'd have...some money. I eventually convinced her to watch and add on what she could. It had to be frustrating to be a ghost in the first place, unable to touch or guide past the sound of her voice.

With my chatty handbook in hand, I was able to start casting basic spells, summoning both hot sunlight and cool, soothing moonlight. The phases of the moon started meaning something to me, as did the positions of various constellations. It was progress.

It'd be enough to show the Crown Council that I had

celestial witches in my family line, and that's what was most important.

The biggest breakthrough of all happened at random when my phone rang early in the morning. I'd answered in a disheveled mess, reaching over Ben's snoring form and pawing for my device. "Hello?" I'd said groggily without checking the screen.

"Good morning," Wren's voice answered. I shot upright so quickly that both Ben and Geo startled awake. "So, our coven is named A Little Wicked now?"

"That's right."

"I like it," she said quietly. "I read your petition." Such things were public documents, if you knew where to look online.

I gestured to Ben that everything was okay and that he could put the knife away. "Yeah?" I asked with a twist of nerves.

"Yeah. I'm going to be there, as will Heath. Don't go replacing us." Her tone was perfectly neutral, and with the subtle crackle of shaky reception, I had no clue as to what she was feeling.

"Okay, um. We're having a meeting this Saturday to go over everything one more time."

"Perfect. I'll bring a gift." She bid me a quick goodbye and hung up.

I eyed the phone, grumbling when I saw that it was still four-something in the morning. "Well, that was weird," I muttered.

The "gift" wasn't, though. She'd rooted through her father's office over the holiday and taken pictures, which she supplied me copies of, all while acting like she was about to attend a funeral, black dress and red-rimmed eyes and all.

"He wouldn't tell me the truth. He's ruined so many lives," she'd muttered. She wouldn't meet anyone's eye during her brief stay at the coven meeting, slinking away once she confirmed the time and place.

Only once she was gone did I review the folder of printed pictures. It was correspondence—messages she'd pulled up on a computer from an odd-looking browser or aged paper she'd unfolded from crumbling envelopes.

I could count on my fingers the number of people I knew who I thought might turn on their own father. But after reading the contents of the secret messages...

I'd sell out Blaize Starsurge, too.

29

BEN

Aunt Jordan opened her pocketbook for the hearing, buying Cress and me traditional sets of clothes to wear. They were...akin to armor, and I felt like I was suiting up the morning of December nineteenth, sliding my hands into fingerless leather gloves. The rest of what I was supposed to wear was leather too, and I'd broken it in from its too stiff state so that it hugged my body perfectly.

She'd also bought me a bandolier that I slid over my shoulder, with needle-sharp knives lining it all the way down. "It's like you want me to fight someone," I'd commented when first presented with it.

"You can never be too prepared. Besides, you look the part of a strong blood witch now," she'd answered, patting me on the shoulder.

Phaeron had bought himself black leather armor at about the same time and wore most of it while we walked toward the campus and our agreed-upon meeting spot before we'd take a portal to Cerris City, Washington DC, a huge pocket dimension metropolis where the Crown Coven held its audiences. We'd only be spending a day there if all went well.

Unlike me, Phaeron had modified his armor, etching runes along the seams one at a time with his claws. He'd fastened his two swords to his hips and carried a helmet dangling from his fingers, alongside a bag full of supplies. He hadn't been convinced that this would be a one-afternoon visit.

One of the buildings that taught celestial witch classes had a teleportation loop, the stone circle they used to create portals to nearly anywhere. Most of our group was already there, waiting. Aunt Jordan wore a formal robe stitched with subtle patterns of falling stars, like the ones etching Evening Guidance, which rested in the case I was carrying.

Next to her, Cress was bouncing the waves she'd styled into her purple hair and adjusting her own robe. I'd seen what Aunt Jordan had intended with the ensemble immediately—it was a shorter robe with wide slits up to her hips, showing the dark pants Cress wore underneath. She'd buckled her belt over the robe, carrying her sheathed sword and handbook on either hip. It was a hybrid of styles, not quite librarian and not quite celestial, but showing both sides of her at a glance. Her three familiars lay together in the grass, napping in the sunshine.

Standing as a protective shadow was Geo in his gargoyle form, holding a new shield made of tempered fae crystal. It was bigger than his torso and sang gently in the sunlight as I came forward to steal a kiss from Cress. "You look stunning today," I said.

She hugged my side, avoiding the bandolier. "Thanks. What's all this?"

"Aunt Jordan wanted me to wear it," I said a little quieter.

"Hmm." Cress's eyes narrowed suspiciously.

I slid to the side to give Phaeron a moment with her, inspecting the rest of our friends and coven mates for a moment. Grant and Heath wore suits, while Wren was in a black robe with dark makeup and a staff in hand. Willow had dressed up some, and Bianca played with a knife, wearing a similar set of leather to me but with her trusty crossbow hanging at her side. Roe was late, as usual, as was Áine.

Grant jerked his chin away from the group and took me aside. "Well, spy extraordinaire," I said in a low voice. "You want to tell me what's going on?"

"I mean, your eyes work," he answered with his usual mocking edge. "But I have figured out a little after you asked me to look into it. Crown Starsurge is still in your blood baron's pockets. The Graygazer witches have been spreading around a heavy-handed rumor that there will be coordinated trouble between them to interrupt your coven's audience before anything too damning can be revealed."

I went a little cold to have it confirmed. We *would* be fighting today. "That doesn't sound safe for Cress. We could reschedule—"

"The augurs are also suggesting that we *have* to do this today. As you can see, it's being taken quite seriously," Grant interrupted, circling his hand to encompass us all.

"Do you fight?" I asked. I cracked my knuckles. Having another chance to kill Garroway, or even punch the asshole politician whose actions had gotten my mother killed, quickly overrode my hesitations.

"Not even a little," he answered with a laugh. "I'll leave that to you and her." He turned his head toward where Roe approached with Áine bouncing after her. The redheaded witch wore casual street clothes, which surprised me, while the faun had a flowing dress that almost hid the fact that she had vines wrapped around her arms that disappeared under the cuffs of her sleeves, which glowed with their own magic.

"Waiting for me? Never fear," Roe announced. "Is this everyone?"

Cress lifted her head. She was pressed to Phaeron's side now, touching the runes he'd put on his armor. "Oh, my mom and sister should be here any moment. They've got an escort walking them here now," she said.

"Are you sure they should be accompanying us, bright soul?" Phaeron asked.

"Mom wanted to provide testimony. It'll help our case," she said.

He frowned and dipped to whisper in her ear. I could tell when they started to argue from here, but her family arrived before he could convince her it was a bad idea. We moved as a group into the celestial witch building, walked into the back by a secretary who showed us to the teleportation loop. Aunt Jordan got to work setting up the portal to Cerris City, ushering the rest of us through until she was the last one in.

I shook off the sense of disorientation as we emerged on a concrete block already full of people. "So lovely to see you all again," Madigan said first, lifting the glimmering visor of her helmet.

She wore a variegated suit of red-shaded crystal, a hybrid of fae style and knight of old, which was instantly recognizable. She wasn't attending this meeting as a concerned mom, but instead as Mad Ash, leader of the guardian witches who'd never failed to protect an important item or person. Her armor came with a matching geode-formed hammer, big enough that she could sling it over her shoulders.

Most of these men and women were guardian witches, wearing variations of crystal and stone. It looked like Madigan had brought as much of Ashbough Protective Services here as possible, but interspersed were a few witches with augury gray auras, including Hana Graygazer herself, accompanied by a man who had to be her husband.

One man took off his emerald-green crystal helm, and I realized he was actually a fae, Prince Orthus. With a startle, I double-checked the auras and armor of the people around us. A good third were Crystal Court fae, some of which had grown armor out of their naturally embedded crystals. I smiled to myself. They were kind folks, going against many of the common trickster stereotypes fae carried around.

"Hey, kiddo. I have your gift right here," Orthus said to Roe. A large pendant hung from the fist of his crystal gauntlet, similar to the one that Madigan wore casually. It gleamed like an orange sun in the light. Roe came over and placed it around her neck, holding up the glimmering pendant with a big grin.

I watched in fascination as he explained how it worked in a low voice, leading her through a spell that ended with her pressing on the center of the circular crystal, pushing it to her chest. It flashed, and crystal grew outward from it rapidly, flooding over her body to form a suit of tangerine-and-yellow-colored armor that broke at the joints to give her range of motion. She flexed her hands into fists, which were exaggerated with an extra-thick layer of crystal.

"Thanks, Dad," she said.

They clasped forearms like warriors of old. "That's my girl," Orthus replied proudly.

Someone tapped me on the shoulder as we got moving

shortly after that, surrounded by guardian witches and armored fae. "Bet you I get first blood today," Bianca said, falling into step with me.

"Sure." I rolled my eyes at her. "If we're going to fight today, I know you'll be right in the middle of it."

"If?" she echoed with a laugh. "You mean, *when*. Bet I get more kills than you, too."

"Well, that's a guarantee. You've got more practice," I said.

I was distracted by the sights. We walked a slowly narrowing path overlooking a bustling city of supernaturals. We'd been teleported to the highest point of the city, where the Crown Coven's grand complex was set as the only structure on a tall hill. I was just glad we hadn't had to climb the steps. Bleached white and softened by the passage of thousands of pairs of feet, they lead all the way up to the front entranceway of the building we approached.

The complex was palatial, built like it housed giants rather than seven important politicians and their staff. Its pointed roof transitioned into a dome ringed with seven flagpoles, each flying the colors and symbols of each witch affinity.

One side, I knew, was for a grand library of knowledge, though Cerris City made it redundant with its own separate library to house dimensional secrets, like NSU had. The other side was for residences. Wren may have been raised here, in the lap of luxury. She lagged behind us, the slowest and most reluctant member of our group.

We filed into the front hall, joining clusters of other witches waiting for their audiences. They eyed our group nervously, not that I could blame them when we were the ones armed and ready for a conflict.

"Look at this fancy-ass place," Bianca muttered.

We were encouraged to sit by the staff, though few did. I stood braced against the wall a few feet away from where Cress paced, muttering her rehearsed lines under her breath. It *was* a fancy-ass place, not that I had time to admire the glitter of the gem-encrusted walls or how grand the chandeliers were. We'd arrived right on time—Cress's audience before the Crown Council would happen at any moment.

An orderly in a fine suit caught Cress's attention, and she nodded along to what he was saying until one rule gave her pause. "It's tradition, miss," he said apologetically. "Only witches can come into the audience chamber unless it's absolutely necessary."

"What if they're providing testimony?" she asked.

"If you identify them, we'll get them in front of a computer so they can do so over a conference call," he replied.

She pointed out Phaeron, Geo, and her mother to him, and he bustled away. With a sigh, she turned to me. "So, we're only allowed one other coven in the chamber with us. I picked Madigan's, but everyone else has to wait out here."

"Kind of bullshit," I agreed, pointing out one of many screens just above eye level to her, which lined the walls. They showed the current audience that was before the Crown Coven, with signs describing how to tune in on a cell phone or computer. "They can watch us, at least."

"I guess." She bit her lip, sliding closer to me. I held her, recognizing the nerves playing over her expression.

"You're going to do great, babe. You're a hundred percent in the right," I reassured her.

She rested against my chest with a sigh and nod, the two of us waiting until a grinding scrape and groan filled the air. Everyone looked to the two twelve-foot-tall stone doors coming unsealed just enough to let the last group of witches filter out. Someone tapped on a microphone. "Up next, the Crown Coven will hear A Little Wicked Coven, accompanied by Mad Ash Coven."

"Let's do this," Cress murmured, standing straight and adjusting her robe before walking straight-backed toward the audience chamber. Her mother caught her hand, giving it a squeeze on her way by, and she exchanged a nervous smile with Carly.

She stood in the center of our coven, with Roe and me following in a step behind her. My breath caught for a moment at how fancy the Crown Coven's audience chamber really was, designed to display the might of all seven affinities.

To the left of the long path leading to the raised dais where the Crown Coven sat, a glimmering lake of blue water churned with waves that lapped the far wall. Intricate statues and carvings lifted from the water, forming elegant ripples through the air. The right held a field of flowers and medicinal herbs permanently stuck at peak maturity, surrounded by formations of rock and crystal.

The domed roof above us could open to the night sky, but right now, it had several flying books circling high over our heads. They were enchanted tomes of magical law, as I understood it. To complete the set of affinities, a set of tarot cards glimmered at the stone base of the dais where we stopped, ready to spring up into the hand of a talented augur. And resting on an ornate loop was the cup and dagger ready for the blood oath every Crown Coven member had to make before they ascended the steps to sit in state above their petitioners.

A man, also wearing a fine suit, stood to the side with a microphone and a tablet in hand as we arranged ourselves on the platform right underneath the stare of the seven most powerful witches in North America. Madigan's coven formed a protective half-circle behind us.

We'd been allowed to keep our weapons only because of the other tradition in this room. Seven witches stood to the side of each politician, dressed in the ceremonial garb of their affinities. In the old days, when it was first formed, the Crown Coven had been required to have one witch of each affinity. Times had changed, and rules were loosened; since they were elected into power, it had inevitably balanced toward celestial witches since it was seen as the strongest affinity. This way, they were at least guarded by one of each.

The suited man cleared his throat. "Let us get this underway. Appearing before the honored witches of the Crown Coven today are the witches of A Little Wicked Coven, accompanied by Mad Ash Coven, one of their sponsors. Their petition involves the circumstances around the untimely death of Eris Darkmore."

He went on to introduce each of us one by one; then he named the seven politicians eyeing us with an assortment of suspicion, eagerness, or curiosity. Seated first in line was the leader of the coven, dark-haired Tempest Wildsong, an oceanic witch wearing an elegant seafoam-colored dress that complimented her honey-toned complexion. "This shall be interesting. Won't it, Crown Starsurge?" she asked with a sharp smile.

"There's no need to assume him guilty so soon, dear," said the elderly verdant witch in seat two, Sophia Greenridge.

The third in line, celestial witch Zander Shadowsoul, crossed his arms and smirked over at Blaize, whose face was reddened as he looked down at us. He'd skipped his gaze right over Cress, his head tilted toward Wren. "Sundrop, why are you here?" he asked.

She tapped a perfectly manicured nail against the wood of her staff. "I want the truth, Father."

A bead of sweat trailed down his temple. "You should get out of here. Now."

She lifted her chin stubbornly, shaking her head.

"Can't say I've ever seen my own kin here behind a petition about me. Rotten luck," said the man in seat five, the only blood witch, Daire Grimsbane. He was a tough-looking Black man with a similar bandolier to mine looped around his shoulders.

"If I wanted your opinion, Crown Grimsbane, I'd ask," Blaize muttered.

"We're all equals here," pointed out the youngest appointee to the Crown Coven, celestial witch Einar Nightwalker. She wilted when both men turned to glare at her.

Silence followed when Kwan Graygazer was announced last, as the man in the seventh seat. He was an older member of the Graygazer family, his features wizened and thoughtful behind the thick rim of his glasses. He shuffled the cards of a tarot deck back and forth in his hands until they were nothing but a glowing blur.

Cress stepped forward when the announcer beckoned, taking the microphone. She drew breath to speak, to begin the speech she'd rehearsed so diligently.

Blaize stood. "Before you begin, there's one thing I want to say."

"Sit down, you bottom dweller," Madigan shouted.

"I should have you evicted for poor manners," he replied with a sneer. "However, whatever you've come here to say won't matter." He lifted the staff he'd had rested against his high seat, casting a quick spell and flicking a superheated missile of magic toward the sealed stone doors of the audience chamber. As they crumpled, I caught the sound of screaming and stamping feet from the other side.

GEO

The moment the doors sealed behind Cress and her witch friends, Hana Graygazer went and snatched the microphone from the coordinator outside the audience chamber. "Listen to me, everyone," she said, her voice raised to a boom as she leaned into the device. "You are in great danger. You need to leave *now*. Escape the pocket dimension if you can!"

"We could use your help, friend," Orthus said to me. I cast him a bewildered look, but he was already pushing confused and panicking witches out the front door. I followed his lead, using my shield as he did to make a wall no one could say no to.

"What's happening? I have to testify for my daughter!" Cress's mother shouted. She was one of the few that weren't being herded outside. Phaeron had her by the shoulder instead, with his tail looping around Carly before she could complain. They disappeared into a curl of smoke together.

I turned to Orthus, brow drawn low. "Explain," I said.

"I'm sorry for keeping you in the dark," the fae prince replied. "One always takes the word of a Graygazer, and Hana was insistent we be here to stop what comes next."

"Which is?" I demanded. My stone heart raced faster, and I thought of Cress, sealed in a room with all of those unknown people and the man she wanted to embarrass and expose live on camera.

"Even Hana wasn't quite sure. She sensed a danger so vast only the best were meant to face off against it," he said. "We'll talk later. These civilians need to be cleared out as soon as possible."

He, his fae, and the guardian witches who hadn't made it into the audience chamber worked as one unit ushering people outside. I followed their lead, clumsily reassuring strangers where I could but inevitably shoving them toward the doors with questions still on their lips.

The last stragglers and most stubborn were still here when the air shimmered. I turned, recognizing the feeling of dimensional magic, but it was white shadow that unfurled and slammed talons through the nearest person. Blood sprayed everywhere, and the Hungering Darkness's wolfish maw formed, opened in rapture as it sucked up and consumed the soul of its victim.

"We have company!" I shouted.

Magic swirled behind us, more and more people equipped for combat appearing. They'd teleported between us and the sealed audience chamber doors, inciting screaming panic amongst the last civilians still in this space as weapons were drawn and magic started to fly. I didn't waste time in forming my crystal club, swinging it at the grinning face of the Hungering Darkness and knocking some of its shadows aside.

It raised its talons to catch my weapon, smiling at me with a pale face so similar to Ben's yet so different, seeming waxy and slack. There was little glimmer of Lucas's humanity within the monstrous enjoyment the Hungering Darkness was taking in this moment. No hesitation, either, as it threw off my weapon and followed through with its claws aimed at my gut.

"Hello to you too, Morgana," it hissed.

My new shield sang a higher note as I caught its strike. "You've made a grave error," I said, determined to crush it once and for all.

Bang! The stone doors leading into the audience chamber shuddered and started to crumble in a fall of rubble and thick dust. The Hungering Darkness grinned viciously as its shadowy white maw reformed over Lucas's face. "No, *you* have, by being here," it replied with a cackle, disappearing in a curl of smoke.

Garroway's army was still teleporting in, but one of the witches aimed a trident at the collapsing doors and blew away the dust with a harsh gust. Witches of all kinds rushed the audience chamber in eerie, robotic silence, leaving the rest of us to give chase.

Ahead of us, the protective semi-circle of Mad Ash's coven turned, weapons brandished. They formed a solid wall of crystal, shields raised, as the first onslaught of mixed magic hit.

"What is the meaning of this?" a man dressed as a blood witch demanded, starting to stand from his high seat amongst the Crown Coven.

The Hungering Darkness took form again behind him, sinking its talons in his chest before anyone could react. "Destiny," it hissed.

I spread my wings, taking flight to get up there faster. A balding celestial witch, who I recognized as Blaize Starsurge, turned his staff toward me, throwing a blistering hot wave of magic in my direction as I arrowed toward the dimensional creature now fighting one of the other witches up on the dais.

My flinch was enough time for it to kill the guard and tear into the woman who'd extended her own trident toward the lake of water within this chamber. The tongues of water she'd been weaving into heated whips fell when she died next.

"Father, what are you doing?" Wren's scream echoed off the ceiling.

"Come up here, sundrop. You'll be safe," he replied in a begging tone.

I circled in for a landing on the dais, but a blur of shadow was quicker in taking form and tackling the Hungering Darkness away from a screaming man crawling away from the bodies of his peers. Phaeron grabbed his brother, rolling both of them off the dais. I checked my momentum and landed next to them instead, club raised.

"I have this. Protect Cress!" Phaeron shouted. His black talons were wrapped around the space over Lucas's shoulder, trying to tug the Hungering Darkness free of him. I grunted and turned, seeing her with her handbook floating just over her shoulder, sword clutched in both hands as she dueled with another librarian witch with dead-looking eyes.

Most of Garroway's army had that blank look to them, no spark of intelligence or free thought on their faces. I swung my club over her head and bashed the skull of Cress's opponent, who crumpled.

"Thanks," she said, taking a moment to cast a shielding spell in front of her.

I stepped in front of her with my physical shield raised and slammed my weapon at the next dead-eyed witch that came forward. It seemed like they were endless, the sheer amount of them creating chaos in the audience chamber, but they were weaker than the assassins we fought in Garroway's manor.

With my height, I could pick out the trained assassins from the crowd and the vampire that lurked amongst them, shredding through all but the toughest crystal with enchanted blades of his own. Most of these people Garroway had brought were bodies—distractions from the few big threats hidden amongst them.

"There's an emergency exit behind the dais," Blaize was saying behind me, still begging his daughter to join him. I picked up on the possibility of escape and started trying to map ways around the crush of bodies crowding us in on all sides. I had to get Cress out of here by any means possible.

Garroway looked up, flicking blood from his weapons. He was the only person here with enough space to think, standing over the dead body of one of our allies. With a lurch of my stone heart, I recognized the suited young man he'd cut down. Heath. Wren hadn't noticed yet, judging by the argument still ongoing between her and her father.

It happened so fast. Garroway took a running leap, boosting his back leg off the shoulder of one of his enslaved witches. I watched his trajectory, tightening my hand on my weapon and reflexively raising my shield, should he come for Cress. Instead, he landed on the dais and had his dagger through Blaize's forehead in one smooth thrust of his arm.

"No one escapes today," he said in a slow cadence, smiling viciously as he retrieved his weapon from the man's skull. "And you've outlived your usefulness, Crown Starsurge."

30
PHAERON

THE HUNGERING DARKNESS thrashed within Lucas, evading the pull of my claws. I could barely feel the life force of the boy it latched on to—a sign I recognized grimly.

"Dance with me, brother," it said, grinning. "One last fight before we bend the knee eternally." It shoved me off and sprang to its feet, drawing twin swords and gesturing for me to do the same.

I didn't pay its words much mind, knowing it'd long passed into the abyss of insanity from its eternal soul hunger. I unsheathed my swords and muttered the trigger word for the spell I'd etched into my armor. It hugged me a little closer and hardened, ready to deflect its claws until the spell failed.

"We need more space, though," it mused, turning to leap onto a lace-like fixture of metal suspended over the lake of water. With bodies starting to float in it, it'd gone from a placid blue to a gore-streaked red. I jumped onto the fixture, bracing as it shook beneath both of our weights.

It hadn't lashed out at my mind yet, leaving us both in peak condition to duel. My shadows coalesced to cover me head to toe, and I released a wailing roar as I assumed my shadowborn form. Our weapons were black and white blurs as we twisted, turned, and struck at full, vicious power.

Endaeron, in his prime, had been the superior duelist, the stronger, more beloved prince. I saw a glimpse of him again as he got past my guard and the edge of one blade swiped the side of my armor. The spell held, but I'd have a bruise from the force of the strike. The fixture wobbled below us.

"What?" it hissed.

"Borrowed an idea from you," I said before cutting the nearly invisible metal thread that kept this platform over the water. We both teleported to a different piece of metal a few yards away, a fountain with a rigid U shape. I gained the high ground, cutting bloody lines across its torso.

"You never could think of your own tricks, could you, Phaeron?" It taunted, smashing both blades into mine and shoving. I turned into smoke before I hit the water, reappearing behind it. But it'd already twisted around, shoving the point of one blade into my belly. I felt my armor strain to keep it from piercing straight through me.

"One of us is still alive," I pointed out, turning into smoke yet again and reappearing with precarious balance on another part of the fountains. I lifted one blade, channeling shadowy magic through it and chopping it toward where the Hungering Darkness still stood. It became a wisp too, and the sharp blade of shadow I'd sent toward it broke the fountain instead, sending a pressurized jet from its newly blunted head.

"But we will both serve. It is Myuna's will," it answered next to me. Our swords locked again, sending up sparks.

"Why mention that harlot?" I snarled, sweeping its feet

out from under it. It went down hard, breathing an *oof* as its borrowed body bent around the pipe we stood on and went sliding into the water. I reached out with several tendrils of shadow, catching its swords and flexing them viciously with my magic. I managed to snap one before it came surging out of the water, talons first.

This time, it parted my leather armor like butter, sending fuchsia blood flying as it scored deep furrows across my chest. "She rules all. And she has always wanted a full set," it hissed, leaning in. "To be served by me *and* you."

"Never," I snarled back through the surge of pain.

That was when it reached out and sank mental claws into my head. Corruption blossomed in the black flames over my body as I fell to my knees, wobbling on the thin metal below me.

"*Cress!*" I called desperately, feeling darkness closing in.

"Get away from him!" A shrill voice pierced my awareness, accompanied by a jet of water. I blinked dark spots from my vision, gasping when I spotted Willow at the edge of the water, balancing two globes in her palms.

Her eyes glowed an icy blue, and power pulsed from her. Her *soul* grew, both sides finally intertwining into a harmonious whole. Blood wept from her cheeks like tears as pinkish scales burst from her skin.

"Monster! You killed my friend!" she screamed, turning her palms toward the Hungering Darkness.

The water churned out of control around it, reaching out with ice-lined arms. I helped him down with a kick to the shoulder, and he landed with a splash, enveloped instantly and pulled to the bottom of the lake. Around Willow, other witches started clawing at their necks, eyes bulging. Water and blood leaked from their lips and noses until they fell, spasming and struggling.

I clutched at my throat, struggling for air. "Willow," I rasped, feeling my lungs bubble with the liquid filling them. I reached for her, choking as her soul pulsed again and coral-pink fins and scales rippled down her arms and tipped her fingers in delicate claws.

She was losing control of her magic as it grew and changed with her shift toward a mer form, and there wasn't a damn thing I could do about it. My shadows faded, and my swords splashed into the water below me. I pitched forward with a desperate gasp, trying to get even a sip of air as the wrong kind of darkness closed in on my awareness.

A flash of red came behind Willow in my blurring sight, and I drew a desperate breath as the water in my lungs vanished. "Sorry, kid. Couldn't have you killing our friends," Madigan murmured down to a crumpled Willow.

I lost precious seconds recovering, struggling to catch a breath and get my shadows to obey in retrieving my swords from the bottom of the lake. A soaked Hungering Darkness erupted from the water before I was ready, claws extended toward me.

CRESS

Wren was screaming behind me, crying over her father's body. It'd tumbled over the edge of the dais while the rest of us fought. Even though it was Blaize Starsurge, I still couldn't imagine her pain.

The remaining Crown Coven witches and their protectors were caught in a desperate fight with Garroway and a couple of his assassins as they picked off the important officials one by one. Some of his enslaved army had blocked the emergency exit, or so I thought when Einar Nightwalker rushed that way and didn't return after releasing a high-pitched shriek.

"This isn't how it was supposed to go," said Eris hollowly, though I was the only one who heard her. Men and women fought *through* her transparent form. I'd summoned her ghost to witness this moment of triumph, just to show her a charnel house as our forces clashed with Garroway's.

I was in a position of relative safety, behind the defensive line of Mad Ash Coven and between Ben and Geo. I borrowed from Bella's senses, the cat hunkered down in a sheltered nook with my other two familiars. We'd practiced, so I heard the rasp of weapons over armor and through flesh at an unpleasantly magnified rate, but also the taunting between Phaeron and the Hungering Darkness.

Phaeron seemed to be losing, especially once Willow started acting strangely. I backed away from her as the men and women around her, both friend and foe, started to choke as her magic surged. That was how I tripped over the case lying forgotten where Ben had placed it.

I bent and freed Evening Guidance from its box, my pulse rocketing in my throat. "I need a spell," I shouted at my mother's ghost. "Something that will burn a dimensional monster!" While I'd take anything, I was hoping for some miracle, something that would save us all.

It was a desperate request, especially since I'd had to set my bloodied sword down to take up the staff in both hands. But I couldn't do anything for Phaeron at the back of this group and crush of people. I'd noticed that celestial witch spells were designed to be long-range, however, unlike the close and personal nature of magic cast from a sword.

"There is one," she said, reading the spell tags dangling from the staff and nodding. She followed as Geo and Ben covered me and Willow collapsed, knocked unconscious. The combatants around us got back to their feet.

"Repeat after me," Eris said, positioning herself on the other side of the staff and laying her static-filled hands over mine.

She shifted her weight, and I mimicked her, lining up the tip of the staff toward the shaky sculpture where Phaeron barely kept his balance. Latin flowed from her mouth, and I repeated it, feeling the wood warm in my hands. It felt like it was sucking on my palms, the feeling transferring up my arm and to the book that'd come in for a landing on my left shoulder.

My ancestral magic flowed down that arm and into the weapon like a coursing golden river. The star pattern on the wood lit up. It vibrated in my hold as the spell I'd activated waited to be released. "Steady, girl!" Eris exclaimed. "Aim and fire!"

I did. When the Hungering Darkness emerged like a razor-lined fish, talons extended to rend Phaeron in half, I shouted the trigger word and sent a laser of concentrated light streaming right at it.

Its head turned, golden light reflecting in its eyes before the spell slammed into it, knocking it backward with an otherworldly howl. My jaw dropped as the Hungering Darkness went visibly tumbling out of Lucas's body as it hit the far wall and slid downward. The monster fled the intensity of light from my spell.

"Lucas!" Ben called, dropping his weapons and diving into the lake without hesitation.

Phaeron launched himself from his perch, shadowy claws extended. The Hungering Darkness was just clipped by his reaching talons, turning into white smoke as it wound over our heads and surged toward the dais. I turned my head, watching it slam into Garroway's body. The vampire jerked his head to the side, frozen for a moment above Kwan Graygazer lying prone on the ground. The elderly man scooted away, crab walking backward to a safer spot.

"Trying to control my magic, Garroway?" the Hungering Darkness hissed from the vampire's lips, clawing at his side to expose a red-rimmed blood rune etched there on his skin. It was unlike Ben's, three rings thick and lined with spiky runes. He'd nearly covered the whole right side of his body with intricate spell patterns. "Don't you know it's *my* magic that makes this possible?"

It grew talons of white shadow over Garroway's hand, and they jerked back and forth for control of the body. Unlike with Lucas, Garroway had some struggle left in him, but that was before the points of those claws raked across the face of the rune. Garroway's body went slack with a sibilant sigh.

"Bright soul, this is nothing good. We need to leave at once." Phaeron appeared in a curl of smoke next to me, his otherworldly eyes feverish with pain. The front of his armor was stained with his fuchsia blood.

"Let us end this farce, shall we?" the Hungering Darkness was saying, drawing the black knife-like shard from its pocket and crushing it in a shadow-lined fist. The sudden collapse of dozens of bodies had me startling. Like puppets with their strings cut, every single member of Garroway's unwilling army and his trained assassins fell.

"They're dead," announced one of the guardian witches, looking as shocked as I felt.

The Hungering Darkness raised its arms, chanting in another language. Phaeron wavered on his feet, his gray skin paling to a sickly shade. "Run. All of you, run!" he shouted.

My mother's ghost looped her arms around me. For a moment, it was like she was tugged toward the chanting dimensional monster. "You can't see it, can you?" she asked. "The souls...everyone who's died..."

The bodies were twitching briefly before going still. It must be using souls for some kind of awful spell.

"This way's faster," came the hoarse voice of Kwan Graygazer as he limped his way down the stairs from the high seats, supporting a blood-soaked Daire Grimsbane, who had healing runes hastily painted across his chest. They led the rest of us behind the curve of the dais, where the emergency exit was clearly marked with a closed metal door and keypad, along with the fallen bodies of several people.

He keyed in a number on the pad, and the grate-like door swung open. Madigan and Orthus took places on either side of the opening, shoving people through. I watched as the elderly man shuffled to a box set right inside the exit tunnel and opened it, pressing on a giant red button. The air in the room shifted suddenly, like an increase of pressure along my spine.

Ben was amongst the guardians protecting our escape, dripping water with his brother slung over one shoulder. He was joined by a fae in cracked armor, who carried Willow, and others who helped our wounded and unconscious to safety. Geo was toward the back of this group, meeting my gaze grimly. He supported Wren, who stumbled along with a deeply stunned expression, and a battered Áine clip-clopped a few steps behind him.

"Phaeron?" I said, lingering when the dimensional stopped mid-step toward safety, a tremor passing through his body. He turned and took a step back the way we'd come. I tugged on his arm, trying to stop him. "What are you doing? We can't stick around."

"It's too late for me, bright soul," he said softly, his expression shifting to obedient blankness. "Leave me behind. Save yourself."

He shook me off his arm with a frown. His eyes flared with aggressively bright white shadow, which persisted even when I pressed on his mark of protection and called his name. It only seemed to annoy him, as he cast one last inscrutable glance over his shoulder.

A gauntlet of red crystal closed around my shoulder, pulling me back. Madigan pushed me into the tunnel as I cried out, reaching for Phaeron anyway, who marched his way back into the death-filled audience chamber.

The whole structure shook, showering dust over us. A voice, great and terrible, rose from nearby. It seemed incomprehensible at first, speaking in dozens of languages before finally settling on English.

"Endaeron? It has been so long." It was feminine but vast, with the kind of power that made it feel like my head was being crushed just by hearing it.

"Myuna," I breathed in horror. The soul-consuming deity that'd destroyed Soiluire, *here*. Tears stung the corners of my eyes as I imagined the same level of depravity seizing Earth. But first, she'd taken Phaeron, and there was nothing I could do about it.

It's too late for me, bright soul.

"What is this place you've summoned me to?" the goddess asked.

Cress and her men's story concludes in Bright Soul!

Consider joining my Facebook group: Ella Hendricks Library Nest! Stay up to date with planned releases, chat about favorite books, and enjoy the occasional giveaway!

Please remember to review! Reviews help other readers find stories they may love. Consider leaving a review for Shadow Slayer on Amazon and other websites.

ABOUT THE AUTHOR

Ella Hendricks is an author of romances with dark roots and steamy twists. She loves getting lost in fantasy worlds, especially if the monsters are naughty and the lady saves the day in the end. When Ella is not writing about swoonworthy men, she's off collecting video game achievements. She holds a master's degree in journalism and lives in Texas with her family.

Find out more about her books at: www.ellahendricks.com

www.ingramcontent.com/pod-product-compliance
Lightning Source LLC
Chambersburg PA
CBHW021235190726
48289CB00005B/1333